PAYMENT IN KIND

(2nd Revised Edition)

Editorial Reviews

The Columbia Review of Books & Film

PAYMENT IN KIND – A Novel

REVIEWED BY: AVRAHAM AZRIELI. *Avraham Azrieli's most recent novel is "Deborah Rising" (HarperColllins 2016), the story of the first woman to lead a nation in history. www.azrielibooks.com*

<u>**Payment in Kind | The Columbia Review**</u> (Summary): "A realistic novel that spans across borders, oceans and continents, yet succeeds in remaining solidly anchored in the lives of interesting, genuine, flesh-and-blood characters. Highly recommended!"

<u>Payment in Kind | The Columbia Review</u>

Payment in Kind by Joseph M. Luguya is a novel that centers on Africa, yet takes readers on a journey both geographical and psychological, exploring complex issues of culture, politics, religion, justice and race. The novel is told in several layers, each complementing the other, in a highly ambitious structure that excels in keeping the reader's interest.

While the novel encompasses multifaceted intellectual disciplines, historical dramas, and social-justice discussions, the author often hones in on human emotions and conflicts with a sharp eye and sensitive perceptions that result in rich imagery. For example:

"The hairs on Father Campbell's dome stand on end as he mentally seeks escape routes from the difficult position he sees looming up."

The tackling of serious and complex issues, which is quite ambitious here (and could be challenging to some readers), is lightened up by observations that touch on the comedic. For example:

"The seminarian's face wears a quizzical air. His wide-eyed stare is briefly interrupted when he becomes overwhelmed by an unexpected urge to yawn. His struggle to stifle the yawn is futile."

Perhaps most exceptional in Payment in Kind is the wonderful intermingling – and contradictions – presented in the context of African culture and traditions, contrasted with Christianity and its adherents. For example:

"But even as they turn to leave in the face of the

practical problems that beset their mission, the representatives of the tribal elders in Namwinkholongwe predict that worse will befall the lad. They are supported in their prediction by not a few of the practicing Christians who watch them leave."

An especially fascinating thread in the story is the exploration of psychology and, more specifically, sanity and madness, which is even more engrossing in such cross-cultural novel. For example:

"Without pausing, the balding professor adds as an aside: "I keep telling my students that insanity could well boil down to a trait of the mind – an aversion for thinking in cheerless straight lines or an avowal that one's thinking will be in abstruse vicious circles!""

In summary, the author's unique point of view, extensive familiarity with his subject matters and a talent for lively storytelling combine to create a realistic novel that spans across borders, oceans and continents, yet succeeds in remaining solidly anchored in the lives of interesting, genuine, flesh-and-blood characters. Highly recommended!

The Columbia Review

Original Books
14404 Innsbruck Court
Silver Spring, MD, 20906
USA
Visit Amazon's Joseph M. Luguya Page
Website: www.originalbooks.org
(Under construction)

Library of Congress Control Number: 2016918757
ISBN-10: 0-9713309-9-9
ISBN-13: 978-0-9713309-9-3

June 2017

Created and written by Joseph M. Luguya

First Original Books Edition
Printed and produced in the United States of America
First published 1985 by The Kenya Literature Bureau

ABOUT THE BOOK

Payment in Kind is a novelty in this genre of novels. It is at once a tragi-comedy exploiting to very good effect the popular African-culture-versus-Christianity yarn and also a monograph dealing with an important but hitherto little explored subject – alienation from the self. The ultimate "Roots" book, it traces the insanity of Kintu, its hero, back to his "psychic" roots. A delightful read for the literary scholar, the social scientist, and the connoisseur alike.

ABOUT THE AUTHOR

Mr. Joseph Luguya received his early education in missionary schools in his native Uganda. He studied Philosophy and Theology at St. Mary's Major Seminary, Gaba. Mr. Luguya later attended the University of Nairobi, the Stanford Business School, the CII College of Insurance in London and, for a brief spell, the University of Dar es Salaam. He has lived and worked in Uganda, Tanzania, Kenya, Canada and the United States.

Mr. Luguya is also the author of *Inspired by the Devil: Part 1 - The Gospel According to "Judas Iscariot"* (3rd Revised Original Books Edition 2007), *The Forbidden Fruit* (Original Books 2011), and the riveting three volume theology-fiction thriller *Humans: The Untold Story of Adam and Eve and their Descendants* (Original Books / CreateSpace 2015).

Disclaimer:

This book is a work of fiction. The characters, names, businesses, organizations, places, events, incidents, dialogue and plot are the product of the author's imagination or are fictitiously used. Any resemblance to actual persons living or dead, names, events, or locales is entirely coincidental.

Acknowledgements:

To my family, for being a great inspiration, and for their support; and to the many individuals who genuinely could not wait to see *Payment in Kind* in print.

TABLE OF CONTENTS

INTRODUCTION

1. The Colored Couple

Ibrahim Mjomba was not normally given to voicing harried expressions. But that morning, as he bade his wife good day before hopping into his battered Ford to drive to work, her appearance had caused him to exclaim suddenly: "What is the matter now, darling!"

It was not characteristic of Jamila either to hurl words at her husband. But in what seemed to him at least to be a fit of anger, she had shot back: "You are the one who looks like you have a problem! What is biting you?"

Encircling her outsized tummy with her ordinarily slender but now somewhat beefy arms, she had added nonchalantly: "For the whole of last week—for quite sometime now in fact, you have been acting queer...as if the entire world's worries had all of a sudden been eased on your shoulders!"

Mjomba had felt considerable relief seeing his wife of six years, ostensibly well pleased with herself after she had mouthed those last words, settle back in the settee and stare out the window in the direction of Oyster Bay. Almost immediately afterwards, however, she had inclined her head to one side casting what he concluded was an accusing glance in his direction.

Thinking back on the incident as he sat in his office, Mjomba admitted to himself that he had indeed been conducting himself during the past several months as if he had a responsibility to the world! He had fallen into the habit of spending his lunch hour at the office instead of heading home as he had been doing previously, ostensibly to save on gas!

Years back, Mjomba, who secretly but consistently harboured the weird notion that he had made a very important discovery relating to the phenomenon of insanity, and believed that his discovery was likely to make psychiatry turn a new leaf, had commenced work on a book. At the time he met and married Jamila, then a private secretary to Professor Claus Gringo, a renowned psychiatrist, he had been about to complete the task of documenting the details of his "discovery". He had been surprised to find at the same time that his "dossier" contained the ingredients of a plot for a first class novel, the sort of novel that would set trends in addition to leaving fame as well as fortune to its author - or so he imagined!

He had allowed his ideas an almost limitless period to hibernate, moving to complete the expansion of the material into a full-fledged historical novel nearly half a decade after he set down the initial plot.

A father of two, Mjomba was determined to complete the book before their third child arrived. But he was also determined to keep his ambitious project concealed from his wife until its completion. Since he could not do any script writing at home for that reason, he had found it necessary to use his luncheon breaks for that purpose, affording himself a quick sandwich for lunch instead of the usual three course lunch Jamila insisted was essential to maintain his health. But he was racing against time, and he really didn't have any choice now.

Like Innocent Kintu, the book's hero and supposed lunatic, Mjomba had once aspired to become a Roman Catholic priest. A tonsured cleric, Mjomba had already had conferred upon him the Minor Orders of Porter, Lector, Exorcist, Acolyte and Subdeacon pursuant to the Code of

Canon Law in preparation for receiving the Church's Major Orders of Deaconate and the Holy Priesthood, when Innocent Kintu, a fellow tribesman who hailed from the same district as himself, entered St. Augustine's Major Seminary.

It had been Reverend Mjomba's view that Kintu was a nutcase long before he was suspected of being one, and certainly before he was declared one! That had been his view almost from the very first.

Since that time, a lot of things had taken place, the most significant of which was Mjomba's conversion to Islam and subsequent marriage to the ravishing quadroon he met in Professor Gringo's office. Previously known as Christian Mjomba, he had likewise discarded his first name and adopted his present one to emphasize the importance he placed on his new circumstances and the change of his outlook on the world.

Ibrahim Mjomba's thoughts were now far from all that - and the book - as he reflected on his domestic life. He felt he had to admit to a kind of fear that the sight of his pregnant wife invariably aroused in him starting a couple of weeks back. He had already become so prone to it that he now recoiled instinctively whenever she came close. Even so, he had not imagined that his face could be a mask of fear as Jamila's reaction that morning had seemed to suggest.

The cause of the fear was fairly obvious. But Mjomba, acting impulsively, refused to let himself be confronted with the subject. He was loath to admit that he had not been paying enough attention to his wife' needs even though the size of her tummy clearly suggested that the baby could arrive at any time.

It was precisely during the previous week that work on the book had been most demanding. After chronicling all the events that led to his hero's mental collapse, Mjomba had found himself faced with the almost impossible task of reconciling certain obvious formal conclusions with some of his own pet theories on the causes of insanity. It had in fact only been through the most exacting and supreme of efforts at concentration that he had succeeded in balancing his arguments in favour of Theory "R", the theory he hoped would advance medical science!

After a good deal of soul searching, Mjomba finally decided that both Jamila and himself were fairly worried - as, indeed, they were entitled to be. Following the months and finally weeks of waiting, it had begun to look like the baby really could come any time!

Mjomba felt slightly unnerved as he remembered that Jamila no longer ventured outdoors as often as she used to or might have wished. He shied at the idea that, while he himself still went to work as usual, he was visibly weighed down with anxiety for his wife and the unborn infant without being conscious of it.

A couple of days earlier Mjomba, the less worried of the two no doubt despite his appearance, had reluctantly agreed that he would arrange to take a month's leave from work without further delay. He had taken such leave on the occasion of the birth of Musa two years earlier. If the circumstances had permitted him to do so when Ali, now four, was born, he would probably have done the same thing.

On the present occasion, he still had to observe signs of childbirth, and was as a result inclined to maintain a wait and see attitude. He would accordingly have preferred to take the vacation when signs showed that childbirth was imminent. Although he loved his wife, he also valued his job at the World Trade Center, and wasn't the kind of person to walk away from his desk - and stay away for a whole month at that - lightly!

2. An Exceptional Kid

Mjomba let his mind wonder back to the time, four-years earlier, when he had sat through his Winter Quarter examinations at the Bay Area Institute of Technology on the American west coast while Jamila was being prepared for the theatre at the nearby BAIT Medical Center. He had been sponsored for a two year MBA program at the prestigious college that Americans referred to simply as BAIT by his employer in conjunction with the African-American Institute, and had decided to take his spouse of four months along at his own expense.

It stood out as the only time he had felt doubts about the wisdom of having Jamila accompany him on the overseas trip. After sitting what later turned out to be one of his best papers, the youthful scholar from the Third World had jumped on his bicycle, and had made it to the hospital's maternity ward barely in time to embrace the still bloodstained and slimy little Ali as he was being transferred from the theatre to the nursery in a nurse's arms.

Mjomba's mental processes were accustomed to revert to the family's sojourn in America whenever an occasion presented itself. His wife was two months into her pregnancy when they jetted into "the land of the free and the home of the brave", also dubbed the "exceptional nation" by Alexis-Charles-Henri Clérel de Tocqueville, the eighteenth century French political thinker and historian.

That was before the Brits burned down the White House at the behest of the Canadians to avenge the attack by the "separatists" on Fort York (present-day Toronto) - the Brits who were already at that time bragging about the reach of the

British Empire, and were certain that British exceptionalism was going to endure forever!

Mjomba would always remember the huge hospital bill that he had had to personally foot because there were no insurance products from any company anywhere in America that would cover Jamila's maternity expenses at that late stage. For that young African couple (or as Americans themselves preferred to say "colored couple"), bringing Ali into the world would turn out to be as costly as purchasing a fully loaded BMW! And the cost would have doubled if they had tried to get him a babysitter for the remainder of the time they were in the States!

In contrast, upon returning to Tanzania (where it would have been inconceivable for any one to refer to them as a "colored couple"), they would enjoy the luxury of engaging the services of a live-in nanny for Ali, a second maid who would double up as cook, and a houseboy to do the grunt work (or "donkeywork" as Tanzanians preferred to call it) around the house. That donkeywork would include chores such as window cleaning, washing and shining their automobile every morning, and doing the family's laundry.

And they would afford this even though their policy was to pay their house help at least twice the going rate in that "abode of peace" which the name "Dar es Salaam" signified. They always did that to be assured of the loyalty and trust of their employees, and they never regretted it.

Mjomba beamed with pleasure at the thought that Ali, a United States citizen by birth, would always be an ever-present symbol of the happy days he and Jamila spent in California - more so, he had once told a friend, than the coveted diploma he bagged for his academic endeavors!

And, on occasion, especially when he was being bugged by the thought that the health system in America, like America's political system and everything else there, was actually "rigged" in favour of the so-called one-percenters and against regular people amid the reportedly stifling and at times quite spectacular gridlock on "Capitol Hill", and what some believed to be a wholly dysfunctional Congress, he would trot out Ali's passport and he would take his time to stare at the Great Seal of the United States atop the large head of the "American Eagle on the wing and rising".

He had the habit, on such occasions, of turning his thoughts to America's claim to being an exceptional and indispensable nation. He was actually tempted on one occasion to say "Yes, this guy is exceptional along with the rest of them", only to cringe at the thought that his son's exceptionalism could potentially be marred by the blight of racial segregation in America, and the documented history of discrimination against "people of color" by the white communities there.

Still, Mjomba typically refused to allow such negative thoughts to ruin the fun he was having celebrating the Exceptionalism of the land of the free and home of the brave with which his son's fortunes were now intertwined. Going that route was something that was definitely a non-starter. There were so many people out there who were prepared to sell everything they had if doing so could buy them a Green Card, which was a far cry from a U.S. passport!

Mjomba had gone further and frequently fantasized that one could not talk about American Exceptionalism without inferring that Americans themselves, and at the very minimum those who called America home by virtue of being its natural-born citizens, were exceptional! It had to be that way. You

18

could not have an exceptional nation without a citizenry that was also exceptional in the same way you could not have a constitution without a nation to go with it!

Mjomba was, of course, aware that there were people who denigrated American Exceptionalism, with some of them going as far as claiming that it only existed as a figment of the imagination of those who believed in it. The thing that really mattered though, Mjomba opined, might be establishing if the prophets of exceptionalism, be it British Exceptionalism (and the belief of those descendants of the Celtics, Anglo-Saxons, Norsemen, Normans, *et cetera* that imperialism was a noble enterprise of civilization and they were "bearing the white man's burden"), or Roman Exceptionalism (that saw the Etruscans conquer the barbarians and subject them to the rule of their "Holy Roman Empire"); French Exceptionalism (that was based on the conviction that France had "*la mission civilisatrice*"; German Exceptionalism which envisioned a world over which the race of Übermensch (Superhumans) held sway; or Greek Exceptionalism, Japanese Exceptionalism, American Exceptionalism or what have you, were true prophets or were false prophets purely and simply.

Deep down, Mjomba himself suspected that the doctrines of exceptionalism, whenever and wherever they were promulgated, amounted to nothing more than myths. And he usually liked to dial back to the days of Rōmulus and Rĕmus, the twin brothers who founded Rome, the Eternal City and soon to be capital of the Roman Empire, to try and understand why the notion that America was exceptional was so popular.

It was notable that the *Sacrum Romanum Imperium* ("Holy Roman Empire") at one time extended all the way from *Roma* ("Rome") to Mesopotamia to the east, to the North African city of Carthage to the south; and well beyond the

Danube to the west, with the provinces of Gaul, Hispania and Britannia forming its western flank. With inhabitants numbering between fifty million to ninety million, it accounted for roughly twenty percent of the world's population. At the zenith of its power, the Roman Empire controlled two and a half million square miles!

Mjomba was taken aback by the fact that the Roman Empire was now "history", and that even the language that was spoken by Caligula (Emperor Caius Julius Caesar) and other emperors before and after him, and that was used by Roman Senators in politicking in the Forum, and in which the Roman consuls, prefectures and provincial governors penned their missives in the golden days of the *Pax Romana*, Latin, had joined the list of those languages that were now "dead" or extinct!

This had happened despite the fact that Romans prided themselves on their time honoured "values" which derived from their *mos maiorum* ("ancestral customs"). But he had also noted that, as they evolved, those values had come to include some things that seemed plainly weird. It came as quite a surprise for Mjomba to learn that, even as the *Pax Romana* was unfolding, Romans habitually jammed the Colosseum in Rome to savor the spectacle of exotic wild beasts brought to Rome from the far reaches of the Empire, including big cats like North African lions and Bengal tigers (also known nowadays as the Royal Bengal tigers), as they were let loose on prisoners on death row and on others who were deemed "deplorables" in the *venationes* shows (wild animal hunts), with the poor wretches permitted only daggers or spears to ward off the starved man-eaters!

And then there were the *Ludi Circenses* or chariot races in the *Circus Maximus* (greatest or largest or biggest circus) that was situated in the valley between the Aventine and Palatine hills and could seat as many as three hundred thousand spectators.

After seeing the flick "Ben-Hur", Mjomba thought he had an idea what went on in the Circus Maximus. And, as if that was not enough to satisfy the bloodthirsty crowds, there were the gladiatorial duels in which the gladiators fought to the death in front of the cheering crowds in anyone or other of Rome's amphitheatres.

These were among the exceptional qualities that gave the Roman Republic the moral right to go out and conquer and civilize the world. The goings-on at the Colosseum were so central to the values and qualities of life that underpinned the *Via Romana* ("The Roman Way") that Venerable Beda, a medieval monk, even went as far as writing in his famous prophecy that Rome would exist as long as the Circus Maximus, that amphitheatre which was founded by Vespasian in the year 72 AD and completed by Titus in 80 AD, did!

Oh Yeah! Values! Mjomba had already convinced himself that American values and the qualities of life in that land of the free and home of the brave, which gave it the moral strength - and the moral right - to venture forth and conquer and democratize the globe in Mjomba's own time, were far superior to the values and qualities of life that had guided the Romans in their own adventures from the days of Gaius Octavius, who had crowned himself *Princeps Civitatis* ("First Citizen of the State"), to the time of the decline and demise of that pseudo "Holy Roman Empire" under Emperor Romulus Augustus.

Mjomba thought that it was notable that Romulus Augustus was himself allegedly a usurper who was eventually deposed by the German "barbarian" King Odoacer only ten months after he himself had deposed the then Emperor Julius Nepos.

During their sojourn in America, Mjomba and his wife Jamila, both of whom were quite new to American politics, had found themselves being treated to a different kind of theatre. The presidential and congressional elections were scheduled to take place in about a year's time, and the "colored couple" was shocked to hear the presidential candidates call each other all sorts of names in the run-up to the elections. They trounced each other again and again as "incompetent" or "corrupt" and "crooked", or as "totally, thoroughly unqualified to serve as President", or as "most corrupt candidate ever," or as "unfit and incapable of serving as President of the United States", or as "physically and mentally unfit to be President of the United States", or as "morally unfit to be POTUS", or as "temperamentally unfit to be President, unbalanced and dangerous", or as "a pathological liar who has taken a short-circuit in the brain and might not at all be mentally fit to be president", or as "a weak person who is actually not strong enough to be president and who is pretty close to being unhinged", or as "a weak person and a monster who is unfit to be POTUS", or as "a shameless habitual liar who would put the Oval Office up for sale", or as "too dangerous to be Commander-in-Chief", or as "thin-skinned and a demagogue who is unfit to be President", or as "a narcissist at a level that America has never seen", or as "utterly amoral and a bully", or as "a first-rate con artist and a clown act", or as "a serial liar", or as "a criminal", or as "The Devil", to resounding cheers from their respective supporters.

And then one of the presidential candidates decried the Supreme Court's landmark decision in the Citizens United v. Federal Election Commission case. The learned justices had apparently agreed that it was actually a good thing for the electoral system to be "rigged" by big money; and their 5-4 decision effectively allowed the so-called "Super PACs" (or Political Action Committees) to spend unlimited amounts of money to get their preferred candidates elected to the Legislative Branch on Capitol Hill, and above all to get their preferred candidate for the position of POTUS into the White House in order that he/she may in turn do their bidding upon becoming POTUS. A majority of the learned members of SCOTUS (the Supreme Court of the United States of America) had concluded that "money actually spoke" and deciding otherwise would have been tantamount to curbing "free speech"!

It did not help Mjomba when, on checking Wikipedia, he found the following astonishing statement: "It has long been commonly assumed that the votes of Supreme Court justices reflect their jurisprudential philosophies as well as their ideological leanings, personal attitudes, values, political philosophies, or policy preferences. A growing body of academic research has confirmed this understanding: scholars have found that the justices largely vote in consonance with their perceived values..."

Whereas an independent judiciary was a crucial component of any democracy, the opposite was apparently true in America! The U.S. Supreme Court justices, who were entrusted with resolving disputes about how the United States Constitution and other federal laws should be applied to cases that had been appealed from lower courts, were themselves *ideologically* divided! And then, as if to seal the deal, Mjomba almost by chance also alighted on an article in one of America's most prestigious news magazine headlined "Dark money buys state supreme court races"!

Suffice it to say that Mjomba was thoroughly scandalized, and not just taken aback but dumbfounded and quite flabbergasted by what he was witnessing! Of course if there were even the remotest hint that these sorts of things were happening in an African country, particularly if it was a country in Sub-Saharan Africa, every Tom, Dick and Harry in the "advanced" world would be screaming that he or she was witnessing "corruption in the extreme"! Worse still, if this was what was going on in America, he had reason to fear for his own continent, because the leaders of the nations that were just then emerging from the throes of colonialism were being handed the perfect template for corruption!

Before setting off for America, Mjomba had seen pictures of the Mount Rushmore National Memorial with its sculptures of the heads of George Washington, Thomas Jefferson, Theodore Roosevelt and Abraham Lincoln in the National Geographic; and he had come to America hoping to see democracy at its best! He was stunned, and said as much to Jamila as they watched the saga of the American presidential election unfold on their telly! Jamila had chimed in and said that she was wondering how Ali would take all this as he came of age! Mjomba had responded by saying that Ali, a U.S. citizen by birth, might be the one to right all these things - if he mounted a successful campaign for POTUS and got away with it before he was shot in the process, that is!

"But how?" Jamila thought that her husband was joking, and sounded quite incredulous.

"Well, one way - if he was in a position to count on support from two-thirds of the members of both the House of Representatives and the Senate, or if he could get two-thirds of the state legislatures to call a constitutional convention - would be to make the decisions of SCOTUS subject to appeal

24

to a new and completely independent layer of SCOTUS or SCOTUS II!" Mjomba was poker-faced and unsmiling as he made the pitch.

Mjomba let Jamila know that in light of the checkered history of politics in America - four U.S. presidential assassinations and seven known assassination attempts - they might have to advise Ali to think twice about joining the race for POTUS with or without those altruistic goals!

It was now Jamila's turn to make her suggestion: "I have an idea", she started; "Look, Ali will be, not just a known unknown, but a completely unknown entity when he notches the age of thirty-five, the threshold for running for the Office of POTUS. Look...this could be a great opportunity for us to make some money. As soon as he announces his candidacy, we could rush and auction off his baby photos for a couple of million bucks to the American media houses, many of which reputedly are into peddling fake news any way. But we will have to persuade him to get out of the race for the world's most powerful office as soon as we have made our millions - and before he gets shot!"

A terrific actor, it was now her turn as she made her own pitch to put on her best poker face. She was unsmiling, and for a moment Mjomba, caught off guard by her stern visage, even conceded that her suggestion was a terrific idea!

"Well, talking about money..." Jamila had cut in, a sheepish smile on her face. "Is it not true that to win seat in the House of Representatives, a candidate has to go begging and come up with at least two million bucks? And candidates for Senate seats need to raise at least twenty million bucks apiece!"

"Yah, that is about right, darling," said Mjomba in response, adding: "But I must wonder how they manage to recoup those outlays given that what they earn in salary pales by comparison…"

Jamila looked and sounded glum and woebegone as she said: "I think there is something mysterious that we do not know; and Ali must somehow figure that something out if he is to make a run for the world's most powerful job! Clearly one must be prepared to dole out substantially more than candidates for the House or the Senate dole out if one is aspiring to become President of the USA! Also, I think I read something somewhere to the effect that seats on the Congressional and House Committees come with a price tag, not to mention leadership and committee chair assignments. Sounds a little strange. This must be what is meant by 'the almighty dollar'!

"But you remember the orientation, Ibrahim? We were specifically warned about the culture shock that awaits newcomers upon their arrival in America. Perhaps this is what the Cultural Attaché at the Embassy in Dar es Salaam had in mind. …"

Information on the historical events surrounding the deposition of Romulus Augustus, also known as *Romulus Augustulus* ("Little Augustus") was scanty to be sure. But Mjomba supposed that he was seeing those events mirrored in the American presidential campaign; and, aware that his son's fortunes and the fortunes of the land of the free and home of the brave were now intertwined, he accordingly worried to death about a repeat of that history. It was not really far fetched, in the circumstances surrounding the American elections saga that was unfolding right in front of their eyes, for someone to start wondering if a loosing presidential candidate might not be tempted to regard the new commander-in-chief and leader of the so-called free world as a usurper!

It was as Mjomba was mulling the events that were taking place on America's political scene and the candidates' respective promises to do this or to do that upon assuming the coveted position of POTUS and becoming the "most powerful person in the world" that something else had threatened to dash the hopes he was holding out for his son. Just around that time, a footnote in his local paper's editorial proclaimed that, even though America was home to only five percent of the world's population, twenty-five percent of the world's prison population were locked up there! That caused the high-minded Mjomba to exclaim with righteous indignation: "There sure is something not quite right going on there!"

For her part, Jamila, even though aware of the commandment that said: "Thou shalt not take the name of the Lord thy God in vain", found herself unable to resist exclaiming: "Christ!"

Of course, as far as Mjomba was concerned, that footnote alone wouldn't have bothered him that much. It was the last sentence in the editorial's footnote that really bothered him, and it simply stated: "The nation's criminal justice system is broken. Forty percent of Americans who are incarcerated are blacks! People of color, particularly African Americans and Latinos, are unfairly targeted by the police..."

Mjomba's initial reaction was that the periodical had made a mistake. He could not immediately bring himself to accept that such a thing could be happening in America! These were things that belonged in an apartheid regime like the one in South Africa, not in a western democracy; and certainly not one that boasted that it was the leader of the Free World.

It took Mjomba a while to take it all in. And he couldn't resist asking himself if there indeed was anything like

"American Exceptionalism" - or "Exceptionalism" at all for that matter! He felt numb and helpless, as he recalled the words that had been attributed to the Pontiff of Rome around that same time albeit in a different context: "Those responsible will have to answer before God…"

Clearly, therefore, regardless as to whether exceptionalism merely existed in people's imagination and was accordingly a myth or whether it was something that did in fact exist objectively and was real, whatever "it" was, it came with built-in self-destructive properties, and the list was long: the exceptional people's reluctance to look themselves in the eye and admit that some egregious things actually went on unnoticed in their midst - things that would not be expected of a self-described "exceptional" nation; the propensity of the exceptional nation for "overreach" in order to prove that it was also an indispensable nation; the inability of the nationals of the exceptional nation to see that, in the final analysis, they were actually a lot like everyone else excepting for their fixation with the notion that they were "exceptional"; the tendency (as one commentator aptly put it) to exaggerate differences and to conveniently overlook similarities between themselves and the rest of humankind; the inability to see that their claim to being "exceptional" and essentially better than others actually entailed a character flaw and a vice; the reluctance to acknowledge the unique strengths of rival nations however obvious; the stubborn refusal of the exceptional nation to accept that it too had limitations like any other nation, or the fact that it too was subject to the provisions of international law *in toto*; and the stubborn refusal to acknowledge that when such melodramas unfolded and things started to unravel, they invariably did so ignominiously.

28

There was also this inability of the characters who were presiding over the nation they loved to present as exceptionally exceptional and indispensable to the survival of the world to take a leaf from history; their inability to see and admit that many characters exactly like them at some point in history strutted proudly on the world stage, revelling in group think and self-deception, and believing that their empires were going to last for ever, but were now long gone and forgotten; and the inability to understand that this was the fate that awaited them as well!

And finally there was always this certainty that the gods themselves were - nay had to be - on the side of the self-proclaimed exceptional nation. In the case of the Romans, the divine support did not pan out exactly as expected in the end despite the commitment to expand the "Holy Roman Empire" to the ends of the earth; and also despite the fact that Romans were intensely religious to the point that the Roman emperors and even the proconsuls were regarded not merely as "godsend" to the citizens of the Roman Republic but "divine" as well.

Mjomba was a realist, and reminded himself that he would have been surprised if those who trumpeted American Exceptionalism for instance acted differently from their counterparts in Roman times. The self-destructive properties of "Exceptionalism" were rooted in human nature. The defenders of exceptionalism regardless of its mould or brand were all human; and it was only natural for Romans, Britons, Germans, and others who had carried that banner at one time or another - who thought it was now their turn to be its bearer - to pull the wool over their eyes so they would remain focused on their ambitious goal, and to pretend that their exceptionalism was going to be an exception to the rule.

Mjomba supposed that it was quite natural, as the belief that a nation was exceptional and indispensable took hold and that nation started moving in full gear to transform the rest of the world in its own image and likeness, for folks to stop calculating the risks of their unilateral actions - until it was too late!

Mjomba worried that, in an era that had seen the emergence of so many nuclear-armed nations, and in which the real prospect of mutual assured destruction of both attacker and defender in a nuclear conflagration, the era in which nations could proclaim themselves exceptional and merely end up with bloodied noses - or just vanish off the world scene entirely as happened to Gaius Julius Caesar Octavianus's (Emperor Augustus's) Roman Empire - was long gone.

Well, two millennia ago, the Redeemer of humans, a Deity, who by his very nature could do no wrong, had been "neutralized" by them. Mjomba noted that foretelling the impending destruction of the temple in Jerusalem and the approaching end of the world had allegedly been among the "misdeeds" He had committed! But Mjomba also noted that the Messiah (or "Son of Man" as He called Himself) had predicted the destruction of the temple and the end of the world almost in the same breath, and this according to all the synoptic gospels of Matthew, Mark, and Luke.

Some of the folks who heard the Nazarene predict the siege and fall of Jerusalem, and with it the destruction of the temple, were in fact still alive in the year of the Lord 70 (*Anno Domini LXX*) when that prophesy was fulfilled. Even though he was only four or five years old when the Nazarene was "eliminated", Joseph ben Matityahu who became known later as Titus Flavius Josephus, and whose historical works "The Jewish War" (c. 75) and "Antiquities of the Jews" (c. 94) attest to the biblical Jesus and as well to some of the evangelists and their New Testament accounts, was there in the thick of it. Himself a Jew, he not only had acted as a negotiator between the defenders of Jerusalem and the Romans during the siege of the city in which his own parents and first wife died, but had bequeathed to the world what was perhaps the most detailed and authoritative account of the fulfilment of that prophecy.

And it now came as a shock to Mjomba that it was looking like he himself along with his wife Jamila and their little son Ali were going to be witnesses to the fulfilment of the second part of the prophesy, namely the prediction concerning the "Abomination of Desolation standing where it should not be (let the reader understand)"!

Well, with the Holy See occupied by someone who hailed from Argentina (where the Atlantic Ocean and the Pacific Ocean met and a nation that even included parts of Antarctica), one could say that the "Gospel of the Kingdom had been preached in the whole world as a testimony to all the nations". And then, with earthquakes an almost everyday occurrence now, and the strangest plagues, like for instance the Zika virus that some said was the worst thing since the Bubonic plague, afflicting the world, it was looking more and more like the end of the world was imminent all right. There was of course no denying that there were already false Christs and false prophets galore in the goddamned blasted world; and they were seemingly capable of showing signs and wonders in order to lead the masses astray. Armageddon was alas all but inevitable, Mjomba had concluded; and he was now also resigned to the fact that he could not fight Fate.

According to him (Mjomba), the very worst thing that humans could attempt to do while they were still kicking was to turn on a Deity, and one that had gratuitously willed them into existence out of nothing at that, and try to consign Him to hell - as they indeed attempted to do two thousand years ago. They were, of course, doomed to fail. But, endowed with free will, try they nonetheless did.

Now, two thousand years later, it looked like His second prophesy concerning "Doomsday" was on the verge of being fulfilled as well. After causing the heavens and the earth to bounce into existence out of nothing, the Prime Mover (as Aristotle called Him) saw all the things that he had made, and pronounced them all very good. Contrary to what stupid humans thought, it wasn't Him who was now about to do something to trigger the Armageddon described by Daniel two thousand five hundred years ago, and again by John in his Apocalypse. It was the stupid humans themselves who were again about to do something horrible in fulfilment of those prophecies. Mjomba supposed that if humans were so bad as to condemn their Deliverer to a grisly death on Mt. Calvary, seeking out opportunities to go head to head and engage in something that leads to mutually assured destruction (MAD) was not just within the realm of possibilities; it seemed to be something that nations of the earth one and all were itching for - to deliberately and knowingly trigger human extinction!

And for sure, this time around, there was nothing that was going to stop them succeeding in triggering Armageddon. They had the means, and they were also free to choose to go ahead and do it or not do it. The choice was entirely theirs, and there was nothing that was going to stop them if they decided to do it! And, of course, since people everywhere generally got the governments they deserved and also deserved the governments they got, Mjomba thought it didn't really matter if the decision to go ahead and do it or not do it was the result of a referendum or was made by politicians or, as he preferred to call them "the charlatans who happened to be occupying the seat of power". He was prepared to hold everyone in the so-called exceptional nation that would finally trigger Armageddon equally blameworthy.

At one point, while chatting with Jamila, Mjomba had even gone on to suggest that were it not for some people imagining that they were exceptional, humans would co-exist in peace. Recalling stuff he had covered in his Philosophy class years earlier, he had made the argument that the earth's population would then be one happy family of "social animals" - exactly as Aristotle wrote in his *Politics*. And that was what humans effectively were, he pointed out, by virtue of sharing in the same human nature (or *esse* as Thomas Aquinas put it in his "*Summa Theologica*") even as they enjoyed each his/her own *exsistentia* ("existence").

But with Adam and Eve, the father and the mother of humankind (and naturally also the "fall guys" in the same way Judas became the natural "fall guy" for human perfidy), falling from grace even before they had any issue through the exercise of their God-given free will, it became natural (starting with Cain) for some humans to try and distinguish themselves from the rest by imagining that they were exceptional humans; and this was perfectly understandable. Mjomba had added that some, aiming to set themselves apart using religion, ended up promoting *religious monopoly* instead of *religious liberty* at the same time as they were pursuing their supposedly "God-ordained" exceptionalism.

Actually, all in all, this suited Mjomba quite fine. The eternal optimist, he took to reassuring himself, with regard to American Exceptionalism, that this was all the more reason for his son to celebrate it while it could be celebrated, and also

33

to enjoy the benefits thereof while they lasted. It didn't really matter at least for now if the landscape did not guarantee that his son was going to enjoy *all* the benefits of American Exceptionalism. And he was accordingly happy for his son Ali who of course *was* undoubtedly exceptional by virtue of being born in the land of the free and home of the brave.

More than at any time before, Mjomba was nonplussed that the Americans, with all their gadgetry, had failed in their attempt to pinpoint his wife's exact due date! It did not surprise him when, on their return to Africa, Musa's expected date of birth as forecast by the doctor at the Gorofani General Hospital also turned out to be wrong.

We at least learnt not to bank too much on doctors' forecasts, reflected Mjomba, slightly bemused. They might be founts of lifesaving knowledge, he told himself mentally; but their knowledge had proved deficient when it came to forecasting the birthdates of Ali and Musa at any rate!

Mjomba reflected ruefully that neither his wife nor himself seemed to have learnt from their experiences how to control their anxiety. Just as on the occasion of Musa's birth, Jamila was registered at Dr. Mambo's Clinic and at the Gorofani General Hospital as well for her prenatal care. He remembered vividly that he was the one who had insisted that she attend both clinics on the two occasions.

The idea that Jamila had been visiting two hospitals for the same thing now looked decidedly crazy. Still, the fact of the matter was that the cost of that crazy arrangement still amounted to a mere fraction of what a similar arrangement would have cost them if they had been in America which was easily the most expensive place on the globe to be born or to die. Even though Mjomba himself didn't believe it, lore had it that, in a move that was aimed at guaranteeing free universal primary education and free universal health care, Tanzania, under its policy of *Ujamaa* ("family hood" in Swahili) and with the help of a grant from the Swedes, had actually succeeded in constructing primary schools and health centres all across the nation, even in places where there were no roads!

What Mjomba knew for certain was that health care in Tanzania was the exact opposite of health care in America. It was cheap and within everyone's means. Tanzania was therefore also exceptional in that married couples could beget as many children as they wished without the risk of bankruptcy! And, miracle of all miracles, the treatment and care that Tanzanians received, whether in public hospitals or in private clinics, was first class!

Not unlike many of the supposedly moneyed city folk in the Tanzanian capital, Mjomba had a bias for the treatment that privately owned and managed clinics and health centers dispensed, and accordingly preferred them to the Government hospitals in spite of the added cost that went with it. Mjomba knew that the care and treatment provided by doctors at all hospitals and clinics in the country in the Tanzania of *Mwalimu* Julius Nyerere's time was first class; and this was regardless of whether the health facilities were publicly or privately managed. It was no a secret that doctors who worked at privately managed health centers also consulted at Government health facilities and vice versa; and the World Bank had not yet intervened to compel the Tanzania and other "developing" countries to switch to the *Via Americana* (American Way) to be eligible for its loans. The real problem was that Mjomba wasn't about to admit that he was a snob!
He now made a half-hearted mental attempt to justify his insistence that his wife see the doctors at both places and

abandoned it almost as soon as he had begun. As if in confirmation of the stupidity of his action in that regard, it suddenly dawned on him that Dr. Mambo had given February 26, three days away, as the expected date of delivery while, according to the doctor at the Gorofani General Hospital, the expected delivery date was February 29!

3. Folder with a Legend

Attired in a close fitting, lilac colored Kaunda suit and rocking gently in a swivel chair, Mjomba, who had already completed the formalities for taking a month's vacation - or "maternity" leave as he put it jokingly to his secretary - effective on the morrow, looked the typical up-and-coming young executive. Jerking himself to attention, he steered his medium-sized hulk the few inches it had strayed from the glass topped mahogany desk.

Mjomba's mind was still wandering as he turned to pore over the sizable mass of papers littering his desk; and it took the wail of the siren announcing the three o'clock shift at the docks to bring him to. Staring at the papers - all of them neatly typed on quarto sheets - he felt for the first time a sting of guilt, albeit only momentary, for having employed his secretary as well as office stationery in their preparation. The fact that the last batch had been typed and delivered to him only earlier that morning heightened his feelings of guilt.

The whine of the siren was at its highest pitch when the buzzer went off. With a practiced movement of the arm and a flourish, Mjomba picked up the telephone receiver and listened to Primrose's affected, almost lyrical, voice.

A typical "siren" and still single at twenty-seven, Mjomba's secretary apparently deemed it permissible whenever she addressed her young, dapper and genteel "overseas educated" boss on the intercom to "put on her charm". The language of the material she had typed for him lately had tended to be of a standard that put the proper appreciation of her boss's work beyond her general capabilities; but she had been content to regard it as her privilege to have been able to help in bringing his dream of becoming an illustrious author closer to reality.

Predictably, there had never been any doubt in her mind regarding the fact that Mjomba took delight in listening to her affected tones. While he enjoyed the treat all right, Mjomba had decided that it would serve him best in the long run if he gave the appearance of "tolerating" his secretary's behavior without either openly approving or disapproving.

When she had announced that a Mrs. Killian was on the line, Primrose deliberately took time to replace the speakerphone at her end, and was able in the process to catch the words "*mama Ali anaumwa vibaya sana...*" (Ali's mom is in labor).

Mjomba was on his legs when Mrs. Killian, who lived next door to the Mjombas on Msasani Peninsula rung off with a click. He felt an irresistible urge to take off running and was surprised that he remained stationary. His hands were instinctively groping about in his trouser pockets for his car's ignition keys at the same time as he was trying to figure out in his mind if there wasn't anything else of importance that he was about to forget behind in the rush.

It was then that his eyes alighted on the blue folder besides the papers strewn all over his desk. The folder had been cut to size and spotted a plain white sticker on its topside with the legend "THE PSYCHIC ROOTS OF A NUT".

In spite of his quickening pulse, Mjomba seemed in absolute control of his reflexes as he gathered up the typed pages and carefully shoved them into the folder. But it wasn't until he was half way through that he remembered! The car was at Ocean View Motor Garage and not expected to be ready until four in the afternoon.

Mjomba sat himself down heavily and dialled the extension of Office Services. Finding it engaged, he resolved to wait until the line was free. But before he could try the number a second time, he decided that it was crazy of him to expect to get a staff car at short notice from the "bunch" on the ninth floor! The idea crossed his mind that he would deserve to be damned if he put any reliance on the people of Office Services in an emergency.

He had the distinct feeling that these folks did not work for money. Since they certainly did not work for the sake of it, he wondered what it was they had on their minds every morning as they set out from their homes for the Trade Center. It suddenly struck him that there probably wasn't any need for the rush any way: the earliest due date was a clear three days off!

Stuffing the folder in a large manila envelope, Mjomba, his face expressionless, bade Primrose farewell and set off from the Trade Center. A bus ride to the Old Post Office and a stroll from there brought him to the Ocean View Motor garage in just under an hour's time. The car had in fact been waiting for him, having been attended to in double-quick time in deference to his entreaty when he checked it in earlier that day for the regular maintenance. The service manager apologized that he had not succeeded in locating genuine auto parts for overhauling his Ford's shock absorbers which, he emphasized, were in really bad shape; and he explained that he did not recommend using second hand or recycled auto parts for his "luxury" sedan.

The good news though was that Ford Motors (T) Ltd., the Ford dealer in Tanzania, had let the service manager know that a consignment had arrived at the Port, and was waiting to be cleared through Customs, an exercise they said might take a week or so. Miraculously, the Ford dealer had succeeded in persuading the *Benki Kuu* (Central Bank), which had a strict policy of doling out the country's scarce foreign exchange only for what the government deemed "essential imports", to finally, albeit reluctantly, approve its application to import the auto parts all the way from the United Kingdom. The bad news was that those Customs duties were going to price the auto parts well beyond the reach of most Tanzanians, the reason owning a car was reserved for the elite in these parts.

The good service manager, a Kalasinga or *"muhindi wa kilemba (turban) and thick beard"* whose parents had come from the then British India to East Africa to build the Uganda Railway or "Lunatic Express" as it was fondly referred to in the British press at the time, had attached, for the fifth consecutive time, a note to the Ford's repair bill advising that the shock absorber were (as he put it) "nearly gone". Mjomba would never forget how much fixing the Ford's shock absorbers had cost him the last time around, and he informed the Kalasinga through gritted teeth that he appreciated the information.

Before jumping into the driver's seat, he tossed the manila envelope into the back seat. As he steered the sedan into Umoja Wa Wanawake Way to head home, he could not fail to notice the improved performance brought on by the new tie rod ends and the wheel alignment. But, with the shock absorbers almost "gone", the ride was still noticeably bumpy; and it did not help that there were numerous patches in the "paved road" that in fact qualified it for a "gravel road". And the fact that Mjomba was in a "rush" to get to his destination didn't make things any better.

4. The Baby Oil

Mjomba had already sped past the Selemani Stores on the final homeward stretch when he remembered the Baby Oil!

He made a U-turn at the Kaunda/Msasani Road junction and was racing back towards the Selemani Stores when his mind was suddenly besieged with images of the assortment of baby items he and Jamila had been "showered" with by neighbors in El Camino Village in the United States on the occasion of Ali's birth. He became simultaneously aware of a vein in his right cheek twitching at an accelerating pace, triggered no doubt by the flood of images. He had been dismayed on at least one other occasion - the occasion of Musa's birth two years earlier - that baby showers as an institution did not figure in either his or Jamila's tribal customs!

Mjomba closed his eyes briefly as if in acknowledgement of the immutability of that situation, opening them just in time to avoid a head-on collision with an approaching vehicle on the narrow two-way street. But there was no way he could stop his mind from wandering now!

Mjomba felt a lump in his throat as he turned to consider the results of his efforts of the past several days that were intended to make up for what the couple now missed. Armed with a list of baby items prepared by Jamila and a not-too-adequate purse, he had done the rounds of shops in the teaming Tanzania capital, buying an item here and noting the price of another there. Heralding the seasonal rains, the heat and the accompanying humidity had also been quite unbearable and inhibiting. Plagued with this combination of

41

troubles, the results of Mjomba's efforts had been decidedly poor as a consequence.

While a newborn could do without such things as coats and pants in the less than friendly weather of the "Heaven of Peace" in the couple's view in the couple's view, they considered Baby Oil indispensable - a veritable soothing balm in the midst of Dar es Salaam's nigh permanent heat wave. The Selemani Stores did not have Baby Oil in stock, and the revelation left Mjomba feeling like a dumbbell.

If you missed an item at the Selemani Stores for which they were stockists, it was usually a safe bet that the whole town had run out of it. The very idea now made him feel exasperated and really steamed up. The previous day the Asian shop attendant had shaken her head from side to side and advised her eager customer to "make another try tomorrow". The sight of the same attendant shaking her head in her accustomed manner caused him to splutter on his way out: "What the heck...shortages! As if it wasn't bad enough paying a fortune when something happened to be available!"

Mjomba, of course, knew that the solution to the shortages wasn't an easy one. While some blamed the shortages on *Ujamaa*, the humanist vision that defined the socialism the East African country had adopted, Mjomba was inclined to think that it was Tanzania's unequivocal support for the Anti-Apartheid struggle in South Africa that was to blame, and specifically the decision of the country's leadership to involve the Chinese in the construction of the Tanzania-Zambia Railway.

Mjomba had no doubt that the shortages were common place now first of all because the Tanzanians had to find ways to reimburse the Chinese for the cost of laying the beginnings of what Mwalimu Nyerere and other Pan-Africanist leaders

42

hoped was going to be a transformational TransAfrica railroad track, much like America's first Transcontinental Railroad (or the "Pacific Railroad" as it was also known); and, secondly, because of the Cold War that was now at its height between the capitalist West (and their support for the Apartheid regime under the guise of the policy of "constructive engagement" so-called) and the socialist East.

With its peculiar brand of "African" Socialism or *Ujamaa*, Tanzania with *Mwalimu* (Teacher) Julius Kambarage Nyerere, and soon to be declared *Servus Dei* (Servant of God) and Venerable by the Vatican, at the helm, was deemed by the West to have aligned itself with the East in that war, and it had therefore become fair game for the West to inflict as much damage as possible on the economy of that erstwhile Chinese ally, if only as an example to other countries on the African continent. Politics was a dirty game.

Talking about the Cold War, after all he had heard about the long-simmering tensions between the Communist East and the Capitalist West that some described as "the ultimate love-hate relationship" and that had the rest of the world on edge for so long, with many fearing that the Third World War was just around the corner, Mjomba could never have imagined that one could find Chinese and Russian enclaves in the Western Hemisphere, let alone in America, that "bastion and also guardian of freedom and democracy" and "custodian of the new world order".

Mjomba was therefore pleasantly surprised to find, on his arrival on the American West Coast for his studies, not only that "Frisco" (as the City by the Bay was referred to by tourists) was home to the biggest Chinatown outside of Asia but that it was by no means the only big Chinatown in North

America! And it wasn't as if the Chinese were there in hiding either.

He was only a couple of weeks into his studies at the Bay Area Institute of Technology when, lo and behold, the impending Chinese New Year became the talk of town. And it became obvious to the young couple from the Dark Continent that everyone in the environs of that "Baghdad by the Bay" (as San Francisco was also known), regardless of his or her station, was preparing to usher in the "Year of the Monkey" with gusto.

Mjomba and Jamila had both heard about the Rio Carnival, the Toronto Caribbean Carnival also known as Caribana, and others. But as the Chinese New Year (or "Lunar Year" as the Chinese themselves preferred to call it) rolled in, the youthful couple from the Dark Continent immediately saw that as far as carnivals went, this one was going to be a really tough act to follow!

Chinese New Year Parade was a glittering display of pageantry that made everyone who was not an active participant stop to look, and it came complete with elaborate floats, Chinese folk dancers, stilt walkers, acrobats, marching bands, lion dancers and above all the enthralling Dragon dance itself! The three hundred foot-long Golden Dragon itself was a spectacle that had to be seen - and enjoyed - to be believed! Continuing late into the night, everyone seemed to agree that this had to be the grandest nighttime illuminated parade in North America if not in the entire world!

"This is just ridiculous" Mjomba had exclaimed, as he and Jamila and their friends watched the pageantry of the Chinese New Year Parade from their vantage point at the intersection of Grant Avenue and Pacific Street. The joyous revelry was so infectious, they found themselves joining the

44

hundreds of thousands of revellers, and waltzing away into the night, to usher in the Year of the Monkey.

He was shocked that there was so much hypocrisy in the world! So, the Americans and their Western allies were busy trumpeting the narrative that Communists were evil at the same time as they were indulging in pleasures of the East - the "Mysterious East" to borrow James Bond's expression! It did not surprise Mjomba when he subsequently learnt that there were more than twenty towns in America called "Moscow" along with thousands upon thousands of Chinese gourmet restaurants that catered to the American palate. Or that it was China - yes China - that had been tapped to construct the new San Francisco - Oakland Bay Bridge, the largest self-anchored suspension bridge in the world that is billed as quakeproof and designed to withstand the Big One!

Seeing the effect of politics on his ability to discharge his responsibilities to his family, Mjomba thought that nations could not sink any lower than that as they engaged in their dirty political games.

In spite of his woes, Mjomba made it home in time to take Jamila to hospital. In the general anxiety, everyone there had ignored Musa and Ali. They were in the lounge by themselves, their attention riveted to a solitary bag stuffed with baby things, some of them left-overs from Musa's epoch as a nursling.

He bounded past them into the hallway leading to the master bedroom only to be met by his wife in the narrow passage. Waited on by womenfolk from the adjoining homes, Jamila had already taken a shower, and now donned her favourite maternity outfit - a light green pleated blouse worn over a brown spotted *khanga*.

45

Outside the apartment block minutes later, Jamila hesitated as her husband swung the Ford's doors open. She evidently knew about the condition of the sedan's shock absorbers, as also did Mrs. Killian

At the latter's behest, the hospital bound retinue piled into her Volkswagen - Jamila who did so cautiously whilst cradling her tummy, Mjomba, Musa, Ali, Mrs. Killian herself and Priscilla, her three-year-old daughter. Mrs. Killian, who was also with child - and whose own tummy made her look eight rather than five months pregnant - had stopped driving as a precaution, and easily prevailed on Mjomba to take the wheel.

They made it to Dr. Mambo's Maternity Clinic with considerable aplomb, thanks to the performance the kids put up along the way. His wife's labor pains notwithstanding, Mjomba could not resist the laughter each time one of them pointed to the bulging tummy of either Mrs. Killian or his wife and, with childlike simplicity as well as grief-stricken voice, intoned: "Painful?"

When they had filed out of the *Beetle*, Ali, ebullient as ever, led the column to the hospital's reception desk, followed by Mrs. Killian who had Jamila in tow. Mjomba brought up the rear with Musa and Priscilla swinging under his arms. As they trooped in, two smiling nurses surrounded Mrs. Killian and began to steer her towards a wheelchair! Watching the scene from the back of the queue, Mjomba could not help laughing - indeed not even his wife was able not to laugh.

The place, a favourite haunt for patients with middle class incomes, was buzzing with activity. Doctors' paths crisscrossed, and nurses, bursting with mysterious enthusiasm, darted here and there. As soon as several of their number laid their hands on Jamila, they whisked her away into the examination room and out of sight.

About fifteen minutes or so after his abrupt and all too sudden separation from his wife, Mjomba, anxiety written all over his face, busied himself with the children in an endeavour to hide his own strangely sharp feelings of expectancy. Dr. Rachel, Jamila's regular doctor, spied him and made a beeline for him.

"Your wife is almost ready now," she whispered in his ear.

"Is it a boy or girl?" Mjomba asked, quite excited. He was convinced he had noticed a reassuring smile flash in the Semitic, decidedly charming, oval face.

"Jamila is almost ready to start delivering the baby," volunteered Mrs. Killian in explanation. She had overheard the exchange and immediately decided that she stood considerably less chance of being misunderstood by the distracted Mjomba than did the doctor, who also happened to be the one she herself was seeing for her prenatal care.

The doctor's reassuring smile was still playing on her face and the laughter restrained as she said: "Next time, make it to the hospital a little bit earlier or it might be in the taxi!"

The doctor's warning caused memories of a scene to which Mjomba had been a witness scarcely three weeks before to come tumbling back into his mind. He had volunteered a lift to a neighbour who was delivering breakfast to a patient at a Health Center on the other side of town, and was waiting by entrance to the hospital's emergency department for the good lady to emerge from the wards, when a taxi cab pulled up next to his battered Ford with its complement of two female passengers and a worried looking male passenger roughly his own age. The cab driver had hardly brought his weather-

47

beaten Peugeot 403 to a standstill when he leapt out and scrambled for the reception desk. But by the time he emerged from the building with a nursing sister close on his heels, the number of his passengers had grown to four!

It had been a painful sight that met Mjomba's eyes as he stood helplessly by and watched the sister sever the umbilical cord joining mother and baby using what looked like a common pair of scissors right there in the taxi. Recalling the incident, he found himself experiencing the same sharp feelings of anger and anxiety for the child that the sight of the naked and crying newborn being rushed up the hospital's staircase in a nurse's arms had evoked in him. It seemed an appropriate time to relate the incident; but Dr. Rachel was gone before Mjomba could engage her in further dialogue.

5. Kunta Kintu

Mjomba had a mind to maintain vigil at the hospital for at least those crucial hours of the count down to the baby's birth. On the way home, therefore, he called on in-laws who lived along his route to request help for little Musa and his brother Ali. The seven o'clock news was being announced on the Broadcasting Service when, leaving the children in the competent hands of Fatuma, a cousin of Jamila's and a favourite with the kids, he jumped into the Ford and headed for Dr. Mambo's Clinic heart pounding.

Jamila and her hubby openly dreaded childbirth by C-section despite the fact that it probably saved Ali's life at birth. The team of distinguished doctors at the BAIT Medical Center in California had initially let Jamila natural delivery. The baby's head had started to appear when readings on the battery of scientific instruments there by the bedside began to signal danger with respect to the baby's condition. The readings, which had already established the child's gender, had been none-too-encouraging for some time—a reflection on the unprecedented level of hypertension to which Jamila was an unfortunate victim. The doctors had decided to transfer her to the operating table right there and then.

Mjomba had been informed days in advance of his wife's confinement at the Medical Center that he not only was free to attend the delivery but could also photograph the proceedings if he so wished. Predictably it had taken Jamila some persuading to agree to be photographed while giving birth, but as usual she had yielded to her husband's entreaties and consented to his proposal to record the different stages of their child's development on film starting right from he moment of

49

his birth. The couple already owned a variant of the famous Polaroid Land camera that Mjomba had bought as a present for his wife at Orly Airport during their stop-over in Paris on their San Francisco bound flight a couple of months earlier.

But Mjomba was so consumed by the idea of recording the child's history he even deemed it worthwhile to invest in a reasonably good movie camera. In that way they would both be able to sit back in their old age and view daylong movies featuring their kid instead of having to flip through hundreds of still photos! He had accordingly proceeded to the Emporium downtown and procured a Kodak XL 360 Super 8 Movie Camera, and a Kodak MovieDeck 435 Projector to go with it, charging the cost against his Triple "E" Account which he opened for the purpose at the Emporium.

The knowledge that he could not be permitted inside the theatre in the event of his wife's delivery by a caesarean section had laid the ground for Mjomba's somewhat irrational aversion for that form of childbirth. In the course of time, the disappointed Mjomba had gradually come to lose track of the fact that his exam schedule had in any case already precluded him from picture taking; and his pathological dislike for C-sections had become coupled with his natural dread for bloodletting incisions in general to make it the last thing he could wish for his wife.

Jamila, for her part, had had a longstanding dread for caesarean operations. Her mother had once said within her hearing that a woman could not very safely bear a second child if she had her first by caesarean. The old lady's words had had a lasting effect on the then immature and highly impressionable Jamila.

To the couple's immense relief, despite the C-section that Jamila had had for Ali's birth, she gave birth to Musa two years later through natural and uncomplicated delivery. On the present occasion, the doctors had said that the odds against a caesarean outweighed those against a trouble free natural delivery. In spite of the assurances, the couple's anxiety had remained boundless. Not even the growing excitement, as the days of Jamila's confinement wore on, had seemed able to affect the gloom that characterised everything they did.

All that notwithstanding, Mjomba's mind, as he sauntered casually into the now desolate reception hall of Dr. Mambo's Maternity Clinic had somehow already ruled out the prospects for a caesarean. At that juncture he merely expected a nurse to emerge from one of the corridors and overwhelm him with the news that his wife had delivered a baby, preferably a girl this time, and that both mother and child were doing fine.

He met with unexpected disappointment, though for a different reason. The nurse, who approached, as he stood there erect in the center of the hall, belonged to a new shift; and her gaze told him even before she spoke that he looked very much like an intruder. It also occurred to him just then that visiting hours for the day had been over for sometime now!

The nurse allowed the inevitable smile to form on her face as she confronted him. "Evening. What can I do for you, Sir?"

Mjomba faltered repeatedly as he struggled to explain himself. He had hardly concluded when she vanished into a corridor only to reappear shortly afterward. *"Bado...bado kidogo"* (not yet). With just a hint of sympathy in her voice, she added: "Could take another one or two hours!"

"Fine...I will call later," he said, his manner businesslike. As he said so, he turned and set out purposelessly down the darkened street. His throat was scorched and he felt badly in need of a drink. But, on a strange impulse, he fought to keep thoughts relating to his own comfort from his head. Summoning all his willpower, he endeavored to resist the wonderings of his faculties of the intellect and the imagination to considerations pertaining to the welfare of Jamila and nothing else! Like a mystic contemplating the sufferings of a divinity, he even attempted putting himself mentally in his wife's position and enduring the labor pains along with her! But the result, perhaps predictably, was total confusion.

He regained control of himself presently however and, turning left into India Street, quickened his steps in the direction of the Solar Clock. He was hoping, as he approached Independence Avenue, that he could kill time window-shopping along the famous tree lined thoroughfare.

Mjomba found that he was the only one dawdling about on the street. It was then that, bewildered and confused as ever, he considered downing a beer or two at the rooftop Moonlite Bar down the road. The red and blue lights of the establishment cast an enigmatic pall over the street and its surroundings as he approached.

Mjomba climbed wearily to the top of the dingy staircase. The bar chatter, a mere distant hum of voices when he began the ascent, was now a thunderous drone that invaded his ears from all sides. Intending to pause only briefly in front of the swing doors before gaining entrance, he took in his breath and readied to brush them aside with his arms. He even allowed himself the indulgence of letting his imagination run ahead of him, so that he now already saw himself occupying a high stool at the bar, and a suitably cold, if unlabeled, bottle of Kilimanjaro Premium Lager and a glass before him. He had filled the glass – in his mind – and was all but feeling the cold beer begin to trickle down his parched throat when he snapped out of his doldrums.

Regaining his presence in front of the swing doors of the bar, he could not help wondering why the thought had not crossed his mind earlier! How on earth could he possibly be thinking of revelling in booze, and on an empty stomach at that, just as his beloved Jamila was in labor!

Mjomba did not stop to consider the possibility of treating himself to a Fanta or a Coke, both of which were a rarity at drinking places and unlikely to be in stock at the Moonlite any way. Turning away from the hubbub, he made straight for the Ford. Jumping in, he adjusted the reclining angle of the driver's seat, lowering it to its extremity. He eased himself into it, determined as ever to complete his vigil as planned.

It was forty minutes or so later when Mjomba, blinking wearily and looking thoroughly flustered, once more sauntered into the Maternity Clinic's reception hall. Several nurses, including the one who had interviewed him earlier, were relaxing on a bench. They all seemed to stare at him with knowing look, but it was their colleague who spoke.

"Mr. Mjomba?" Her voice and face were familiar enough and her manner polite if cautious.

A casual glance at the girls, and the speaker in particular, and he became convinced that he had been the subject of their chatter shortly, if not immediately, before he made his reappearance. Staring back at them, he imagined their countenances, so prim and undemeaning now, enveloped in giggles and he thought: "How pert of them!"

Aloud, Mjomba said, "Yes"; and waited for the news he already knew would not be forthcoming.

"I'm sorry" the nurse went on after a pause; but we don't have any news for you yet. In fact, as it is already pretty late…"

"I know, I know," Mjomba cut in. With full anticipation of what she had been about to say, he continued: "I think I will be better off waiting at home."

"You want us to telephone you if there is news?" she piped in his general direction. Her tone was rhetorical and she seemed to expect no more than a nod. But Mjomba raised his voice and began thanking her profusely for the idea.

"Oh, we will be glad to do that" the nurse said cheerily, her mates nodding approval the while. Another nurse consulted a chart she took from a shelf and read out Mjomba's residential telephone number inquiringly.

"That's it, that's it", he said with a wan smile.

Before retracing his steps to where he had parked his auto, he turned to the first nurse and, wringing his hands, said: "*Nitashukuru saana*" (I'll be much obliged).

The hands of Jamila's Omega watch which Mjomba had borrowed indicated 9.45 p.m. as he started the car's engine to drive away. He half expected to find a message at home instructing him to head back to the Clinic on arrival, but none had been received.

The kids were comfortably in bed. Fatuma had laid out his dinner on the table, which he left untouched for lack of appetite. He took a cold shower instead, after which he selected a settee by the telephone, tuned his Satellite receiver into the Voice of America and settled back to listen to the African Panorama Show.

As he recalled later, a male announcer on the "show" had give the time as 10.30 p.m. Then a sprightly female voice had come on the air to announce: "Tis request Time!"

Apparently weariness had overcome him in the minutes that followed, sending him into a deep slumber. For beyond that, his mind registered nothing - apart, that is, from the dream.

When the telephone rang, the fifteen-minute programme was still continuing. But in that short space of time, Mjomba had not only traveled in his dream to far away California and back, but he had also made it to the nearby Gorofani General Hospital and back, the places of birth of Ali and Musa respectively.

At the BAIT Medical Center off the panoramic Highway One, Mjomba found himself gazing through a glass partition at his day-old son. Freshly circumcised and naked, poor little Ali had his tiny leg held apart to allow the bulb's heat to dry the wound. And now he whimpered ever so piteously as if to say that no more and no less than the return of his foreskin could persuade him to make a truce with the world!

The only one of African stock among the nursery's occupants on the day in question, Ali was possessed of a hue that made him appear no different nonetheless from his "white", "red" and "yellow" comrades. He was recognizable only by the nameplate that was pinned to his crib and his wonderfully rich crop of hair!

Closer home at the Gorofani General Hospital where Mjomba was transported in his sleep for the final leg of his phenomenal trip, he had slipped into the nursery disguised as his wife Jamila, so he could take a stealth look at the day old Musa.

Mjomba was shocked to discover that two and some cases three infants were being made to share a crib! But before he could recover from his shock or locate the boy in the crowd of the nursery's wailing inmates, the plot was uncovered. The guard, a wretched looking old man who had pretended to be fast asleep, had in fact been awake and quite alert. But, apparently a deaf mute, he proved quite impervious to the intruder's pleas and even offer of bribes, and proceeded to set off the alarm!

Even before the old guard's emasculated hands had found a proper grip on the mechanism's lever, there was a pealing sound not unlike that of a fire alarm. The sound promptly merged with the telephone's muffled purr as Mjomba, his forehead ringed with beads of sweat, awoke.

If the anxiety precipitated by the neighbor's telephone call that afternoon and the exhaustion from the subsequent events had dulled the expectant young father's mental faculties, the events of the dream, so nightmarish and livid, had tended to sharpen them. But Mjomba's wits were still a shade blunted as he stirred to answer the telephone. His bruised nerves were screaming for more relaxation, and it was not until he heard the faintly familiar voice of a girl talking that he completely awoke to reality, which now burst in on him like a clap of thunder.

Even so, when the nurse's voice came crackling through the earpiece, with the new that his wife had given birth to a baby boy, the couple's third, it all sounded like another dream to the awakening man. The nurse said he weighed seven pounds - a giant of a baby, Mjomba thought, considering his mother's size.

The nurse had added: "A beautiful, chocolate colored little thing with an ample tuft of negroid hair on his dome!"

As with Ali and Musa, the color of the new arrival's skin apparently took after their mom's, a ravishing bronze beauty herself. The clear tone of Jamila's skin combined with the classic dimensions of her head, body, and legs and the

56

tantalizing natural grace she exuded to make her a veritable lily in Mjomba's life. But, strangely, it was upon a black and white photograph he acquired during his courtship of the daughter of a Hajji that Mjomba frequently gazed to keep himself reminded of his "lily flower"!

To his artistic mind, the abstractness of a black and white portrait of his darling Jamila, because it left more to the imagination, was more preferable to the brightness of a colored portrait. Mjomba fancied the picture of his then smiling bride-to-be so much that he continued with the habit of carrying with him the old picture, tucked away inside the covers of a notebook, everywhere he went long after they had been wedded.

Standing there shouting excitedly into the telephone, Mjomba scarcely noticed the figure of Fatuma who had been aroused from her sleep by the commotion and now looked on from the passageway, her complexion wrapped up in glee. A strange elation took hold of her when she noticed that his gaze trained on a faded but still expressive black and white photograph of her aunt.

Setting down the receiver, Mjomba nearly ran into Fatuma. But he realised almost at once that the Ford's ignition keys were in his trouser pocket and made and an about-turn that prevented a collision left the girl dazed all the same. With gestured had signals and muttered words that fell far short of a comprehensible manner of speech, he attempted as he backed out of the bungalow to direct her to close the door after him. He bolted for the garage door before he could finish.

The pain and pangs of childhood behind her, Jamila was nestled contentedly in the trim hospital bed and sipping tea to quell her rising desire for food when her husband came swaying into the recovery room. Mjomba could see that she was thrilled and utterly mirthful, a complete contrast to her appearance early that morning as he was readying to head out to work.

In reply to his "Hurray!" she plunged into a vivid description of the ordeal she had been through only minutes before—how she had "pushed and pushed" and come close to giving up in her exhaustion! She had scarcely finished when he too began to describe how he had kept vigil and how he had come close to abandoning it in despair!

When he had finished, Jamila revealed that the baby had really started to come as her husband took off in their battered Ford less than an hour earlier! She not only had overheard the conversations in the reception hall but could tell when he drove off because the Ford's exhaust pipe did not have a muffler.

Their chatter, seemingly endless, did not appear as if it was about to bore them in any way. They continued to vie with each other in recalling anecdotes from the day's huge store of events. Mjomba, bubbling with joy, had all but forgotten about the other hero of the day in the course of the chatter. But now, as the nurse who had broken the good news to him over the telephone appeared in the doorway a small bundle balanced between her arms, the atmosphere in the room changed visibly.

Gingerly, he took the "bundle" in his own arms and stared down at the pink, round face. Still wrapped up in his swaddling clothes, the newborn babe looked like an angel and far from being battle scarred, despite his gruelling and traumatic entry into the world.

The nurse watched as Mjomba turned to his wife and, eyebrows upraised, said half in jest: "Love, one more,

58

perhaps-not-so-tough task this time for you. Will you choose the name by which this young chap shall be known?"

"Kunta!" The syllables came automatically from her lips and for a fleeting moment appeared to hold Mjomba dumbfounded. The previously garrulous World Trade Center executive made no effort to hide his surprise.

The nurse flexed the muscles of her well-rounded curves and brushed away imaginary dust from her satiny white skirt, an eager expression on her comely face.

"Kunta" had sounded faintly familiar to Mjomba; and, like so many things about which one has only a partial recollection, the defied association with every object his groping mind resurrected and remained a mere sound with no apparent meaning to it.

"Honey" Mjomba said finally his mind still swimming in the world of imagery; "If I had been the one searching for a name for the baby and had come across this one, my choice would have been no different!"

The nurse, who had held her breath at the sound of Mjomba's voice, emptied her lungs of the stale air with an audible hiss when he finished talking. Visibly relieved, she now stood relaxed once more. She tuned a rare, totally fond look full upon him concurrently. Jamila's long eyelashes meanwhile flickered up and down in quick succession as she shed imaginary tears of joy!

Mjomba blushed and felt rather awkward in the silence that followed his meaningless utterance. He hardly felt relieved when his wife, eyes misty and heart-beat racing, rested her hand on his lap and, her gaze intent on him, said: "Darling, you must find Kunta a middle name so he will be just like his buddies!"

Mjomba felt a lump suddenly form in his throat and breathing became difficult as he tried to think of a name - any well sounding name - only to find himself stuck! Jamila meanwhile edged closer to her husband so that their cheeks all but touched. There was at that time, however, nothing that Mjomba would have wanted more than to be miles away from his wife!

Severely embarrassed, Mjomba was on the verge of turning to the pretty nurse for help when, suddenly, the single word he had been trying to pin down in his mind's innermost recesses materialised from out yonder and settled on the edge of his mind. To his weary mind, the soft white LED 40-watt bulb lighting up his wife's recovery room - had it been lighting up his inner sanctum - might as well have been replaced by the sun itself in that fraction of a second as the word "ROOTS" formed in his thought processes.

The unbroken silence persisted for another uneasy second. Then it was promptly shattered as Mjomba announced triumphantly: "Kintu…Kunta Kintu Mjomba! That is what he is going to be called!"

Aside and out of earshot, Mjomba mumbled: "Kunta Kintu Mjomba…they do rhyme after all! Kunta Kintu Mjomba…"

Jamila's face registered puzzlement; and, as if in sympathy, the dimples that had hitherto played on the nurse's cheek also vanished.

"O.K.! Honey" said Mjomba, brightening up. "I guess I cannot keep the secret to myself any longer…"

"Secret! What secret?" Jamila said methodically. The nurse shared her quizzical expression.

"Guess what! 'Tis you yourself who has lead me to it with your very appropriate choice of name for this guy! Over the past nine months, I've been engaged in writing a book…"

"A book? You don't say!" intoned Jamila, a look of disbelief in her eyes.

"Yes, and wait - it is going to be quite a book! T'will be dedicated to you and the children. It is designed, naturally, to be a best seller…"

"Best seller!" she echoed, cutting him short.

"Yes. It'll top the best seller lists." Mjomba's voice was vibrant and a shade emphatic.

"And …here - just listen to the title: *The Psychic Roots of a Nut!*" he added, his gaze transfixed to a dot in the ceiling. "'Tis laden with stuff every literate person just has to know! It is about madmen, but it'll appeal likewise to ordinary folk like us here struggling to stay on the rails…"

As Jamila and the nurse broke out into hearty laughter, he continued: "I predict that Kintu, the book's hero, will become an even greater celebrity than Kunta!"

Jamila recovered from her laughter in time to say: "What is all this nonsense, Ibrahim?"

In response, her husband snapped his fingers. "Hey, hold it!" he said, half shouting. "I think I've got the manuscript in the car!"

Mjomba scrambled off the side of the bed and, thrusting the little "bundle" he held into the nurse's waiting arms, scampered off towards the parking lot. The laughter was mildly restrained when he whizzed back into the room second later flourishing a small blue bulging with neatly typed pages.

"Here it is" Mjomba said, breathless. "You see, not many books have been written about nutcases, leave alone the mental roots of nuts…"

61

"Darling" said Jamila, an expression of obviously contrived earnestness enveloping her well-rounded ebony face; "Are you sure you re not going haywire yourself?"

When she saw that her husband remained unmoved, she feigned an exaggerated appearance of despair and cast an awkward glance in the nurse's direction.

When Jamila and the nurse, the latter's deep-set eyes clouding with an all too noticeable and patently effusive lustre, stopped giggling, he pursued: "The narrative is fairly adequate as it stands now. I still have to find a publisher; but even so I do not expect they will edit away very much..."

"Now you are talking!" Jamila interjected. "First get a publishing house to accept your manuscript for publication and stop counting the chicks before they hatched - or is it Jane here you are trying to impress?"

The nurse, whose participation in the proceedings had so far been confined to giggles and diffident eyewinks, interrupted herself imposed silence.

"Your husband has already won me over as his literary fan" she broke out in a soft, exquisitely mellow voice. Then, her eyes fastened on her newfound idol, she continued: "It sounds a very interesting book you are writing; and, although I am no great reader of novels, you can already be sure of at least one customer..."

The sound of the nurse's voice made Mjomba feel a good deal more relaxed following the burst of energy he had expended dashing to and fro to get the manuscript and his subsequent verbal exchange with Jamila. He took the opportunity afforded to take in the figure, which he suddenly found to be strikingly well proportioned and captivating. He did not wait for his newly found fan to finish.

"Not a bit of it, Jane" he chortled; "I can safely promise you a complimentary autographed copy." Dragging his gaze away from the large shadowy eyes, he added: "I can't even believe I have finally succeeded in pulling off something so…so ingenious! Until this moment, only my secretary knew I was preoccupied with the book project. I gave myself a deadline to accomplish the task as part of the fun, and all the time I had to keep Mama Ali here – well, Mama Kunta now – in the dark about what is probably my life's most important single achievement. I cannot recall the number of revision I made…"

In a voice shorn of all reticence now, the nurse cut him short: "Would you mid telling me what *The Psychic Roots of a Nut* is about, Sir?"

Black as coal and some ten years Jamila's junior, Jane's dark handsome features now loomed up in the young executive's mind as both a devastating contrast to his wife's and no small challenge. He was bugged by the fact that the nurse had looked just like any ordinary girl when she accosted him for the first time not long before.

The nurse's direct electrifying gaze and the mesmeric quality of the youthful, innocent sounding voice meanwhile left him only partially in control of his motions. He became conscious of a hitherto fettered spell being loosed upon him! In order to conceal the effect it was having on him, he backed to the edge of the bed and, clasping his sweating hands together, seated himself down by his wife's side.

Jamila nudged her husband in the side with a forefinger to draw his straying attention just as he was beginning uncertainly to proffer a condensed version of the material of his literary work.

Feeling a good steadier, Mjomba went on: "Born of parents who first converts to Christianity, Innocent Kintu sets out to observe the precepts he is taught strictly from the very beginning. He is determined to pursue the dictates of his faith to their logical conclusion - never mind that the tenets of the strange new religion are in apparent and fairly outrageous conflict with the traditional beliefs and customs of his people.

"For a time, he succeeds in fulfilling his heart's wish and is even regarded as his tribe's standard bearer. Then the unexpected occur - Kintu is taken mentally ill!

"Just as Innocent Kintu, a senior seminarist by now and a favored candidate for the priesthood, is sliding into insanity, one Moses Kwentindio, a fellow seminarian and a tribesman, also finds himself all of a sudden fighting to keep his own scruples and misgiving from driving him over the edge! The 'Rod' as he ha been nickname by his brethren, avoid a crushing depression only to land in a baffling triple dilemma. If his tribesman's brand of Christianity is the right one, then his own practice of religion, which (he supposes) is liberal and unpretentious in contract to the blind and almost impulsive spirituality of his 'brother in Christ', is ill-founded and sham! But his realization that Brother Innocent and himself could still both be fakes leaves him in a trap.

"Thus, unless and until he succeeds in resolving the mystery surrounding Brother Innocent's behaviour, there may well be little likelihood that he will ever fully realize his own identity in the mystifying circumstances of the New World!

"It is this equally strange set of circumstances which prepares the ground for a giant leap for science - the discovery by Brother Moses of Theory 'R'! That theory not only solves the mystery of Brother Innocent's malady, but also helps Psychiatry turn a new leaf!"

At the end of the narration, all three, oblivious of their problems at the start, burst into mirthful unrestrained laughter. Mjomba's laughter fizzled out presently, and he intoned even as the others struggled to bring their spasms of laughter under control: "But there is a catch! Moses Kwentindio, the Rod, is me. The true life 'Innocent' is another story altogether. The perfect madman who would normally exist only in theory…he is entirely my creation. A one-faced character, incapable by definition of leading a double life; and he lives up to his reputation…"

Mjomba waited for the wail of laughter to recede before he said: "Innocent Kintu's psychiatrist, Dr. Claus Gringo - he features elsewhere in the book a Dr. Schizof Quack - had a secretary…a quadroon! Jane, do I need to say the rest?"

The fresh spurts of laughter petered out only to become thunderous once more as he added: "I'm sure you already recognize it - the old story of the scramble for Africa! It started off as a scramble for Africa's wealth; then it became a scramble for our bodies with slavery. The advent of the churches turned it into a scramble for our souls!"

They were still jittery with laughter when the drone of bells, as a distant clock struck midnight, brought them to attention. It was also just then that little Kunta Kintu Mjomba lost his temper for no apparent reason and flew into a violent explosive rage. He began flaying about with his tiny but tight fisted hands in an apparent effort to connect to Jane's head! He tried to kick the sides of his captor but only caused his unpractised legs to become entangled in the web of the swaddling bands enfolding him.

As if determined to exercise his autonomy and personal freedom, he also began to scream in his squeaky voice, which was not unlike a kitten's. Finally, defeated, the nurse bid the couple good morning, and reluctantly retreated with her charge into the sanctuary of the nursery.

As soon as he was left alone with Jamila, the senior Mjomba kissed his wife on the cheek before carefully dropping the folder in her lap.

"Put it away until tomorrow, Honey" he said, turning his own cheek. "You need all your rest as of now - and, besides, my book is really meant to be read in perfect peace by the fireside!"

Jamila felt well enough to go home the next day. There was, moreover, nothing she wished for so much as to be joined to her family and to be able to share her joy with her neighbours, relatives an friends in the snug comfort of her home. She was therefore heavily disappointed when Dr. Rachel, doing the rounds at dawn herself, insisted on detaining her for at least another twenty-four hours in a different room.

In the wake of the doctor's departure, she was disconsolate, and all the more so for want of something active to do. As always happened at such times, she also felt irritable; but, rather strangely, it was her husband, not her condition or Dr. Rachel, who loomed up in her mind as the apparent cause of her misery! She ate her breakfast, consisting of scrambled eggs on toast, bacon and black coffee in sullen silence. Even as she was being transferred to her new room and a new bed not long afterwards, her charm and good looks were overshadowed by her melancholy.

About an hour later, she was all but resigned to her gloom when the blue folder on a stool by her bedside caught her gaze. The ordeal of the previous day and everything else that had happened, including her husband's late night visit - and the manuscript - had all gone of out her mind, wiped out by her uninterrupted five hour slumber and the morning's events. But now everything came tumbling back.

The Psychic Roots of a Nut! The idea of her husband writing a book now all of a sudden seemed so plausible! Yes, for all the bustle and activity that characterized his everyday schedule - for all his inexhaustible fountain of love for her - Mjomba was, she clearly realised now, the "thinking type of man"! That was the impression he had given her when they met for the first time at her place of work years before, and it now seemed to find confirmation in his fling at being a published author!

For some reason, Jamila's memory of that first meeting remained fresh - almost as if it all had taken place months rather than years before. She still could have told, even after all those years, the exact type of attire he wore including the color of his shoes. The picture of him in the majestic apparel of a traveling clergyman had stuck fast in her imagination, seemingly not to be erased even by the passage of time.

An only child of a trader who financed his way to Mecca and the title of Al Hajj long before her birth, she had been brought up in strict Islamic tradition. But the ascendancy of Christianity in the region and the growing impact on her of foreign cultural influences had caused her adherence to the Moslem faith to gradually wear off.

Jamila Kivumbi, as she was then known, had taken an instant liking for the brash churchman. She had been prepared to become a Christian for his sake and as a prelude to exchanging marriage vows. She had been pleasantly surprised to find him keen to embrace Islam. But the adoption of Islam by the former Reverend Mjomba had meant little in practice, apart from his subsequent change of name from Moses to

Ibrahim using a deed poll and the fact that he stopped going to church.

Secretly she had been happy that Mjomba continued to collect and read scholarly works on Christianity in general and Catholicism in particular, and generally kept away from religious gatherings of Christians and Moslems alike.

Jamila had always felt a little shy about extolling her husband's intellectual endowments. But there had perpetually lain at the back of her mind, nonetheless, the thought that he was potentially if not actually a genius. If he were writing a book, she now reflected, he would of course use the opportunity to delve into the most obscure subject of them all - namely insanity!

Indeed she could not think of a better sounding title for a book dedicated to herself and her children than that which her husband, staring fixedly at an imaginary point in the ceiling of her recovery room, had announced. *The Psychic Roots of a Nut!*

Jamila suddenly felt that she had to read the manuscript and finish doing so before facing her husband later that day. All signs of dejection were gone as she settled back between the fresh linen and began leafing through the leaves of the blue folder. She found the material, which was split up into three parts and numerous sections, gripping from the very first.

Told in the present tense, the story of Innocent Kintu's psychological development, comprising the first and second parts of the "novel", was replete with interesting twists and turns. In contrast to Alex Haley's famous work, which sought to establish the ancestral roots of Kunta, her husband's study went all out to establish the mental or psychic roots of Kintu, his unsung hero.

It was a formidable task that, she nonetheless finally decided, he had acquitted himself of admirably. The third part in contrast to the first two was abstract and full of philosophical erudition. As if that were not enough, the rhetoric in that final part was so thick, she could at times hardly "see the wood for the trees" as they say! But it contained the biggest stock of surprises - she, Jamila, indeed featured in it!

Quite early on as she devoured the paragraphs, then pages, and eventually sections of the *Psychic Roots of Innocent Kintu,* something rather uncharacteristic of novels began to unveil and to suggest that it was the most unusual novel she had read and probably would ever read. Although the characters in the in the first and second section of the book were mute and spoke not a word, her husband had somehow managed to ascribe to them thoughts in a way that stripped all mystery from their actions. Although he had heard before this the truism, popularised by Charles Darwin and Mark Twain, that actions spoke louder than words, she had never imagined that it could all be so true!

Then, the "novel" aimed surely enough at explaining the unexplainable - insanity! But could Ibrahim Mjomba, the man she had known as her husband for a full five years now, really unravel the mysterious subject as she had earlier been inclined to think?

She was suddenly incredulous. This in turn gave rise to suspicions that the accounts she perused were possibly entirely fictitious in character! But as she delved deeper and deeper into the material, she gradually began to realise that it was a question he had to answer one way or another before the day was out - and on the basis of the account before her rather than her wifely feelings for him.

69

Still, the more she doubted his ability to do so, the more the material she had already covered impressed her with its realism and logic! The biblical clarity of the first two parts of the "novel" caused the lurking suspicion that the work might have been intended as some sort of joke by her husband to remain at bay. But as Jamila turned to the last part in which she featured, the pieces of the puzzle seemed to fall in place all at once.

Nudging herself into a comfortable seating position on the bed as her wandering eyes picked her name from a page, she quickly became engrossed simultaneously with her role in the book. Memories of the events of that morning, almost half a dozen year back when Professor Claus Gringo and a brash young cleric were locked in an abstract discussion centering on one of the professor's patient, came tumbling back into her mind.

She easily recalled how their voluble chatter had aroused in her a strange curiosity, causing her at one point to abandon her post at the secretarial desk so that she could indulge in eavesdropping.

Observing the performance of the young "padre" through the keyhole had suddenly evoked in her the most unimaginable, all too wanton, feelings of lust. Bewildered and ashamed at her spontaneous reaction, she had slunk back to her desk and attempted in vain to banish memories of the experience from her mind by banging away furiously at her IBM Selectric typewriter.

Jamila was light-hearted and curiously happy as she came to the concluding page of the manuscript. Turning over the last page, she kidded herself that, for all it's rhetoric and abstruseness, the final part was the best by far. It all just seemed so much evidence, if indeed she needed any more, of

Ibrahim's complicated nature; and she found her husband all the more worthy of her admiration.

While the former Jamila Kivumbi's mind was preoccupied with the sagacious material of her husband's novel, not many block away, events were being enacted with Ibrahim Mjomba at their center - events that might have come straight from a James Hadley Chase thriller!

The needle of the Ford's speedometer seemed to be jammed at the forty kilometer per hour mark as the battered car roared along past the New Post Office and approached the Askari Monument. The din caused by the absence of a silencer was now supplemented by a rattling sound not unlike the clatter produced by a quartet of cows wearing bells moving at a canter!

In his final bid to stock up on baby oil following a tip-off volunteered by a neighbor's houseboy, Mjomba had spent most of the morning searching for a backyard store on the city's southern outskirts. He had had to motor over roads that, even though listed on the map as major thoroughfares, turned out to be rough tracks filled with potholes big enough in a few instances to conceal a six-year-old.

Mjomba's inability to skirt all the potholes in his path had proved rather telling on the Ford's low-lying suspension. His sympathy for the machine as its undercarriage again and again scraped the road surface had in time given way to gloomy resignation.

The auto must have shed the rubber bushes as he approached the shack that had the baby oil, an undoubted slow mover, among its wares.

The mercilessness with which the lower ends of the auto's rear shock absorbers, no longer insulated from their metal housing, beat out the strange new rhythm as he set on the journey downtown, had caused him to soon forget his newly acquired taste of sweet success. The sweet taste, derived from knowing that he had overcome every obstacle in his way and had succeeded in getting every single item on the list of baby items his wife had prepared, had turned to bitterness as he tried to imagine what it would cost him to get the car fixed!

Mjomba had listened in confusion to the violent and as it turned out non-stop clanking noise originating from the car's rear, and had fought the temptation to stop the vehicle and seek out the cause with stubborn determination. He had however not noticed the strange fact that the medley of clangs increased in their intensity as the speed of the auto decreased - and vice versa!

The city sounds in the vicinity of the Askari Monument were drowned out completely by the noise as the Ford slowed down behind a queue of cars. One and all, the milling crowds stopped to stare. Disappointment became visible in the faces of the majority of onlookers as the source of the din turned out to be a slow moving, if somewhat battered, Ford and not a fire engine in full throttle. Mjomba, his form rigid in the driver's seat, seemed unconcerned by all the attention.

Next to him on the front seat was a gigantic bouquet of flowers neatly wrapped up in gift paper. In the back seat, Fatuma struggled to keep Ali and Musa in check. An unusually joyous and expectant atmosphere prevailed, and it received a periodic boost from Mjomba's ingratiating backward glances. Every time he looked over his shoulder, the children ogled at the image of a crested crane embroidered just below the knot of the blue-grey BAIT tie he had on for the occasion.

If Ali and Musa had seen their dad in a tie before, they evidently no longer had any recollection of it. In Dar es Salaam's stymieing weather conditions, only magistrates and the attorneys who argued cases before them donned ties, and Mjomba had never had any reason to go against that sensible tradition. Indeed apart from an odd collection of ties and western suits that were leftover from his grad school days in America, his wardrobe consisted of Kaunda suits, fancy Afro shirts and jeans.

6. The Hot American Sun

Talking about stymieing weather conditions, this was one of the areas in which they had not been prepared for the culture shock upon their arrival in America. The BAIT scholar, along with his spouse, was shocked to see the extent of the role played by the New York Times, the Los Angeles Times, the Washington Post and other media houses in America in forming perspectives of the folks there on the world outside their borders in general, but especially with regard to the weather conditions in Africa! Jamila and Mjomba found that the media, whether by design or through ignorance, loved to use expressions such as "the hot African sun" or "sizzling heat" to represent the moderately hot climatic conditions that one found in parts of the "Dark Continent".

And Mjomba accordingly wondered what an average American would be imagining when told about the "stymieing weather conditions" that prevail in the "Haven of Peace"! Actually, to be fair on Americans, Jamila and Mjomba noticed that, by and large, they went out of their way to express their sympathy for what they imagined to be absolutely hellish weather conditions in Africa; and this applied especially to folks who had not had the opportunity to visit the "Dark Continent" either as "hunters" or as "tourists".

During his sojourn in America, Mjomba had attempted to explain the situation "back home" to a group of 2nd grade schoolers on one occasion saying: "I mean, someone in Africa could get by - and I'm not talking about the elite who drive big cars and live in the European quarters in the cities - by and large by constructing a grass thatched hut and by clearing the surroundings to keep snails and snakes at bay; and then live

74

off the land just as Adam and Eve did. This was especially true in the days before the onset of the "scramble for Africa".

Mjomba had asked the young people what they thought would happen if the City of Dar es Salaam was suddenly exposed to the snow storms and the heat waves that continually walloped Upstate New York or the American Midwest?

Jamila, who was accompanying her husband on the study tour of the small town in Indiana, had helped the young ones out by suggesting that, without air conditioning while the heat waves lasted, and without heating to keep the foul winter weather at bay, many people would die!

Their visit to Indiana was in the first weeks of spring, and actually occurred just a month or so following their arrival in America. They already knew from their geography class, and also from reading novels whilst in Africa, that spring was one of the four conventional temperate seasons, and that it followed winter and preceded summer; and that winter was caused by the axis of the Earth in the hemisphere being oriented away from the Sun.

But they were caught off guard when one of the grade schoolers alluded to the "Daylight Saving Time" in a question. They had never heard of such a thing; and the idea of tinkering with clocks sounded so funny! And they did not at first believe it when the class teacher for the second graders stepped in to explain that this was necessary because the days were shorter in the winter and longer in the summer. They looked askance at her as she explained that days got shorter in the fall because as the winter approached, less and less of the northern hemisphere was tilted towards the sun, and so the earth saw a little less sun each day! The bombshell came when she said that in the winter the light wanes at four o'clock; and it doesn't get dark until around nine o'clock at night during parts of the summer!

Mjomba would later explain to Jamila that he'd probably seen stuff in books and even in movies regarding Daylight Saving Time (DST). But, in the exact same way so many folks read one thing in the bible but believed something else and quite often the very opposite because of prejudices, it would have taken a miracle for him to accept that there indeed were places on earth where the days got shorter in the winter and longer in the summer! He suggested to her that it would take a leap of faith for most folks who had been brought up on the Equator - and who were accustomed to divining the time of day, not by checking their watches worn on their wrists, but by checking the position of the sun in the sky - to even try to imagine something like that happening! He tried to imagine the sheer disruption that would ensue if folks there were told that they had to set the clock forward an hour in the spring (when DST started), and back one hour (when DST ended) in the fall!

Jamila had weighed in that half the country would probably do the opposite, namely set the clock *back* one hour in the spring (when DST started) and *forward* one hour (when DST ended) in the fall!

She had added that she couldn't imagine the scale of robberies as winters dragged on (if, instead of sitting on the equator, Tanzania was located either in the Northern Hemisphere and was subject to the vernal or March equinox and the so-called Summer Solstice, or in the Southern Hemisphere with its autumnal equinox and the Winter Solstice so-called) since robbers, thieves and other characters like that loved to operate under the cover of darkness! Her husband agreed.

The Bay Area Institute of Technology was located in San Francisco's so-called Mission District or "The Mission" as the locals preferred to call it. And, if truth be told, neither Jamila nor her husband had ever touched snow. And hence their disappointment when, on their arrival in San Francisco in early January, they learnt that most folks there had "never lived through winter"! Apparently here, in the city that takes its name from St. Francis of Assisi and is famous for its bicycle paths and lanes and bike routes and boasts a population that is ranked among the fittest in America, the only experience the residents had with winter was celebrating the "winter solstice" which marked the longest day and the shortest night of the year.

It was not too long following their address to the grade schoolers that the "colored couple", apparently still intent on proving that it couldn't possibly be that the hottest spot on the globe was in America, joined a party that was heading to Death Valley down south. Mjomba was still struggling to understand why correspondents of American news outlets seemingly couldn't help referring to the "hot African sun" in their news despatches from Africa, and he regarded their planned visit to Lake Tahoe in the Sierra Nevada and thence to Death Valley in America as one that wasn't just obligatory, but a sacred duty to be performed at some point during their sojourn to the continent that Amerigo Vespucci discovered in the late Middle Ages.

It was in mid-September of their first year in America that the couple hopped onto a plane for their East Coast study tour. They stepped off the plane at New York's JFK International Airport only to find the Big Apple literally sizzling in a heat wave that some blamed on "greenhouse gases" (or GHG) and others on the so-called "global warming" or climate change. The New York Caribbean Carnival was ongoing, and the young couple from Africa were shocked to see so many other people of color! Because of the very hot and humid conditions that were plaguing New Yorkers, they easily excused the revellers, many of whom were so scantily dressed, one could have said that they just had on the proverbial "Adam's suit".

This was so funny! Before coming to America, Jamila and her husband had got the impression from reading news articles by Westerners on the Swazi people with their Reed Dances and other "African tribes" that there couldn't be people in the Western world who celebrated their cultures in the nude. But now here they were in Times Square in the Big Apple, watching as thousands upon thousands of revellers danced and pranced virtually in the nude!

"This is just so ridiculous!" Mjomba had exclaimed, while Jamila, wide-eyed in amazement, continued to gaze at the spectacle and to wonder why Westerners made all that fuss about people in Africa participating in cultural activities while attired in traditional garb. And it was always "Westerners", never "Easterners"!

As far as the couple knew, even when Zulus performed their traditional dances like for instance the *Umhlanga* (reed dance), or the Zulu dance, or any of the other ceremonial dances to pulsating Zulu drums, the boys and girls danced separately, and similarly the men and women. And in the case of dances like the *Ingoma* (ishishameni) or the *Indlamu* (where the dancer lifted one foot over his head and brought it down hard, landing squarely on the downbeat), it was the women who danced the *Ingoma* and the men who performed the *Indlamu*.

But despite the fact that the festival in New York was taking place in the public square and in front of television cameras, the throngs of male and female dancers and revellers there did their gigs without in any way being mindful of the need for maintaining suitable distance from each other, if only for the sake of the younger participants, and also to minimize the chances of wrong signals being sent.

The heat wave advisory was still in place when they jetted into Ronald Reagan Washington National Airport or DCA in IATA lingo. Luckily for them they were able to join a school party for a tour of Capitol Hill and the Library of Congress. But they were denied the opportunity to take a peep at the White House from Pennsylvania Avenue because protestors who called themselves Occupy Wall Street (OWS) had caused a security scare there and the place was in lock down. The President of the United States and the First Lady were both reportedly inside with their two children though. Jamila and her husband braved the sweltering heat to visit and ogle the Washington Monument, the Thomas Jefferson Memorial and also the Lincoln Memorial.

As a result of their experiences in America, Jamila and her husband loved to joke that, with all the talk of "global warming", the "hot American sun" was heading their way and could arrive at any time in the city that once went by the name of Mzizima (Kiswahili for "healthy town").

Actually, when Mjomba was growing up in the Tanzania hinterland where rose bushes, dahlias, morning glory and even tomatoes grew and thrived all year round, and where his great grand father lived to be a hundred and some years, he used to imagine that the weather in Europe and America had to be absolutely gorgeous all year round as the people there were reputedly "advanced".

The words "Europe" and "America" evoked images of paradisiacal weather conditions he imagined were enjoyed by folks there all year long. As a teen, he just assumed that it had to be the reason Europeans and Americans were reportedly "advanced". And even after he learnt about the industrial revolution, it still didn't immediately strike him that appalling weather conditions in combination with other factors, rather than fairy-tale weather, were more likely to prod folks into exploring ways to survive.

At the time he told Jamila that story, he had added a rejoinder that it also explained why Europeans invaded Africa with the help of the gunpowder that Chinese alchemists had discovered!

"You must be kidding!" Jamila had retorted. "What stopped them?"

"It is you who is now kidding" Mjomba had shot back. "The mosquitoes...those who were sent ahead as scouts - the explorers - died when they were bitten by the mosquitoes. Of course, at the time, not much was known about malaria, and much less the fact that mosquitoes were the vector for it in humans. People in Europe just believed that the mosquito was the most dangerous animal in the world! And even after it was reliably established that the fall of the Roman Empire was precipitated by the bites from infected female Anopheles mosquitoes, the connection between the mosquito bite and the 'Roman fever' eluded researchers until quite recently. Our ancestors were immune to mosquito bites, I guess."

"You mean we were saved by the mosquitoes?" Jamila always knew exactly how to wheedle her man.

"Yes. We wouldn't have been a match against the invaders with just our slings, spears and poisoned arrows...

The Zulus did, of course, try and quite valiantly albeit with mixed results."

"Interesting…"

"At one thousand two hundred million and some" her husband continued, "the population of Africa today almost rivals the population of Europe and North America combined! And the conclusion that the elements had a bigger toll on Europeans than on Africans before the Chinese invented the rotary fan for air conditioning appears inescapable. And we, of course, know that migrants from Europe flocked to the Sun Belt in the United States only after William Carrier invented modern air conditioning at the turn of the twentieth century."

"Wow!" Jamila had interjected.

In response, Mjomba had pressed: "It is also notable that the first waves of colonists were not just plagued by very high death rates in which the elements played no small part, the death rates regularly exceeded birth rates! With the population in a steep decline, many would be migrants initially freaked out, and resisted the temptation to jump on the bandwagon. Up until then the 'Red Men', as the indigenous peoples of the Americas apparently referred to themselves at the time, had roamed the American continental shelf unchallenged and unfazed by diseases or elements.

"But today, the Western media want everyone to believe that the most foul weather on the globe is to be found only in Africa! And it is not possible to persuade Westerners that reports that all newly discovered diseases have their origins there as well are the best examples of fake news!"

Like her husband, when growing up, Jamila had the habit of leafing through copies of the National Geographic in the local library and, poring over the photo galleries of the National Geographic depicting places of interest in Europe and America, had been quite impressed. And when it came to places of interest in Africa, it was always about the wild animals and invariably the "hot African sun".

An avid reader, Jamila was nearly always moved to tears of joy by the depiction themselves. She could never get enough of the vivid descriptions like for instance:

"Hippos spend hours submerged in rivers and lakes to keep their massive bodies cool under the hot African sun…"

"At this watering hole, you will find hippos basking under the hot African sun or walking into the cooler waters…"

"The giraffe's long legs and neck provide a large enough surface area for heat dissipation that it does not need to wallow in the mud, fan itself with large ears, or stand in the shade to keep cool as other animals do…"

"A beautiful male white lion resting in the hot African sun…"

"A male lion sitting in the shade under the hot African sun…"

"And with the baking hot African sun baring down on them, and a lack of rainfall, the elephants waste no time slapping layers of thick mud and dust over their skin in covering themselves up to keep cool…"

"African elephants have large ears that are shaped like the continent of Africa…"

"Elephants have huge ears that fan their bodies to cool them down in the blazing hot African sun…"

"Retreating from the hot African sun, these lions are resting after a night of patrolling their territory…"

"Each day that the crocodile exposed his skin to the hot African sun, it would get uglier and bumpier and thicker, and was soon transformed into what looked like bulging armour."

"The ferocity of the African Killer Bee...is ingrained from centuries of adapting to the harsh hot African sun..."

Because in Africa folks kept away from wildlife for their own safety, she had never been to the nearby Mikumi Game Reserve that was talked about so much or to any of the other places in Tanzania where wild animals roamed free - and she had no desire to do so. Accordingly, the only depiction of wildlife that she had come across was what was carried by Western news media.

As Jamila saw nothing in these depictions suggesting that there could be anything approaching what could be described as "the hot European sun" or the "hot American sun", she had concluded that life in Europe *and* the weather there could never be anything but awesome! Accordingly, in Jamila's mind, wild beasts and the hot African sun, symbolizing diabolical weather, could only belong on her "Dark Continent", and everything in Europe and in America, including the weather, had to be fantastic.

It went without saying that she had often wondered why, with the exception of the timber wolves that still roam free in remote areas of Eurasia and North America and the American bison herds that she had seen in the Wild West movies, the wild animals - lions, elephants, leopards, giraffes, crocodiles, hyenas, hippos, etc. - were found in Africa in abundance, and why they had apparently eschewed Europe and America. There had to be a reason for that, but it escaped her at the time. The fact that people were into farming cows and sheep, and even kept poultry, came as a surprise.

And as she read more articles and books in the local library as a grade schooler and later on while attending secondary school, she had decided that, with life in Africa being what it was described to be, and life in America and

Europe being the exact opposite by implication, and with no hot sun there to interfere with anything, it had seemed quite plausible that, perhaps by a fluke of nature, advancement *was* indeed a function of the weather. What else could explain why Africa rightly or wrongly was depicted as "backward"! It had to be because of the weather there symbolized by the hot African sun!

7. The Snowmageddon

Because the BAIT welcome brochure had trumpeted the fact that the Bay Area was among the top five best weather and also most pleasant places to live in America, with just seventeen inches of rainfall on average a year and zero inches of snowfall, Mjomba and his wife had initially wondered how that could be. When packing their clothing to head out for the BAIT campus on what was their very first trip outside Africa, they mused that they would definitely be missing out on the snow. Since it snowed in Europe and America, and it did not snow in Africa except on the slopes of Mount Kenya (the mountain where, according to Kikuyu lore, God or *Ngai* or *Mwene Nyaga* lived when he descended from the sky and where he had his throne on earth, and also the place where Gĩkũyũ, the father of the Kikuyus and the first human to scale the mountain, used to meet with *Ngai*) and Mt. Kilimanjaro with its twin peaks, Kimawenzi and Kibo or "snowy dome", which the Chagga who live there described as "*kilemajyaro*" or unclimbable, the impression the couple had, after seeing the disparaging treatment of the weather in Africa by the Western media and the perpetual harping on the "hot African sun", was that Africa had to be missing out on something really terrific in the shape of ice and snow.

They had of course seen snow and ice in movies, but they had imagined that a dusting of snow on the human skin had to be something that Europeans and Americans looked forward to as the spring equinox gave way to the summer solstice, and the summer solstice gave way to the fall equinox and the fall equinox finally ushered in the winter solstice! Ice and snow had to be something that people in the advanced world looked forward to! It was also probably the snow that was responsible for Caucasians being white-skinned. It was therefore puzzling that the BAIT brochure could describe the locale of BAIT as being among the top five best weather and most pleasant places to live in America when it never snowed there.

It was the month of January, and it was looking like the "colored couple" were indeed going to miss out on the snow. But something thankfully, thanks to global warming, greenhouse gases or whatever, something happened in the Bay Area that, according to the San Francisco Chronicle, had never happened there in memory. The snow fell and lots of it, and it caught everyone, including the locals themselves and even the folks who manned the national weather service by complete surprise. No one was prepared for it.

The weather service had at first predicted that the Bay Area would receive some snow…but just a few ice crystals on the grass; or at the very most some snow flurries originating in what they called "stratiform clouds"; but they would be light and no significant accumulation was going to result according to the meteorologists. But those modern seers or diviners were proved to be completely wrong by the events. And as the snow flurries turned into intense snow showers that were initially accompanied by strong, gusty winds, and finally into an "historic" winter storm that devastated everything in its path, a sense of hopelessness and despair in the voices of the television meteorologists started to become evident.

Pandemonium, chaos and mayhem reigned everywhere as the radio and TV weathercasters (who already evidently had a bad reputation as "purveyors of panic and panderers to pandemonium") started to say things on live television and on radio that sounded patently incoherent. The reason was obviously the fact that no one could say with any certitude what was going to happen next. For a tumultuous three days, the blowing snow fell nonstop and in torrents, blanketing the entire West Coast and bringing everything to a halt.

The unprecedented winter storm ravaged towns, cities and the communities up and down the coast. To make things worse, the storm caused a blackout that lasted for hours on end, cutting off all communication with the outside world. Just before the blackout, it was reported that all travel had been grounded, and that included aviation, road, rail and marine traffic. All the interstate highways, including the I-5 that had its eastern terminus in the State of Oregon and its southern terminus in San Ysidro on the Mexican border, and the US 101 that extended all the way from San Francisco to the State of Nevada, had been closed.

There were whiteout conditions in the entire region as the unexpected and historic winter blast swept the region, accompanied by powerful gusty winds that grounded everything from planes to trains to vehicular traffic. San Francisco's cable car system ground to a halt. The streetcars were first pelted mercilessly by snowballs and damaged beyond repair before getting buried in the snow.

Before the Bay Area residents' television sets and other electronic gadgets flickered and lost their signals or just went blank as the winter storm knocked out California's electric grid and threatened to bury its hydro and nuclear power plants under a pile of snow and ice, the news channels had flashed pictures of spun-out cars that had piled into each other on the freeways, 8-wheelers that had jackknifed, and roofs of homes blown away by the ferocious winter storm. One announcer on the weather channel had just named the storm

"Snowmageddon" and labeled it the Storm of the Century just seconds before the station went off the air.

It snowed almost nonstop for three days, and over that period of time the Bay Area received in total a whopping five and in some places seven inches of snow. The system, an El Niño fuelled winter storm and a really fast mover, had apparently raced all the way from north of the border in Canada into the U.S. Midwest, leaving havoc in its path. Even the folks in the Midwest, who were used to shovelling snow during the winter, were reportedly unable to cope with the snowfall there because the system had hopped from across the border into the United States without any warning!

According to the weather service, North Dakota, South Dakota, Nebraska and other Midwestern States were themselves blanketed by up to four feet of snow in some places, and, before going off the air, the TV stations reported that there was misery everywhere with massive power outages occurring across the region. The total number of casualties of the winter storm that one newscaster had nicknamed "La Niña" would never be known.

Mjomba and his expectant wife rode out the storm by staying holed up in their high-rise apartment on the BAIT campus. The classes were cancelled for the entire week; and, at the height of the winter storm, not a soul could be seen outdoors on the campus. BAIT went on lockdown as the precipitation was dumping the first inches of snow. The Governor of California in tandem with governors of four adjoining states declared states of emergency to enable them scoop up the available Federal funds for the "clean up" that would follow in the wake of the storm.

The havoc that La Niña and the accompanying winter blast left in its path would be engraved in the memory of the residents of Baghdad by the Bay, even though it wasn't a guarantee that they would also stop maligning Africa with warnings and advisories about the "hot African sun"!

For the coloured couple from Africa, the surprise unanticipated winter storm had left them with mixed feelings. They had been able to see snow at long last, and lots of it! At one point, Mjomba had ventured out into the snow - to check it out as he put it - against everyone's advice only to regret it. Intending to claw his way through the mountain of snow that had fallen and had made the entire place unrecognizable in order to try his hand at making a snow man just as he had seen kids do in movies, he had stepped on a patch of black ice, and had very nearly killed himself. He had remained sprawled there in the freezing snow for a minute or so, wondering what had tripped him and afraid of sustaining another nasty fall if he got up and tried to use his feet to get back into the safety of their high-rise apartment. And his mien said it all: Mjomba now knew and understood that he could have easily busted his back with his reckless gambit - or even broken his neck in that nasty fall!

Because of the shortage of snowploughs, even after the worst of the storm had passed, some neighborhoods were forced to wait for the hot American sun to reappear and melt the mountains of snow and ice that covered the neighborhood roads and the cartways. A day or so after what the residents of the California now regarded one and all as the storm of their lifetime, Mjomba and his wife noticed that the snow that had not melted or been removed with the help of snow ploughs or shovels mysteriously hardened and actually became rock solid, before melting away gradually.

Mjomba also noticed that there were still patches of black ice everywhere he looked. Even after the BAIT lockdown was lifted, and the BAIT's Quadrangle was filled with crowds who did not want to miss the opportunity to enjoy the clean fresh air, or who just wanted to bask in the sunshine, he seemed contented watching the goings-on from the safety of their apartment's balcony.

Days later when he thought the better of it and also decided to venture out, Mjomba was shocked to overhear one chappie refer to the "freak" storm which, while it lasted, had grounded all travel in the world's sixth largest economy for close to a week, and then joke that it was now time for the United States of America to voluntarily cede its position as Leader of the Free World to its northern neighbor. He explained that Canadians had shown that they were manifestly better at dealing with Mother Nature, while Americans were still too proud to learn from the "Canucks" how to handle "Snowmageddons", "Snowpocalypses", and "Snowzillas"! He added to roaring laughter that it was unheard of for schools and government offices across the border to close shop because of inclement weather! Mjomba suspected that the speaker hailed from across the northern border.

8. The Clown

Mjomba looked veritably like some old-time clown with the noose-like object around his neck. The picture of a bird below the knot made him look all the more clownish, the fact that it constituted the emblem of his Alma Mater notwithstanding. Fatuma blushed many times and even Mjomba himself chocked repeatedly with laughter seeing Ali and Musa bursting with infectious joy.

As he turned into the driveway of Dr. Mambo's Clinic, the thought crossed his mind that the drive from the apartment to the clinic had been accomplished in something like the twinkling of an eye!

It was not as if his mind had been preoccupied with anything in particular. On the contrary, it had in fact been as close to the proverbial *tabula rasa* as it could possibly have been without actually being a "smoothed tablet". He had made a desperate woefully futile effort to get his mind attuned to the clangor produced by the Ford as he set out from home that afternoon, and had decided that he wouldn't let anything disturb his mental faculties for the rest of the day. With his reason relieved of it guiding role, his automatic reflexes had taken charge, and now he came to only to find himself guiding the ageing auto into the crowded parking lot instinctively!

To all appearances, Mjomba's mind was far away as he snatched up the flowers and banged the car's door shut behind him. He strode along, head held high and the bouquet he gripped with both hands looking very much like a fixed bayonet in a soldier's arms - and even apparently oblivious to the fact that he was traveling in the company of Fatuma and his children.

Suddenly he had the sensation of walking into someone! By the time he brought himself to a dead halt, his eyes were already closed and he was nagged by an overwhelming sense of being off balance. He became simultaneously of being enveloped in the fragrance of a perfume the scent from which was simply stunning!

"Excuse me!" The words, spoken in the barest whisper by a woman, caught Mjomba's ear at the same time as he was feeling the provocatively soft touch of fingertips he imagined were also suitably long and slender about his loins.

Jane's hands were still flaying about for support when Mjomba opened his eyes. In the same split second he swung the flowers out of the way to one side and shot out his right just in time to stop the nurse from striking the paved ground.

After clambering out of the Ford, Ali and Musa had merely skirted the colliding pair and raced on, unconcerned, towards the hospital's reception counter in their haste to rejoin their mom. Fatuma, trailing behind them, stopped in her tracks and stared with open mouth as the nurse's white uniform blew up a cloud of dust. Her mouth had scarcely closed when her hands rushed to clutch her chin a second time. She watched literally with her heart in her mouth as her uncle and the nurse first exchanged awkward glances and then burst out laughing!

All three were jolted to attention by shouts that emanated from the hallway and filled the air. Two plaintive voices were screaming: "*Mama! Mtoto! Mama! Mtoto!*"

Mjomba, Jane and Fatuma were drawn to Jamila's room as if by a magnet. Jamila and little Kunta were being mobbed by Ali and Musa when Mjomba's hulk filled the door of the small boxlike room. Jane and Fatuma, the latter's face all giggles, closed in around the bedside as Jamila sat upright in

92

her hospital bed. She took in the flowers and the BAIT tie in a glance, and proceeded to ease Kunta into Jane's waiting arms.

As husband and wife embraced, their lips sought out each other; and immediately they met, hers were heard to make tiny little noises, giving the impression that they were struggling to get themselves loose from his grip! They suddenly did, but just long enough to enable Jamila to hiss: "Darling, I love you...and the Psychic Roots of a Nut - it is the best novel I have ever read! A guaranteed best seller!"

Jamila's gleaming eyes looked like a pair of diamonds as they sought out the blue folder lying on the night stand in the meantime. They seemed to derive similar satisfaction from lingering over the folder to that which their owner was deriving from the man's embrace.

THE PSYCHIC ROOTS OF A NUT

By

Ibrahim Mjomba

To: My wife Jamila and our children Ali, Musa and...

Part One

1

Barren Ground

When he first arrived in the territory on his missionary journeys, Speke himself used the phrase to describe his feelings. The same phrase would in time become a catchword to which the missionaries and converts alike gave utterance out of habit - almost like an act of faith. Not a particularly impressive or original phrase, it said simply: Everything in this place smells heathenism!

In conformity with time hallowed tribal practice, the Welekha people, inhabitants of the Northern and highest flank of the equatorial table-land in Africa's heartland revere and venerate spirits of their dead, circumcise their sons and generally indulge in a great many activities no doubt destined to be adjudged orgiastic and pagan before long.

As the trickle of missionaries grows into a flood, the stage will become set simultaneously for a sure head-on clash between the old order and the new! Christianity, coming in the wake of imperial colonialism, seems to be attempting for now to establish a beachhead in the continent Christianized peoples have already dubbed the Dark Continent, as a prelude no doubt to becoming an independent force in the lives of the people of the continent.

The territory, even so, enjoys a class of its own. Welekha-land might not exactly rate on a par with the biblical Garden of Eden with its tame wildlife, harmless reptiles - and all. But, what with the beauty and splendor of the landscape, the abundance of the terrain and the disarming climate, this land of the Welekha cannot be too far removed in its rating from the renowned arch type.

Ever lush green, Welekha-land treats the unaccustomed eye to a startling and thoroughly delightful view of enchanting valleys, mountain ridges, riverbanks, waterfalls and hills bedecked with the richest foliage. Out of this splendor, blossoms a great variety of edible substances - bamboo shoots, yams, berries, pumpkins, vines, plantains, etc. The vegetation includes diverse healing herbs and flowers the dust from which goes into the manufacture of charms and other herbal concoctions. The land is crammed, besides, with virtually every specimen of animal life, a great many of which make first class veal.

Traditionally, Welekha tribesmen never see any use for granaries, since they only need to step into their backyard or nearby wood to be able to procure everything that goes into the preparation of the daintiest dish. Not even the oldest among the Welekha remembers having experienced famine. Their very tongue does not possess a term for it, the closest synonym being the Kilekha equivalent of hunger and thirst.

Folklore has it that that the land mass in whose immediate vicinity generations of this Bantu tribe have passed their days is the abode of the spirit of Lekha, Father of the Welekha people. The colonizing powers, according to their imperialist custom, have taken measures to have the mountain christened and called something else. But, the new epithet notwithstanding, the citizenry have persevered in the practice of deeming the mountain hallowed and possessed of the spirit of Lekha, their ancestor, just as of old.

With natural grace, Lekha's descendants customarily attribute to their venerable ancestors whatever bounty they see coming their way. As they have always imagined it, Lekha's whitened ghost from time to time emerges from the bowels of the earth by way of the dormant volcano atop Mt. Speke (the new speak for Mt. Lekha) and then proceeds to cast favorable and potent spells over the earth's elements from the commanding heights. The Welekha went on to believe that the elements control everything from the weather to fertility and luck throughout the length and breadth of the land that the Great Lekha bequeathed to them as inheritance!

For generations following the passing of their great and venerable ancestor, food gathering and hunting have been the principal means of subsistence among Welekha tribesmen. Even then, the Welekha can scarcely be ranked together with the primitive food gatherers of the erstwhile pre-capitalist societies. The conditions here existed that made food gathering and hunting attractive as an economic proposition from the beginning, giving the mountain tribesmen comparative advantage over the neighboring tribes in those respects.

Despite the internecine territorial feuds that have flared up from time to time in the region and have traditionally focused on the extremely fertile foothills marking the boundary between Welekha-land and the homelands of the surrounding largely Nilotic tribesmen, there has flourished a barter trade whose boom cycles coincide with the lulls in the tribal wars.

Living in relative affluence compared to their neighbors, the Welekha, by design rather than fortuity, take an active part in the trade. They would even, indeed, have dominated it were it not for the fact that they have a particularly strong attachment to the mores and customs handed down to them by their forebears.

The culture and traditions of the Welekha tribesmen make them inclined to economy and simplicity in their lifestyle. But even after the money economy was ushered in with the planting of the British imperial flag on their land, these people have continued to treasure an impecunious yet dignified way of life.

Everything takes it own course with them. Unhurried and free from visible care or worry over individual personal destinies, the descendants of Lekha always find time to act out with regularity their faith in a variety of ritualistic fantasies. The oblations and libations offered up to the ancestral spirits in accordance with age-old customs more often than not are a accompanied by frenetic displays of rhythmic dance that may be joyous or sombre depending on the occasion.

By the time the monster of imperialism waxed and became strong enough to rear up its ugly head over the horizon at what undoubtedly was a choice piece of real estate, the inhabitants already formed, not unlike the Greeks, a free peasantry, tenacious of its tribal customs. Communal ownership of property, that old Teutonic institution, had already given way to an enlightened capitalism in the shape of clan property relations.

But despite the richness of their traditions and the wealth of their land, Lekha's descendants remain, in the eyes of the messengers of the Gospel, good for nothing except perhaps as a particularly fine specimen of spiritual barren ground.

2

The Crusader

It is just after sunset in Namwikholongwe, a village in the Eastern part of Welekha District. Kholongwe, a renowned village elder and medicine man, is in an unusually high spirits. Not only has the day ended well - he has this day initiated no less than fifteen of the village's youths into manhood through the ceremonial rite of circumcision; he has a predicament that the night too is going to end in a blessed way. He has in fact just learnt that two of his twenty-five concubines are in labor with the village's wizened old ladies reportedly in attendance.

Hours later, the village elder and the rest of the village's population, with the exception of the very young and old, are still very much awake and busy celebrating the approaching end of the circumcision season with rhythmic dance and song in the near total darkness. Then, as the luminous face of the moon finally comes into view above a high mountain peak in the small hour of the night an casts a its radiant glow over the village to reveal a festive people totally caught up in a frenzy of delight, a messenger, strings of bead about his bare chest and loins, and his head framed by an assorted collection of birds' feathers, sweeps into the hut where Kholongwe, by himself now, is dozing over a gourd of banana brew.

Whatever apprehensions the old man still has about the night ending in a blessed way are quickly dispelled by the report that his wives have been safely delivered. Kholongwe is delighted as never before when the messenger announce that the newborns are both male.

Overwhelmed at the prospect of becoming a father of two boys at once, Kholongwe immediately summons before him the two mothers. Obediently they come each bearing her son. In order the better to enjoy the sight of his "harvest", - that is how he has always regarded children born to him - he orders the two women to depart briefly while he gloats over the babies laid out on a mat before him. Had what next happens not transpired the way it did, it is quite unlikely that the rest of the events as catalogued herein would never have taken place the way they did.

Trouble starts the moment the two mothers return. They had left their sons wrapped up in distinguishing bands of bark cloth for easy recognition; but now, as they enter the master's hut, the babies lie naked and screaming in the old man's lap and are quite indistinguishable! The swaddling bands of cloth have been cast by the *mzee* to one side where they lie in a heap.

The two mothers, their faces strained with anxiety, bustle with great unease in their individual endeavors to identify each her tot. And it comes to pass that both women settle on the self-same little one, each of them claiming him for her child!

The old man, disturbed that so small a matter threatens to undo the day's happy ending, commands the women to stand aside. He picks up the screaming babies, one at a time, and dumps them into the hands of the one or the other at random in order to put an end to the dispute.

The two newly born tots are given their names that same night. One of them is named after the medicine man's deceased father who went by the name of Nkharanga, while the other takes after the medicine man himself.

Kholongwe Junior grows and waxes strong and in due course develops into a healthy young man, physically and mentally, in the favorable atmosphere of traditional Welekha life. But Nkharanga, the child neither of the two mothers wanted, grows up neglected, sickly and deprived amid plenty - a virtual orphan. For the concubine to whose care he was assigned never comes around to taking a liking for the boy.

Nkharanga, unlike his half-brother who has it easy all the way to his grave, survives early mortality by dint of luck. He makes it through thick and thin to the age of seventeen when he gets what looks like a break in his fortunes. A white man, whose adventures have landed him in the village, comes upon Nkharanga who looks dejected and unemployed in the village's otherwise busy surroundings. The stranger is direly in need of the services of a porter for his forays into the upper reaches of Mt. Speke and is only too pleased when Nkharanga agrees to be engaged in that capacity.

Nkharanga has not been in the lanky white man' service for long when he begins to plot, with the relentlessness of a desperate person, to run away from his home. With his promotion in the short space of time to the position of Guide, the gods themselves seem to be giving their blessing to his intended flight.

Unknown to his fellow villagers, Nkharanga contracts to continue in the white man's service indefinitely. And so, even as the white stranger bids the village goodbye to continue on his adventures, the distracted youth is already waiting to make rendezvous with him at a prearranged spot outside the village limit, his mind preoccupied with vision of a great many white people who - his new master has assured him - will be on hand to receive them on arrival at their destination.

With the circumcision season approaching, the old man, who considers it a propitious time for Nkharanga to undergo circumcision, has a mind to propose to his son that he start preparing for the rite.

Now, the circumcision rite has not exactly been the kind of thing that Nkharanga, who had sensed what was in the offing, would have wanted to hear about. Since his childhood, the youth has been conscious of the fact that he grew up deprived of a lot of things others always took for granted. The lines on his thin, almost shapeless, forehead bore witness to the fact that he had been feeling alienated from not just his immediate family circle but from the entire tribe! And while youths preparing themselves for circumcision had as a rule found themselves inundated with gifts - usually flocks of chicken, goats, sheep and even cows - intended to give them a good start in their new roles a "men", Nkharanga, true to his capricious, all too cynical nature, had seen the possibility of that happening to him as remote.

The underlying significance of the circumcision ceremony had been lost on him to a large extent too. In his view the rite of circumcision merely reflected the coarse and undoubtedly sadistic tendencies of his old man and the rest of the warriorlike tribal chiefs who governed the villages with an iron-like grip! Nkharanga was thus well pleased with himself as he emerged from the shadows to join the white explorer against whom he had no axe to grind.

While Kholongwe Senior was not averse to his son offering his services to the white man for pay within the neighborhood, the medicine man was not one to suffer the boy to be cut off from his people and customs. His son, who at seventeen had yet to attain manhood through the circumcision rite, was still regarded as being of a tender age. And now, to the surprise of everyone, Nkharanga had defied his father and departed with the longhaired stranger!

The young rebel - or "renegade" as the villagers were more inclined to think of him - and his white boss, after crossing a wild tract of land to the South, meanwhile reach the safety of the white settlement in the Highland after fifteen days of strenuous hiking.

To Nkharanga's amazement, the territory swarms with *Wazungu* as white people are referred to in the *lingua franca*. They include women and children and, inn his view, have transformed the place into something decidedly out of this world. For the first time ever, he sees human riding horses and he stares with astonishment as a few die-hards hop into smoke-belching vehicles and drive away even over hilly ground! Still, jarring as it is, the experience causes Nkharanga, a misanthropist in all but name, to regain a measure of confidence in the human race.

The young lad, in spite of everything, makes headway in the service of the jaunty people from the mythological world that the local populace refers to as *Uingereza*. (Back home, Nkharanga's tribesmen call it *Bulaya*.) Because his skin, unlike that of white men, which is ghost white, is deeply tanned, Nkharanga even earns himself the flattering title of "Mr. Copper"!

Nkharanga is more than content to live in his "box" at the back of his master's garage. Still he feels homesick a lot, particularly in the beginning. And there are times when his homesickness threatens to mar his good work, which consists of gardening and house cleaning chores.

Brooding about his old father as well a uncles, aunts and other relatives whom he left behind, Mr. Copper often feels that he sinned in running away. That is not to say he did not have reasons to flee his home.

He had been well aware that he was due for circumcision. But he had witnessed young men succumb to the ordeal on countless occasions as they underwent the circumcision rite. The experience had unnerved him.

Although it was well known abroad that his father was as skilled in the art of administering circumcision as any one could possibly be, the mere thought of his dad crouching on a stool gripping his member with one hand and a glinting knife in the other in readiness to shave off his foreskin sent tremors of unease through him. He was therefore glad, if for no other reason, to make his escape in the company of the congenial white stranger.

Nkharanga feels deep in his heart that he has done a great wrong nonetheless. As the son of a village elder and a medicine man at that, he understood - or at least was supposed to understand - better than most people of his age the fundamental norms of life that stipulated obedience to elders. It was the one aspect of life that the deprived circumstances of his upbringing did not overlook for some reason!

Even in his changed circumstances in the "White Highlands", the motive power behind his will to work, while being affected increasingly by monetary and other factors, springs from his early training in blind submission to the injunctions of older people in society.

He grew up inclined by instinct to do as he was told. Blind obedience was something that had been ingrained in him from childhood. Being at the core of a person's upbringing in the village, obedience to elders reflected not just reverence to them but the tradition to defer to the wisdom of the older person.

Indeed, as a consequence, the satisfaction he derives from work of any sort has come to depend on his ability to discern whether or not his bosses, be they village elders in his homeland or white people from *Uingereza*, regard the results of his industry as praiseworthy or otherwise.

In the course of time, Nkharanga loses the incipient nervousness his initial contact with *Wazungu* gave rise to. The nervousness, due in the main to the fact that his encounter with the strangers has been taking place outside the secure surroundings of his familiar tribal life, was very noticeable at first and has been the only serious complaint he heard voiced against him. He now feels exalted as he watches his exertions unfailingly elicit words of praise from his delighted boss.

Then, just as everything seems to be going great for him and life in his quarters behind the garage is growing brighter and brighter with each passing day, Nkharanga finds himself temporarily out of employment! The *Mzungu* he escorted from Namwikholongwe some seven months earlier, and in whose continuous service he has been ever since, leaves for *Bulaya*, leaving his property at and the house under the care of a stern-faced representative of a multinational company. The latter has no use for Nkhalanga and informs him of it!

For three days Nkharanga stays holed up in his quarters, which he continues to occupy illegally, pondering what to do. He grows increasingly upset, moody and unpredictable. As hunger gnaws at his middle and the gloom of desperation begins to descend on him, he starts to feel hatred for his former boss. At first imperceptible, the hatred rises with the passage of time until his heart, swollen with anger, is beating and throbbing as if it is a drum reacting to the blows of an accomplished beater.

Venturing out on the evening of the third day, Nkharanga comes upon a pastor and his wife who are out on a stroll. The couple once called to see his ex-boss and were struck by

Nkharanga's eager manner and otherwise benign composure. They recognise him stop to exchange greetings. The hungry Nkharanga sees his chance and starts pouring out his story. His lack of vocabulary, which is more than evident as he attempts to express himself rapidly in the English tongue, has the effect of accentuating the desperate nature of his situation.

Listening to Nkharanga's story, the missionary couple cannot but feel extreme compassion for the distracted youth. The pastor does not need his wife's urging to offer the lad a position as *shamba* boy. Since accommodation and food go with the job, the young man is delighted. He promptly regains his usual benign spirits and, after deciding to let bygones be bygones, settles down to work for his new white boss.

While loudly expressing his belated gratitude to the couple for their "merciful act", he hears the pastor's wife retort with words that, though only faintly familiar, make instant sense. "It is the will of God," she says; "It is Him you should thank!" She says those words with the trust and confidence that remind Nkharanga of the faith his own people back home place in the spirit of Lekha, the Father of the Welekha!

Nkharanga soon meets with even greater and quite unheralded luck. In recognition of the efficient manner in which he despatches his assignments, the good couple give their *shamba* boy a chance to discover "the three Rs". There is not far off a "bush" school run by the Church Missionary Society to which they decide to send Nkharanga.

Although only a part of his mornings are devoted to literacy classes, the speed with which the "native from across the border" learns to read and write surprises the couple. It does subsequently persuade the missionaries to sponsor their African servant right through elementary school!

107

The former Mr. Copper proves to be a brilliant pupil at the "bush" school where he learns, among other things, to read the bible. He is baptised in due course, and given the new name of Victor. Mr. copper would find out later that his patron saint was a native of Africa who enjoyed a twelve year reign as Pontiff of Rome in the late second century and is also credited with making Latin the official language of the Church of Rome. In the meantime, under the salutary influence of the couple, bible reading soon becomes a part of Victor's daily routine.

Victor Nkharanga is half way through the elementary school course when the pastor's wife proposes to him one evening that he consider paying a visit to his people at Christmas time. She reveals that they themselves plan a visit to the Cape in South Africa and will not therefore miss his services.

The young man, who has risen from *shamba* boy to houseboy and cook by this time, finds he can neither ignore nor refuse the bidding of the mistress of the house. The news hardly seems to portend well for him to be sure. He sorely wishes that the idea of him paying a visit to his people so-called hadn't come up in his ladyship's mind. He finds himself having to exercise supreme efforts in order to hide his own anxious state of mind from the couple.

Victor is a changed man as he embarks on the preparations for his journey home. When the departure date finally comes round, try as he might to conceal the plight of his mind, he looks visibly unsettled. The couple are moved to tears just watching him wave back from the distance as he leaves to catch the train for part of his homeward journey, a bundle of clothing strung over his shoulder and his free hand firmly gripping the pocket-size bible they have given him as a Christmas present.

If Namwikholongwe village has undergone any transformation during the two years Nkharanga was away, it isn't immediately noticeable to him as he strides up the path leading to his father's compound. It takes him mental effort nonetheless to gain the realization that e is returning to his home. Indeed, if anything, he feels a quite different person from the untutored and flippant tramp who set out on the journey into the unknown what looks like ages ago in the company of the *Mzungu*!

The prodigal son is received back into his father's house with feasting and merriment. Kholongwe Sr. has acceded to the chieftainship of the clan in the meantime and considers his son's homecoming a good omen. And so, with the resources at his disposal, the chieftain, white-haired and bent with old age, throws a great party for his son. The joy of the women finds spontaneous expression in the Nndimba, a Kilekha victory dance that is traditionally dominated by members of the fair sex and children.

Wearing necklaces of python vertebrae and their arms bedecked with row upon row of ivory or copper bangles, the women, hips swivelling beneath their load of beaded jewellery and scarcely concealed by the sparse strands of banana leaves enshrouding them, lead the minors in a lusty performance of the Nndimba. The banana leaves form changing and spectacular arcs about the quivering loins and fly mostly level with arms that are now lithe and now taut and firm in consonance with the exotic sounding chant bawled out by the surging crowd.

The dance consists in movements of the belly, hips and bosom, and is rendered in strict consonance and sympathy with the rhythmic, deep, resounding throb of drums. It reaches a climatic point as the men, arrayed in hunters' fetish jackets and feather headdresses, spring from the bushes and join the delirious throng of women and children in a captivating display of Lekha eroticism.

Now that he is back in the place of his birth, however, Nkharanga, who now prefers to be called Victor, is saddened and swayed by the fact that his people are still steeped in their heathen beliefs and practices. For the first time in his life, Nkharanga feels sheer zeal for the Word of God well up in him, and with that the least scruples that may have previously troubled him vanish.

Although no priest, Victor reckons that in the absence of those anointed of God, the very least he can do is stand in for them and preach God's word. And so it is that the young zealot, abandoning all thoughts of a quiet and carefree holiday as the welcome member of the chieftain's household, chooses instead the life of a Christian crusader in heathen surroundings, unmoved by the pleas of the villagers and once again in defiance of his father's mighty will.

The enraged old man interprets the novel ideas propagated by his son as dastardly, and he also sees them as obnoxious in the extreme. He reasons that, unless swift action is taken to stay the hold those belated notions have on the young fellow, something dreadful will surely overtake not just the youth but the entire clan!

As far as he is concerned, his son displays a clear tendency to contradict the sagacity of his elders - sagacity such as the boy, uninitiated in the wisdom of traditional life and quite "green" in the self-same, can counterpoise only at the risk of incurring anathema from the spirits of the dead. Anyway, in his mind, the solution to the "problem" posed by such waywardness isn't something to rack one's brains about! Tradition dictates what to do in circumstances such as these.

The old chieftain resolves to order, as a first step, that the circumcision rite be performed upon the young deviant without further delay. There must then follow the various other initiation ceremonies that are now overdue. A she-goat that has a speckled underbelly has to be found and slaughtered as soon as all the foregoing ceremonies are over. The still warm and steaming dung will be extracted from the animal's bowels and sprinkled over the youth's shaven head. The youngster, as everyone knows, is not to taste of that goat meat, it being taboo to do so. Only thus can the recalcitrant youth be cleansed from the ill effects that have resulted from his contact with the white man!

The clan folk, among them the young crusader's former playmates, rising to their elder's command, execute it to the letter without the slightest regard to the pleas and protestations of their former chum.

Nkharanga emerges from these events seemingly insensible to all that goes on around him, including pain. He neither speaks nor eats. He sleeps little and, as he wanders about listlessly and incommunicado by his own choosing, it is circulated on the village's grapevine that the rites that have been performed on him have had their effect, the young man having most certainly "heard" from the spirits and been suitably mollified, no doubt, by their sound advice!

The opportunity is not long in coming enabling the certainty with which the villagers talk about Nkharanga's deliverance to be put to the test. Even before the medicine men are satisfied that the incisions he sustained on his person in the course of the cleansing are healing properly and certify accordingly, their patient is suddenly discovered missing! But

111

he vanishes only to turn up a decade later as a catechist and government agent.

3

Fate of a Royal Child

The sky is overcast with dark, menacing clouds. The horizon to the east of the village is blacked out by the wall of advancing hail and mist, and the rainstorm. A dozen crows freewheel in their dogged fashion high in the Western skies and below them a sea of banana leaves and branches of trees wave and rustle with increasing vigor in the brisk wind. Everything in sight appears to be bracing itself for the imminent storm - the village folk included.

The women are still rushing about to and fro, feverishly trying to get additional supplies of firewood, their basic fuel, under shelter when the first hailstones begin to fall. As they retreat into the houses - round structures of wattle and daub roofed with pleated banana fibre - all but the youngest kids of the settlement sprint out from the verandahs into the village compound to help themselves on the hailstones.

They dart here and there picking up the stones and popping them into their mouths and are all bursting with lusty, as yet untapped energy and mirth. All the kids, that is, except for one little girl - a mere child of five who, however, looks eight or older. She was by herself when the bustle started, and she continues to stand lonely guard in the portico of the village's largest hut, and to stare at the goings-on with only the slightest hint of interest registered on her pale face.

She is Mvyengwa, youngest daughter of Mpakha, famed medicine man and head of the largest clan in Nghashongwe. Nestled high in Mt. Speke amid scenic waterfalls and jagged cliffs, Nghashongwe is perhaps the most picturesque village in all of Welekha-land.

Starry-eyed, Mvyengwa watches the proceedings with an air of one who has just landed in the village from some distant but superior planet. Even so, her gaze portrays, easily enough, a powerful inner longing for some hitherto missed fulfillment that now seems in danger of becoming out of reach altogether. Her sunken face and gaunt expression meanwhile bespeak of want and utter neglect!

Want and neglect - they are the two things with which Mvyengwa's fate became woven starting four years ago in the wake of her mother's mysterious and premature demise.

The youngest of Mpakha's twenty wives, Mrembo, or *Ma* as she was already nicknamed by the then husky and radiant child, was the jewel in the house of the renowned medicine man and clan head. Hefty and dark skinned, she was the most handsome of the women she shared her husband with.

On his part, Mpakha, a septuagenarian when he added Mvyengwa to his flock of wives, seemed to consider it excusable at his age to display openly his doting love for the seventeen-year old daughter of the village blacksmith. Calling her his "black beauty", the old man, who himself is fair-skinned, quickly developed a habit of showing her off to gathering of his patients as occasion permitted.

The young girl's marriage to the medicine man had the effect of propelling her to the top of her social structure. And Mrembo was more than delighted to join Mpakha's already crowded household. Her happiness was not affected in the least by the fact, known throughout Nghashongwe and beyond, that tropical blindness was fast descending upon her idol. For, his growing handicap aside, he was everything that a grand old man his age could attain to in traditional Lekha

114

society - head of the clan, medicine man, and interpreter for the venerable ancestral spirits. The fact that he was a rank polygamist, whose wives had already mothered close to a hundred sons and daughters who in turn had bequeathed to him an even larger number of grand sons and daughters, was just one more additional reason to fall for him.

Mrembo was thrilled to learn, just two months after becoming Mpakha's consort, that she had conceived by him. She saw nothing wrong in being paraded by the *mzee* before mixed gatherings of people that often included Mpakha's senior wives. Later, as she watched little Mvyengwa grow and wax, she took the happy circumstances in which she and her daughter found themselves completely for granted. It neither surprised her when Mvyengwa became in a very short space of time following her birth the village's most envied child, just as she herself was Nghashongwe's most envied woman.

Mphakha, already partially blind when the object of his doting love passed out of this world, let concern for his own health take precedence over everything else. The wellbeing of his youngest and last child figured less and less in his mind from then on.

Meanwhile, as a result of their former jealousies and envy, the chieftain's surviving wives were only too glad to see the daughter of their former rival abandoned to her misfortunes. This situation, which prevailed four years ago, has continued to prevail. Those four years have seen Mvyengwa grow up virtually fending for herself, surviving in the face of the overwhelming odds by dint of luck, and sustained only by her survival instinct.

After what looks like an eternity, the hailstones stop falling. The village kids, their wet black faces glistening in the descending gloom, retreat into the tranquil and warm atmosphere of the huts.

The hollows of Mvyengwa's eyes cloud with tears as she watches five little girls and eleven small boys, their wet sparse clothing clinging tightly to their skins, to come bolting to the shelter of the large hut. She remains immobile like a post as they stampede merrily past her and into the hut's cozy interior. The tiny bare feet, in their casts of alluvial mud, leave elephantine impressions on the cow-dung plastered floor. She knows without looking that, once inside, they all without exception are flopping carelessly into the arms of their respective mothers.

Mvyengwa finds it intolerable to stay aloof from members of her age group. But her instinct tells her that it will never work for her to try and mix with them.

From as far back as the little girl can recall, she has been aware of the existence of an invisible, yet solid barrier, between herself and the other children in the village. It is a barrier that has been woven over a stretch of time from sly glances, muted curses and the like which those kids' mothers traditionally direct at the lone little girl. Although they give the impression of being kindly and gentle when other adults are present, she knows that those women can be harsh if they think that she has at any time participated in games played by their children.

As a cold misty rain sets in, accompanied by a furious gusty wind, Mvyengwa turns to go. She skirts a small throng of socked and chattering kids near the fireside. Timidly she edges her way in the direction of an elderly aunt who only that day arrived in Nghashongwe on a visit. A childless sister of the *mzee*, she took an instant to the obviously neglected child on her arrival. She sits huddled in a corner of the great hut by

116

herself, reclining her back against a pile of firewood and smoking tobacco.

Mvyengwa picks her way cautiously at the far side of the fireplace. As she approaches the visitor, the light from the flickering fames exposes a rickety gait. A bag of bones, she lets her limp form sink to the ground within arm reach of the old woman. She begins to stare with nervous concentration aunt, seemingly unaware of her presence, continues to puff away at the lighted end of the tobacco roll.

4

From Mvyengwa to Annamaria

A decade flies by, helped on by the rapid pace of events as the colonialists tighten their grip on Welekha-land and the neighboring territories. At the end of it, Mvyengwa is no more than fourteen years of age. But her cheeks look hollowed out as if she is forty! Shapeless and languorous in her disposition, her gawky manners appear to confirm the widespread view that she is daft as well as her family's black sheep. For these reasons, precious few pay her any attention.

After a while it so happens that Mpakha, now utterly blind and bent with old age, and everybody else in his household believe that the girl is living with her distant aunt. Unknown to either them or the aunt, Mvyengwa has crossed the border into the Protectorate of Uganda to the East and is in fact staying at a convent with a group of Franciscan nuns.

One of the nuns, returning from a charitable mission on foot, stumbled on the bewildered girl who looked ill, starving and very much lost. The nun encountered little difficulty in persuading the Sister Mother of the convent to afford the poor creature the food and shelter she clearly was so much in need of.

It is not until some three years after Mvyengwa set out from her home to visit her aunt that her whereabouts become known to the villagers back in Nghashongwe - three years spent with the nuns which see her grow up into an attractive young maiden. During that time, she is taught to read and write, and she is also baptised and confirmed in the Catholic faith.

Under the tutelage of the nuns, Annamaria as she is now called develops an irresistible desire to become a nun herself. Although still in the middle of elementary school and not yet in possession of the educational qualifications required of postulants, she easily succeeds in gaining the requisite dispensation from the diocesan bishop to enroll immediately as a postulant.

The very first Welekha candidate for sisterhood, Annamaria learns to be recollected and obedient, and to observe all other imperatives that traditionally bind God-fearing souls favoured with a vocation to the religious life. She is particularly happy that she too is expected to maintain a "respectable distance" from the world. This, her spiritual director points out, is necessary for the cultivation of the spirit of recollection.

Annamaria has additional cause to welcome the Rule's insistence on maintaining suitable distance from things mundane. The requirement that she banish the outside world from her mind and consideration gives her fresh assurance that her decision, arrived at many years ago, to sever once and for all any such link as she had with her people was not only the right one, but one that was also divinely inspired!

Unhappily for the novice Annamaria, the rumors to the affect that she has defected, not just from the distant relatives she supposedly was visiting but right out of this world, finally reach the ears of her old man back in Nghashogwe. The old chieftain thinks it madness that his daughter should have thus eloped. He accordingly organizes a squad of toughs from the village and assigns them the task of snatching back his daughter from "the pit of darkness into which she has wandered" as he puts it.

It is thus that, as Annamaria along with the other postulants and nuns are gathered together in chapel for Rosary and Benediction with the Blessed Sacrament one evening, a band of "natives", some of whom Annamaria seems to recognize, burst into the building and bundle her away amid the terrified screams of her colleagues. Barely managing to wave a goodbye to the convent Mother, she lets herself be hustled away by her unswayed abductors.

From the moment she set foot in the convent to the day she is unceremoniously plucked from the bewildered gathering in the chapel, Annamaria considered herself to be very well qualified for the life of a nun. She was, besides, keenly aware of the fact that she learnt faster than the average novice to adjust to the surroundings from which she hoped to emerge as a full-fledged "spouse of God".

It now appears to ex-novice Annamaria as she is borne away that she will surely find her new predicament too much to endure unless the good Lord hastens to her aid with his graces! Even as she is thus engrossed, she senses the sorrow that descended upon her in the wake of the kidnapping begin to lift, and she soon is experiencing an indescribable peace of mind. She also becomes aware of a mysterious light that materialises in her innermost depths, dispelling all fear and confusion from her mind!

Although all this happens in the twinkling of a second, in that momentary space of time, Annamaria is able to grasp that by thrusting her right back into the world - one that in her experience is thoroughly confused - Providence obviously intends greater rather than lesser things for her.

Annamaria's meditations in the convent made it crystal clear that a place among the virgin brides of God who "follow the lamb wherever he goes" (Rev 14:4) is hers - and hers, she surmises, by divine decree. That being so, she feels she is right in believing that she just has to continue to strive to accommodate Divine Love in as fervent a manner as she may whilst living among the simple common folk out there in the world to be certain of her reward. But to make doubly sure, she plans to intensify her devotions, those to the Sacred Heart of Jesus and His mother Mary's "Immaculate Conception" in particular, following in the example of St. Margaret Mary Alacoque who was her favorite saint.

As Annamaria has anticipated, she finds herself living the life of a virtual prisoner in her own father's house on her return to Nghashongwe. Everyone detests her openly. The older women scald her loudly at the slightest excuse while the men, both old and young, scoff at her. The life she leads reminds her of the hard life she endured as a child following upon the death of her mother of loving memory. This time around her endurance is backed by the unceasing devotions she offers up as well as denials of the self, and the good works that she dedicates principally to the conversion of her "misguided" people.

Not many years after her forcible abduction from the nunnery, Annamaria (who is known to the village folk simply as Mvyengwa) spies a white couple as they lumber wearily up the village path. A well-groomed and strikingly handsome young African man accompanies them. Her attention is drawn to them in part because, since leaving the religious house, she has never set her eyes on a white person let alone a white couple; and her curiosity is aroused in part by the fact that the white gentleman spots a Roman collar!

Her first thought at the sight of the visitor concerns her spiritual life. She recalls with horror that she has not been to confession or received any of the Church's other sacraments in

121

a long while. But even as she is turning these things over in her mind, she observes that the lady clings to the "priest" in a manner that clearly signifies a love relationship!

To say that Mvyengwa is astonished at what she sees would be an understatement. She is clearly aghast at seeing the clergyman passive in the woman's embrace. She has heard about Anglicans and Lutherans, but she has never thought that, "perverted and lost" as they are, they could permit their clergy to marry! In this condition of perplexion, she approaches the couple's African guide for an explanation.

Unknown to her, the Fates have determined that her confrontation with the stranger shape not just her own destiny but that of the stranger as well as the destinies of an innumerable number of her countrymen. The meeting certainly is to prove to be of no small consequence to one Innocent Kintu whose destiny as the first fruit of their subsequent marital union becomes fixed as of this date.

There is a clump of trees close to where the travelers camp. Annamaria, timid and vacillating by virtue of her maidenhood, draws forward from the shadows to accost the tremulous and equally apprehensive and shy Victor. No sooner do they confront each other than a transformation, swift as a bolt, comes over them both. Cupid - if we are to believe Greek mythology - as surely as they breathe sends shafts through their respective cardiovascular organs, veritable seats of love as it turns out, causing the two hearts to bleed for each other.

Victor and Annamaria fall in love at the very first sight that they ever have of each other. As they do so, they are individually convinced that, unlike other common instances of falling in love, theirs is a divinely inspired affair. Their eyes are misty and contemplative as they themselves stand face to face and gaze longingly at each other.

It is not until two years later, however, that the lovers, having triumphed over a host of problems that threaten to mar their happiness and in line what seems unmistakably to be God's will, are finally joined in holy matrimony. By that time, Victor, having bowed to the will of the indomitable ex-novice, not only has embraced Catholicism but is also set to become a catechist in the service of Holy Mother Church.

5

Father Campbell

Having finished reciting the day's Office, Father Campbell sticks the breviary under his left armpit. A towering six-footer, the missionary cuts a solemn figure in his snow-white cassock, which he wears complete with crimson sash round about an enormous waist, as he paces to and fro in front of the parish church. He moves in a line parallel to the church's massive panelled doors. These are wide open and made fast on either side with iron hooks.

Overhead, bats fly missions between a high niche housing the figurine of Christendom's first pope and patron saint of the parish and a nearby grotto overhung with a variety of morning glory. The bats' forms are barely visible in the faint twilight; for it is that time of twilight when the light of day seems to linger on in defiance of the fast descending gloom of night.

The priest glances into the darkened interior of the church. As if drawn by a magnet, his eyes move upward in one sweep, allowing his gaze to settle on the tiny speck of light formed by the sanctuary lamp. His thoughts turn to the Blessed Sacrament of the Eucharist as the all too familiar words begin to crowd his mind. *"Et panis quem ego dabo caro mea est... Caro enim mea vere est cibus et sanguis meus vere est potus. Qui manducat meam carnem et bibit meum sanguinem..."* ("The bread that I will give you is my flesh...my flesh is truly a food, and my blood is truly a drink. Whoever eats my flesh and drinks my blood...")

Those words, spoken mentally, add little to Father Campbell's grasp of the mystery of the Holy Eucharist.

Undaunted, the priest is all but settled on his next move, namely the journey down the long winding flight of concrete steps leading to the convent chapel where he is due to conduct the Paschal novena for the nuns and postulants and perhaps hear a confession or two. His contemplative mood suddenly comes close to being shattered as the sound of distant whistles, mingled with the chiming of bells and the unmistakable voices of women and children in lusty song, catches his ear. There is soon no mistaking the boom created by the frenzied beating of an assortment of drums and gongs!

As the festive party of men, women and children inches its way along the path hard by the church, the bewildered clergyman is able to make out most of the noises including the thumping of many feet, the men's throaty grunts and the lyrical voices of the womenfolk. He himself lets out a wistful grunt as he watches the throng of exuberant natives burst into view round the corner of the church and then disappear down the hill and into the lush green valley below.

Just before his attention became riveted to the group of dancers, the parish priest was in the process of raising his cassock to facilitate his progress down the series of steps leading to the convent below. Caught unawares, he stopped to stare at the procession by accident rather than by design. The procession passed out of view, but the priest remained immobile for a couple of minutes, his weight balanced between his right foot which was still on the church terrace and his left foot which had already gained the first downward rung.

"That's it…the slaves of the Evil One!" Father Campbell murmurs bemused. A wan smile plays on his lips as he resumes his descent. A good while later, as he dons the stole for the novena, he can still hear the insistent drumming of tam-tams and the refrains of the women in response to the drummers' yodelling voices, and the tinkle of bells.

Even as he leads his wrapped congregation in prayer, the churchman, who has done everything to banish the images of half-clad natives in their rhythmic and vigorous dance from his mind, finds himself quite unable to concentrate on the devotions. As he speeds through the Latin phrases and antiphons by rote, he feels grateful to God that he knows the prayers by heart and, therefore, can conduct the novena while at the same time engaging his mind elsewhere.

A seasoned padre, Father Campbell knows well enough how to deal with Beelzebub and his machinations. Instead of fighting to keep the damned images out of his mind, he decides to resort to a line of action that spiritual directors, beginning with the messiah himself, have advocated.

"If you can't win in open contest" the voice inside him repeats, "Join the enemy!"

Thus, instead of battling the crazy images and the suggestions behind them, he now makes them the subject of his meditation!

With his trained mind, he sees at once, however, that there is something the matter with the way things appear to be going on this particular occasion! But he also knows that, whatever it is, it has nothing to do with scruples of conscience.

Throughout his tenure as Rector of St. Augustine's Major Seminary, the post he relinquished only lately in order to preside over what he had heard was a particularly difficult parish, he was known to despise any manifestation of scrupulosity. On receiving reports that a goodly number of the seminarians tended to display scrupulosity of conscience, he promptly made "Scrupulous Conscience" a regular subject of the weekly spiritual conferences over which he personally presided, effectively dubbing it the "plague of the unseasoned"!

Since his return to active pastoral duties, the "P.P." (as he is fondly referred to by his white curate) does allow himself, if somewhat unscrupulously, to occasionally indulge in visions of himself as another Curé de'Ars! His orbit in an obscure part of the Dark Continent seems to him at times to be even more exacting and trying than was that of the original Curé de'Ars!

His parish, with its unenviable record of zero applicants for the priesthood as of this date, is not about to produce a flock of priests - and certainly not in the short period he has been around! But Father Campbell feels it is within his rights to enjoy his reputation as a pillar of the Church in the diocese. This reputation was undoubtedly a factor behind his appointment. Yet, none of these things has made him change his attitude to the phenomenon of scrupulosity.

The reasons for the absence of vocations to the priesthood from amongst his parishioners seem to him plain - the contemptible circumcision rites being decidedly one of them. For the Welekha tribesmen who inhabit the length and breadth of St. Peter's Parish, the circumcision seasons that come and go with each succeeding leap year are as big a distraction from spiritual activities as any that the missionary can visualise.

During his own minor seminary days in Europe, Father Campbell read about the pageants and dances that supposedly abound among Central African tribes. The impression he formed, and which he still retains, is that the dances and the age-old ceremonies constitute pagan rites that the errant and infatuated tribesmen believe in, in much the same way the civilised peoples of Western Europe believe in Christianity.

As he seeks to put the livid and undoubtedly bewitching scene of the natives in their frenzy of delight in perspective, the priest little knows that a dreadful idea, at once nebulous and slithery, is in the making and that in his musings he is de facto sowing the seeds for the abominable thought that is destined to rock the faith of the man of God!

Trouble starts when it crosses Father Campbell's mind that the focal point of the ritualistic extravaganza is manhood. He also notes that, in the event, there cannot possibly be any bounds to the dissipation of the spirit with its implied threat to the imbibed creeds, fragile devotions and whatever else the natives may have been taught to parrot as catechumens.

A very practical man, Father Campbell is not in the habit of letting himself be deceived by appearances. He easily recalls the difficulties he had just trying to have students at the Major Seminary pronounce Latin words correctly. Their failure to use Latin, the Seminary's official language, in conversation pointed to a patent inability to follow not just the Latin mass but the liturgy as a whole in his view. The chances that his mostly illiterate parishioners possess a satisfactory grasp of the Church's teachings were slim indeed!

But he sometimes thought that it was perhaps well that the Curia in Rome was determined to stick with Latin as the Church's official language. He doubted if any good could come from employing Kiwelekhe in church liturgy! For some very strange reason a number of the commonest terms in Kiwelekhe sounded exactly like a few of the "dirty" words in the priest's own European tongue, reinforcing his belief that any move in that direction would be wrong! Father Campbell is contemplating these things when the fleeting though floats through his mind that the salvation of the Welekha tribesmen and particularly their offspring would be greatly facilitated if they forsook their mother tongue and adopted Lain as their new language!

To make headway in the Christianization of the pagan enclaves of the still "dark" continent, thinks the churchman, the youth have to be screened from the bad influence of the folklores, dance rituals and the myriad other weird things relished by the primitive and, he has been told, once upon a time cannibalistic tribesmen. Yes - shielded from their entire blighted cultural heritage! No wonder that after five decades of evangelizing, the tribe of the Welekha, numbering some two hundred thousand souls, has not in all of that time produced a single vocation to the priesthood!

"Damn it!" the priest curses under his breath, staring ahead into the pews that are crowded with white clad expatriate sisters and a sprinkling of native postulants who mostly hail from adjoining tribal lands.

"Christianity and these superstitions they call traditions cannot go together," he hisses. "They are contradictions - the one being godly and the other satanic!" he mumbles, shifting his gaze so that it now rests on the haggard, life-size wooden figure of the crucified Lord that looms over the sanctuary.

No sooner does the priest pass that damning sentence than he seems to sense a ring of untruth in his own verdict, orthodox though it sounds. Although still in the process of sizing up the problem, his racing philosophical mind hits on something that, he suddenly realizes, had never occurred to him before.

True - the primitive *ng'oma* dances, with their uninhibited self-abandonment, and the generally entrancing life-modes of the natives, including acts of libation, magic incantations and

129

such like, were aimed at mollifying the occult. But these pagan rites, he now reflects, have as their object the self-same mundane matter that is the focal point of the Church's own sacraments - birth, marriage, reconciliation and death.

Father Campbell looks a little bemused as he concedes to himself that the inveterate "ancestor worshippers" could very well argue that the church's, not their own, practices represented a departure from the true path! He balks at the implied suggestion that the beat of African drums, and not the drone of his own quaint voice as he recites the Office day in and day out, holds the key to heavenly joys!

He remains kneeling when his disciplined congregation of sisters and postulants rises, begins to file out of the pews singly, and genuflects in the direction of the altar and tabernacle. The movement of shuffling feet and the occasional grating of a shoe as they depart in silence for the refectory does not interrupt the goings-on in the Curé's mind.

Left alone, he feels even less enthusiastic about the other and potentially more dangerous proposition, namely that neither western culture nor Christendom has produced through the ages a heritage capable of stirring a people to heights of mirth and jubilation the way the cultures of the "heathen" and essentially "primitive" tribes of Africa have done.

Whilst Christendom on its part has produced luminaries like Francis of Assisi, Teresa of Avila and a few other mostly strange types whose union with the Redeemer, even prior to their departure from this world, afforded them a foretaste of eternal bliss in their day, these exceptions to the rule are too few and far in between to provide any significant rebuttal of the damaging proposition. As for the so-called Western culture, it is, the priest now concedes, decrepit enough and

130

indeed perverted and too dehumanizing to merit any further word in its defence!

The hairs on Father Campbell's dome stand on end as he mentally seeks escape routes from the difficult position he sees looming up. He recalls involuntarily how, years back as a newly ordained priest, he was wont to cross himself every time he found himself faced with some seemingly intractable problem - to summon some latent brainpower (or will power) as it were. He smiles to himself as he thinks: "This would have been one of those occasions!"

The priest also still remembers how, on many such occasions, he felt inspiration well up in him from nowhere immediately afterward - to buck him up in the nick of time before he uttered some blasphemy or started to doubt his faith!

Now, decades later, it ordinarily would be most unlikely for the P.P., a seasoned member of the Church's hierarchy, to cross himself in circumstances such as those. He now normally crosses himself before meals, when commencing or concluding a prayer, or bestowing a benediction on an individual or an object. But the unexpected happens! Father Campbell stirs from his rigid posture and then, suddenly and without apparent reason, crosses himself once, then again once twice over! He feels neither qualms nor unease about his action. For his mind engrossed with the awful discovery that pagan rituals can be quite a match for Christian liturgy fails to register these mechanical movements!

Part Two

6

The Narrow Path

When Nkharanga, standing stiffly to attention in a cheap black suit and tie, Mvyengwa, her head bowed down meekly beneath the veil of a plain wedding gown, exchange marriage vows, on the occasion of their wedding, they are not exactly of the same mind in all of their intentions right there and then. But they certainly are of one mind and one heart regarding the kind of upbringing they visualise for their children - they do not doubt that the Almighty, in his infinite goodness and power, will bless them with offspring.

The sort of upbringing that the newly wed couple envisage for the fruits of their sacramental bond is, of course far different from that which Montessori and the likes of her preach. Fortunately - or unfortunately - for the couple, they have never heard of Montessori and her camp. The latter doubtless would stand condemned by reason of the doctrines of self-reliance and freedom from control that they advocate for the young, and the emphasis on the so-called "rights of young people". These things, sounding as they seemingly would the death knell of Christian morality, already are the work of the devil himself in the couple's view!

How on earth can one expect mortal man, warped by original sin, to grow into a useful being whilst being afforded opportunities to do as he desires! The very suggestion would seem to them preposterous. By the same token, humans stand to be spoilt by comforts of the body and have to be denied all such.

With an uncompromising sense of self-righteousness, the newly wedded pair have for their part resolved that no sibling of theirs will, God forbid, be exposed to hedonism or similar tripe. Their children will be fostered so as to make obedience to Christian ethics their first nature and the pursuit of individual common sense their second. Their little ones will accordingly be taught to eschew the artificial humility that hypocrites the world over display unashamedly and will be given constant guidance to enable them to follow the narrow path of true humility.

As the earnest couple see it, the greatest talent that normal human beings possess is the ability to conform. Besides, it appears to Nkharanga and his wife - given the backwardness of the Welekha in particular and of black people in general – that the Almighty in His goodness has richly endowed their race in that respect, even though in other respects like technological advancement for instance He sort of forgot them. The couple, aware of the fact that hedonism and technological advancement had for all practicable purposes become handmaids, see that as a blessing in disguise. Anyway, that being so, unlike the unworthy biblical servant who received but one talent from his master and buried it, they are determined to develop that talent to the point beyond which they can develop it no further, and this with regard to both themselves and whoever will come under their influence!

Faithful followers of the Church's doctrines, the couple do not at all feel they need to crack their brains to discover ways of systematically lulling persons who might happen to come within their ambit into acquiescing to the "sweet call of self-immolation and obedience". They are not even about to presume - so they think - that they can command, all on their own, the necessary influence and pressures to achieve this.

Somehow it all seems already figured out for them. In their literal minded way, they believe in the workings of God's grace and, of course, such success - or, indeed, failure - as accrues to their efforts is in their reckoning rightly ascribable to their Redeemer and Saviour.

Before Nkharanga's wedding, Father Campbell displayed a reluctance to appoint the former Protestant to the position of catechist. Now that the proselyte has shown, by his successful courtship of and marriage to a staunch Christian and ex-novice, that he too is determined to be a committed and respected member of the Church's laity, the balding priest is persuaded that no more good will be served by his continued frustration of so ambitious and clearly well-disposed soul. Moreover, the priest, whose own parents were converts from *Svenska kyrkan* (the Church of Sweden) was one of those who believed that Protestant converts to Catholicism typically ended up infusing into the Church a very much-needed evangelical fervour.

The number of people Nkharanga and his matronly wife can count among their true friends at their respective places of birth has never been significant. Thus on their arrival at Khalolweni, which is easily the most far flung of the mushrooming outposts of St. Peter's Parish, the couple only miss the company of their mentors. These consist mainly of priests and nuns who encouraged them along the "difficult" route to what they have described as true and undiluted Christian belief.

The young adventurers do not otherwise care less even though Nkharanga is coming to a truly remote corner of Welekha District for his first posting as a resident catechist. They even consider it advantageous to be as far flung from their own clan folk as possible! As it happens, they are almost immediately confronted with problems not entirely unlike those they seek to avoid by minimising contact with their own people.

The welcome accorded the strangers by the local populace at the new station is chilling for several reasons. The dialect spoken by the *mwalimu* and his stern, evangelically minded wife differs slightly from the local dialect. The sound of the slanted "Northern" dialect of the newcomers scarcely seems to appeal to the ears of their listeners. Then also, the behavior of the catechist and his wife from the first leaves no doubt in the eyes of the local populace about the fact that the couple despise the traditions of the land. Added to all that is the apparent presumptuousness of these "freaks", how dare they imagine that they can successfully propagate the strange new "mythologies" in he strict traditional Welekha society!

What causes the greatest rancor is the indication Nkharanga one day lets slip out of his mouth that he intends to acquire land and to settle in the area perhaps permanently. The people here as elsewhere in the district are customarily wary of strangers, white or black, who might trick them into parting with the soil in which their forefathers lie buried.

The rancor of the population reaches a climatic point with the discovery later on that the catechist, a stranger to those parts, is a nominated member of the District Council, overseer of the machinery the colonial powers have set up to administer the lands they evidently have designs to exploit!

But this also marks a turning point in the relations between the *walimu* and the local populace - the support Nkharanga receives from his wife makes her as much a *mwalimu* in the eyes of the people of Khalolweni as the catechist himself! The turn-around in relations coincides with Nkharanga's success in persuading one of the villagers to sell to him a small parcel of land bordering on the grounds of the catechumenate for cultivation. Following the catechist's advice, the vendor invests the proceeds - a roll of paper money he receives in payment - in a bicycle. This makes the villager in question the only other person apart from Nkharanga who owns a bicycle for miles around. The catechist was given the bicycle he now owns by the Catholic "Mission" which considers it and the catechism to be essential tools of his "trade".

Although the narrowness of the footpaths and the steep gradients as well as other numerous obstacles like rocks and overhanging boughs of trees render bicycles of little use in this part of the district, the outlandish conveyance arouses enormous interest among the inhabitants an ownership of one soon comes to be associated with convenience, modernity and even affluence. But bicycles can only be bought for cash from the bazaar in far away Livingstoneville, the district administrative center and seat of the *Zungumuzia* as the District Council is called in Kiwelekhe.

The tendency from now on, therefore, is to see in Nkharanga's offer to purchase land the chance of becoming moneyed and advancing oneself. And so, more and more folks begin to show their willingness to sell unwanted pieces of land to the new comers. It thus remains a matter of time before more and more residents not just of the neighbourhood but of outlying areas as well begin to "accept" the new comers and what they stand for.

The former outcasts begin to command, in due course, the respect due to a dutiful couple. For their part, the Nkharangas have no intention of letting down people's expectations. They now feel enjoyed, in their dual capacity as leading citizens and teachers, to educate the masses in matters pertaining to the world and to the spirit no less, but especially, they feel, the latter.

The policies pursued hinge on the couple's desire to ensure that their offspring, and all such as become their disciples, grow up to pass on to future generations the Christian tradition that is reflected in their own living style. This policy is guided by the belief, shared by both of them, that nothing redounds to a Catholic home more than bringing up children dedicated to the Lord's service. Indeed, they are no sooner blessed with their first child, haply a boy, than they set upon their young charge with close to fanatic fervour, intent on seeing him imbued with Christian sentiments in the same manner and degree as is the case with themselves.

While they outwardly seek rapprochement with the local populace, the walimu are actually undeterred in their resolve to maintain what they consider a suitable distance from it, particularly as regards social practices. The couple's segregationist policy is an open secret from the start. But with the arrival of their first child, the grizzly details of their chosen course begin to emerge.

From the outset - and more unconsciously than consciously - they take to systematically lording it over the hapless creature, determined to see him imbibe the religious beliefs they themselves hold dear in their original, supposedly undiluted form. Initially they approach their task by recourse to pictorial representations of scenes from the bible and the lives of saints, and use other worldly-wise methods they know to be effective for the purpose.

The influences and pressures, often quite crude, have varying effects, some of them obvious and some not so. One not-so-obvious effect of the treatment is that of narrowing the range of the child's object-awareness - to use a bit psychiatric jargon - so that he consequently is capable of only a dim awareness of the objects that fall outside the scope of the directed response. If the psychiatrists are to be believed, the impressionable little one will finally have no choice but to submit to the control of the couple's inescapable psychic omnipresence!

To cap it all, the couple throw up a veritable iron curtain around the boy. Even though the enraged neighbours and others inveigh them for their seeming distrustfulness, the *walimu* persevere in ensuring that the boy has minimum contact with children from the surrounding homes. They are infinitely glad that Providence has not made them work in the immediate vicinity of their own next-of-kin, where it would be impossible to resist the invectives their relatives would most certainly direct at them. They proceed to carefully screen their growing child from the influences of his "heathen" surroundings!

As need arises, the lad is physically kept away from the "bad" influences. Such need does arise from time to time as when country-folk, for instance, abandon their implements to join in *n'goma* dances at traditional weddings and during the circumcision seasons. It is deemed harmful for the impressionable kid to view the vulgar and uninhibited displays that have little about them, morality-wise, to commend them. During the circumcision season, with its pageants, dances and orgiastic extravaganza, their young charge is never permitted to leave the house!

Even the maids, who usually double as babysitters and cooks, are vetted prior to being taken on. Their engagement is, in any case, subject to an undertaking that they themselves agree to adhere to a prescribed code of conduct. Troublesome relatives who take it upon themselves to journey all the way from either Namwikholongwe or Nghashongwe to see the couple and then make the mistake of voicing criticisms concerning the couple's practices are turned outdoors and curtly told not to return again.

The couple's firstborn and the offspring who come after him thus grow up understanding that it is bad to mix with other children, to eat away from home, to be found lingering in public places or people's homes without lawful excuse, and generally unaware of the need for people to have roots in a social setting of some kind.

If there are some who object to the result, there are many who approve even if indirectly, and these range from His Grace, the Most Reverend Bishop of the Diocese and Right Reverend and Very Reverend Monsignors, who finds himself drawn to Khalolweni and inevitably to the Nkharanga's homestead by some strange force, the P.P. in the person of the Reverend Father Campbell, to simple folk, both Christian and pagan. But never is the reality of this brought into shaper relief than when the couple, driven by their avowed love for fellow men, stir to dispense their heavenly inspired hospitality.

Since their first arrival at the bush station, the walimu have considered it imperative upon them to ensure the comfort of the parish priest and his assistant when they call at the outpost to give catechumens supplementary Christian instruction or to administer the sacraments. It does not take very long, however, before the couple find themselves playing host to touring priests, nuns, religious brothers and even bishops in their modest house facing the ramshackle edifice that provisionally serves as the church.

The shack, conspicuously located on the hilltop, is due to give way to a more permanent, albeit far from sumptuous, structure put up with the assistance of a wealthy Irish couple.

The gleaming white painted exterior thereof and the rooftop cross fashioned from a pair of massive concrete beams will be visible for miles around and will, in time, become an even better landmark than either the hill itself or the sunbathed cliffs that adorn the neighborhood.

There are likewise not a few seminarians from distant lands (Welekha district has yet to send its first representative to the seminary) who, on return to their communities, can boast being acquainted with the couple, a pair (as they tell it) who radiate a thoroughly Christian spirit, encircled though they are by heathens and unbelievers! And if there is one thing that their memories invariably retain, it is the fascination with which the couple's children (whom they will have promptly nicknamed "angels") received them.

Observing the gaily-clad little ones step forward to greet them with characteristic humility, a guest does on occasion succeed in remaining detached and unimpressed by the evidently atypical performance. Possibly wary lest the young people are just putting on a show with regard particularly to their physical appearance, and mistrustful of the demonstration of shy modesty, the suspicious guest soon finds himself/herself weighing the chances that the couple may in fact be in the habit of "dressing up" their children and themselves at the first sign of an "important" visitor!

It is a trite matter thereafter to reach the conclusion that the couple's children, by nature tatterdemalions who are normally prevented from going about bedraggled as well by incessant warnings of the most dire consequences, now instinctively substitute shy modesty for their usual gawky disposition; that they adopt, as occasion demands, artificial muffled tones in place of the pealing, supplicating refrains that customarily represent speech when "important personages" are not around to be reckoned with; that they repress at will the impulsive motions (that characterize relations among love-starved children), assuming in their place the subdued composure that is supposed to pass for self-respect!

But it is only very occasionally that this happens, for many guests who find themselves thinking in these critical terms usually soon choose in the face of their hosts' solid reputation as first rate persons, to stifle all such demeaning notions. Indeed in conversations with the couple's children, atypical diversionary tactic employed by many an esteemed guest is to take the young people aside and let them know in no uncertain language that they are lucky to have such wonderful people for their parents!

During their visits to that "Christian home", the reverend guests are always made to feel as comfortable as they can wish. They have food to eat - delicious meals washed down with bottles of beer or mineral water.

Even if the eminent personage is making only a brief stopover (the district's road communications network has been expanding catechumenate), and is unable to tarry long enough to enjoy the couple's bounty to the extent described, a wad of notes squeezed into the palm of the visitor "for petrol" can usually be counted on to do the trick. Only a single experience of that kind is necessary to persuade the Right Reverend Bishop, the Reverend Monsignor, Father, Deacon, Brother, or Sister to pay the good couple another visit.

The visitors are usually not told of the fact that the house in which they sit and feast is consecrated to the Most Sacred Heart of the Redeemer. But after seeing the myriad pictures of saints the frames of which literally cover the walls of the living room and the statues of Christ, the Blessed Virgin Mary, and of St. Joseph amongst others, they are as a rule never left in doubt as regards the deep spirituality that reigns in their host's home. "Here is a couple at long last" they declare among themselves, "who are zealous for the Word of God without reserve!"

Not all who so declare are even aware that not one day passes on which the Holy Rosary and the *Angelus*, as well as the daily morning and evening prayers aren't recited in that home. This constancy on the part of the couple and their children is matched by good works, pre-eminently the giving of tithes and visitation of the sick. These activities, combined with the couple's reputation as leading Christians, make it fairly inevitable that people from near and far come to look upon the inmates of that home as high-minded individuals deserving of the most special regard. The devotion of the couple to the education of both young and old and the development of the district in the meantime grows to be a talking point not just in Khalolweni but in the neighbouring regions as well.

7

Beyond the Reach of Beelzebub

He is hardly a fortnight old. Yet, even at such a tender age, he stands out for the peculiar alertness he seems possessed of. He is far from used to all the sounds around him, but the tremendous clamor for his attention that has been building up does not fail to drive the point home. He clearly is the center of special attention! Innocent Kintu, as the little infant is called, finds himself persistently and most ruthlessly assailed by meaningless mumblings and other like hocus-pocus that his parents, and eventually the maid, as well as guests, direct at him.

The neighbours who flock in to share the couple's joy constitute a particularly disappointing rabble. Without giving as much as a wink to the greasy condition of their rough, germ laden hands and clothing, they invariably rush to grab hold on him - as if not to do so would signify ill will!

Little Kintu's learning faculties become debarred from setting their own pace in the hurly-burly in which he finds himself thrust at birth. While they prompt and approve of their child's alertness, Kintu's parents deeply resent what they feel is interference on the part of the neighbours who call to express their good wishes on Kintu's birth. Victor Nkharanga and his wife are predictably wary lest the affectionate embraces that the neighbours for instance shower on their "angel" result in over-familiarity and an uncontrolled relationship impinging on his spiritual development.

On their part, the neighbours, amongst them converts to Christianity whose intense traditionalism makes them in the couple's view Christians only in name, hope that the *walimu*'s cute little boy will grow up to convert his "misguided" parents back to traditionalism.

Innocent's honeymoon on earth is long by ordinary standards but short-lived when compared to that enjoyed by the majority of kids born. But it is intensely enjoyable - much more so than the average honeymoons enjoyed by little tots following upon their birth into the world.

After being cuddled excessively and with unimaginable fondness for some three or four months, the child Kintu soon begins to know fear as no other little one his age has known. For, tiny as he is, it soon becomes clear that his baby cries and the bursts of emotion that he gives vent to from time to time are destined to miss their object which is none other that the unvarnished sympathy of his dad and mom. The fact that his effusions spring from the raw animal instincts in him makes the frustration and pain of his infantile mind sharp and unbearable.

Consistently denied the sympathetic regard his puerile nature has predisposed him to expect, he too gradually begins to suppose that perhaps his nature, rather than the machinations of his earnest and otherwise admirable guardians, is over-demanding. This point of view seems to be fully borne out by events that, young as he is, he cannot fail to notice. And that view grows to become immanent in him and seemingly incontestable as he gains in maturity over the months.

To be sure, the laudable deeds of the "personages" in question (Innocent Kintu will never know his parents except as lofty, infallible and fathomless messengers of God!), where his survival in general and his "last end" in particular are concerned, are only too well known among the populace.

Notable among these deeds was the timely decision by the couple to have their child not only baptised but also consecrated to Mary, Mother of God, barely hours following his birth.

Although accompanied by the usual pangs and pains, the childbirth was smooth. The good lady remained with all her wits about her throughout the delivery and was quite alert. Trouble started when the senior matron, her features drawn in what seemed to be a look of concern, let slip from her lips something to the effect that the baby, unlike all others she had helped deliver, skipped his post-natal whimper!

While the stray comment would have meant little or even nothing to other mortal souls of the lay world, it was not to be so with the couple. The anxious look on the matron's face as she worried aloud worked on the newly delivered mother's mind unabated until, racked by uncertainty regarding the child's welfare, she confronted her husband and explained to the baffled young father the basis for her fear. When they finally asked the matron to elaborate, the surprised lady told them firmly to ignore the "meaningless and unintentional" remark and urged that they dismiss their fears.

Their minds were already made up, however, and they proceeded to have the infant baptised without further delay. He was christened Innocent after the Holy Innocents who were murdered by the so-called Herod the Great. The former ex-novice, looking distracted as ever had determined to put that first fruit of their marriage beyond Beelzebub's reach, easily prevailed on her husband and on the hospital chaplain (who had once paid the couple a visit and was therefore not a total stranger) to have little Innocent consecrated forthwith to the Blessed Virgin.

The couple's kid was discharged without any sign that he had been in any danger for his life. But on arrival home, the *walimu* systematically and with characteristic callousness painted quite a different picture, leading the neighbourhood to believe that, but for the grace of God, the couple's beautiful little baby would perhaps not have survived to be with them!

The subsequent behaviour of the child's parents had led the neighbours to infer that his "miraculous" survival posed a challenge to the catechist and his single-minded wife to live both inwardly and outwardly as behoved "persons who had found salvation". On their part, the couple proceeded, as a matter of course, to have the very cottage in which they lived sprinkled with holy water to signify that the lives of its inmates were concentrated to the service of their Divine Master.

And so, the couple now are fully confident that their boy, protected through the intercession of none other than the immaculately conceived mother of the their Divine Redeemer, is safe from the evils of heathendom - evils that abound in the otherwise picturesque and richly blessed mountain ranges that together make up Kiwelekha District.

Indeed, whereas another couple might be persuaded to suffer poor little Kintu to indulge, even if only in a small way, in his strivings - a harmless tug at Father Campbell's beard, a determined endeavour on his part to escape the embrace of a visiting nun, or a sudden refusal to cooperate with his mom at feeding time - as a lawful way of calming his incipient temper, Victor and Annamaria, with consummate devotion, seek to stamp out from the very first each and every propensity on Innocent's part that points at self-assertiveness or, as they think, self-love!

The success of their efforts, which are more often than not accompanied by a show of insensate rage, soon become manifest in the speed with which the impressionable and hapless little thing deserts his inborn hubris and, instead of merely rising to the occasions when a demonstration of his sense of submission is called for, the little one clearly feels forlorn when no one fusses around him in the overbearing fashion to which he has grown used. There is now finally nothing on which poor little Kintu thrives or that gives him the kicks as does servility. As he grows and waxes, nothing arouses his rancor as does the sight of self-centered behaviour and the self-assurance that invariably goes with it.

As a kid and subsequently as a teenager, Innocent never thinks of these things consciously. For, his indoctrination in that somewhat peculiar ideologue - indoctrination that people of lesser ambitions would be inclined to consider an idiosyncrasy of a possibly terminal kind even - and the loathing he feels for anything frolicsome has began when he is but a toddler.

But while Innocent Kintu is outnumbered by kids whose life's aim seems to be what he would describe as the senseless display of brazenness and unbounded cheek even in front of persons of note, his own peerless disposition and touch of idealism multiply the number of his admirers at least among "people who matter" and confound potential detractors. This is ample compensation for his early decision to forego what he certainly would term "self-love" but others more likely would deem self-respect!

It becomes fairly plain in the course of time that apart from the children of the couple, there are very few souls abroad whose sublimation in the course of growing up is so nearly complete. Still, as far as Innocent, the eldest and also most committed of the couple's children is concerned, neither his brother Gideon nor Francesca and Josepha, his two sisters whose feminine nature predisposes them so to dare individuals of respect including their own parents, possess the combination of singleness of mind and unwarped disposition that sustains godly souls in this "vale of tears". Inclined to frivolity and quick to grieve what Innocent Kintu always thinks of as imagined misfortunes, they are plainly, in his view, a shame to the family!

It is past question that Innocent, whose self-effacement dazzles the imagination of even his father's most ardent critics, one day will be persuaded to speak about these things. But assuming the impossible takes places, there is no doubt that he would be explicit and most candid in what he would say. He might, for instance, tell of the fact that he shares fully in the "rational consciousness" of his wise and respected parents, and that through them he has become possessed of an undying faith in his Lord and Redeemer. And he also might proceed to give his inquisitor intelligence to the effect that, being truly in love with the Most High, he passes his days (by the grace of God) unfettered by base worldly cares. He might likewise tell of the unutterable peace of soul and other consolations that this condition ensures for him.

Innocent Kintu's relationship with his esteemed dad and mom and with God's representatives on earth reflects his spiritual relationship with his Divine Master. Years later, as he prepares himself for admission to the seminary, he will indeed look back and rejoice in the fact that it long was his resolve to do in life the bidding of the Most High with at least the same, if not greater, assertiveness and devotion as he performed the bidding of his venerable "elders".

8

Breakthrough

As they grow up, the *walimu's* children exhibit a most peculiar attitude to that well-known purgative - pain. The attitude to the phenomenon of pain and suffering is reflected in many of their actions. Retiring in manner and as docile as lambs, nothing touches the foursome and particularly Innocent (whose leadership role in these matters is matched by constancy and zeal) like the sight of a suffering being, only that they are touched in a varying manner depending on the background to each case.

Take the occasion when some notable person pays a visit to the cottage and they are desired to kill a chicken for the visitor's meal. The act of slitting open the bird's throat and bleeding it to death, while heart-rending and pretty unsettling in the beginning, in no time loses its grisly overtones and begins to feature in their thoughts only to the extent that it represents an occasion to practice the virtue of obedience. Additional assurance as regards the propriety of their action readily comes out of their awareness that the principal beneficiary is a person of note!

The fact that the bird suffers pain, if ever it crosses their minds, remains just one of those trite things in their view and one that the mind is better left unencumbered with - a veritable distraction. The chicken, in this instance, may as well be shorn of all capacity to feel pain!

Innocent in particular sees nothing unusual in such an attitude and tends to react vehemently if he suspects that someone charged with such a duty is tending to become "chicken-hearted". Their views regarding when to commiserate with a victim of suffering and when not to do so reflects in a direct way the notions they have about such fundamental things as the "purpose of creation" and the "value of material vis-à-vis spiritual things". For example, they tend to regard their own physical selves as so much foreign matter that will in time disintegrate practically of its own accord.

There is in fact nothing about the human body that merits useful consideration in their estimation. More than anyone else, Innocent tends to live according to the theoretical or better, philosophical ideal! He fact that his body registers pain just goes to prove that his earthly life (which has never seemed worth living in any case) is de facto ephemeral and not worth an instant's thought. In his understanding, man's earthly existence has value only to the extent to which it can be held in fief to others in humble obedience!

The phenomenon of pain and suffering are thus considered meaningful only in relation to the notion of punishment and cleansing. It may indeed be said in this connection that nothing delights Innocent more than the sight of a "delinquent" being disciplined. This is so in spite of the fact that he never brings himself to gloat openly over any occasion it happens. That naughty individuals, being as they are under the vassalage of Prince of Darkness, deserve to be cast in hell fire for instance seems to him pretty obvious. Conscious as he is of the evil all around him, the future seminarian would never have been able to conceive of creation without a bottomless pit of some kind into which the unrepentant - and they abound to be many naturally - are cast for everlasting retribution. Earthly pains and suffering are, in contrast, this much easier to justify, being wages of people's sins for one!

Talking about hell, if there is anything that Innocent loathes and which he is prepared to fight with everything in him, it is the biblical hell. Is it not, after all, a dogma of the Church that there is this place of damnation! Besides, he is not about to set himself up in opposition to the infallibility with which the doctrines of Holy Mother Church are taught. Still - all pious sentiments aside - it is rather unlikely that any of the *walimu's* children will ever forget the punishments they individually take at the latter's hands for even the most minor lapses in discipline. The catechist and his wife have always firmly believed that to spare the rod is to spoil the child, and they have never had any scruples about applying the stick liberally where it hurts real bad. And, while at it, there is nothing they detest like the noise of a culprit whimpering!

As long as the unruly streak in Innocent or any of his kindred shows signs of revival, the conscientious couple do not hesitate to wallop the culprit on his bottom, ankles, knuckles, or even scalp. This foretaste of hell has predisposed Innocent to assume that the real hell (which was originally intended for fallen angels according to the catechism) is not the sort of place he can fancy.

But he also knows that the "earthly" hell he went through before becoming "saved" through submission and a godsent knack for blind obedience is nothing compared to the crucible of pain and suffering that Gideon and, to a lesser extent, Francesca and Josepha have gone through. The trio have always tended to provoke the most unsavoury tempers of the couple by the way they deviate from established norms.

Innocent learnt extremely early on in his life that it is foolish to act counter to his parents' will. His birth order has undoubtedly served him in good stead; and, similarly, the feminine roles of Francesca and Josepha have helped them.

Gideon, who will turn atheist in later life, has borne the brunt of the couple's ire, and has on occasion displayed what is tantamount to "lunacy" through his refusal to conceal his own spite.

Innocent has guessed (correctly as it turns out) that this is all due to the negligence of his esteemed parents in giving Gideon free reign and permitting him too many opportunities to interact with the neighbourhood's children. These children are adjudged by him as "thoroughly and irredeemably misbehaved" and "very bad" indeed for the simple reason that their misguided and "ignorant" parents allowed them "excessive liberties" from their infancy and failed to "discipline" them the way he himself was disciplined!

While punishment by whipping with the cane has been rampant, the use of other forms of "correction" has by no means been neglected by the good *walimu*. A favourite non-corporeal form of punishment for example is the couple's use of stinging epithets on the habitual offender in public. The ensuing isolation, particularly give the fact that the couple have been careful not to let their children mix freely with others in the neighbourhood as they grow up, cannot be expected to be anything but unbearable!

It is not uncommon for the culprit to be sent to bed supperless or to be locked out for part of the night. What with the blood-curdling tales of man-eating bats, of witches and sorcerers who pursue their craft under the cover of night, and other horror stories culled from the vast Welekha lore, not even Gideon with his spiteful nature can desist in these circumstances from coming to terms with the rebellious self in him if only out of desire to appear acceptable to his indomitable and unflinching parents.

The decision to fall in line always proves to be the wiser course. The neighbours and the populace at large now hold the walimu in high regard, and it can never do for Gideon or any of his siblings to show that he or she disagrees. For one – instead of being seen as self-respecting individuals whop are willing to suffer for their faith in "human reason", and "self-reliance", they would just stand to be dismissed as failures who now are seeking to be no better than other good-for-nothing Welekha youth.

Respect for the *walimu* has in fact become a cult and it is common to hear exclamations such as "Here are children brought up in the Christian tradition!" or "Such well behaved, dependable and gracious youngsters!" Without the slightest doubt, people in the neighbourhood regard the couple's children as having been emancipated from the fetters of heathendom and hence quite unlike their own offspring who, they fear, are likely to remain tradition bound.

While they themselves cannot get down to giving their children the same treatment with the cane, for instance, they are generally well disposed to admire and even to wish they were in a position to emulate the actions of the couple. Some have even wondered whether there is a couple anywhere in the world that is so steadfast and devoted to the "correct" upbringing of their children. And so, when the *walimu's* eldest boy declares his intention at the young age of seven to apply for admission to the minor seminary in order to commence his studies for the priesthood, the majority of people receive the news with not a hint of surprise. And there is many a Christian then who cheer on the catechist and his matronly wife for the spectacular breakthrough.

9.

The Minor Seminarian

At eight, Innocent Kintu, who regards himself as a pillar of virtue, is set to begin his career as a seminarian. If it wasn't for his deep humility, he would undoubtedly be the first to admit that deep in his heart of hearts he knows that in all of Welekha-land, there is not another of, or about, his age with credentials that can be considered suitable for admission into St. Paul's Minor Seminary. The hurdles he himself has had to overcome along the route to the seminary career are proof enough of this.

A year ago his parents, nudged by their son's frequent and to all appearances sincere averments of intention with regard to the sacred calling, battled unsuccessfully to have him admitted to St. Paul's. The normally voluble albeit indulgent Father Campbell had to face the couple and tell them matter-of-factly that the Diocesan rules did not permit seven-year olds and under to be enrolled as seminarians.

The *Omukhulu*, as the parish priest is referred to in the Kiwelekhe tongue, is eager to redeem his pledge to have the keen lad join the institution that he himself founded not so long ago, and he would of course very much like to see his chilled relations with the pioneering family return to normal at the earliest opportunity.

Kintu's record at the bush primary school that the Church operates in conjunction with the catechumenate has, meanwhile, been quite impressive. From elementary class one through four, he has never once ceded first place to any other pupil. That would, for one, have implied slackness and inattentiveness, and would clearly not have presaged commendably for a lad of his ambitions and stature. For another, such a development would have conceivably led to a crisis with his stern parents. Even the newer generation of teachers manning the ever-expanding Khalolweni education centre have been highly impressed!

Lean and a shade too tall for his age, Innocent Kintu continues to maintain his record as he graduates from Prep (as the beginning class at the minor seminary is called) to Low Figures, High Figures, Grammar, Syntax, Poetry and finally Rhetoric. He does so despite the fact that he is regularly engaged in such extra-curricular activities as playing the harmonium and lawn tennis, occupations at which he is likewise growing to excel.

The young pioneer from Welekha-land, who prefers to wear his hair "natural" or uncombed, has an effusive, almost contagious sense of humour. His humour often even appears to belie the devout figure he cuts in chapel particularly while clad in his white cassock.

But it gradually comes to be known in the course of time that the retiring, self-effacing youth neither welcomes discussion of his praying habits nor entertains people's curiosity about his attitude to the world at large. After initial attempts to talk everyone he met into agreeing with his mostly pious notions proves futile, he simply clams up in so far as those notions are concerned. Thus, perhaps not surprisingly, the subtlest suggestion on the part of anyone with regard thereto now tends to evoke his direst ire in addition to making the usually happy-go-lucky and mesmeric seminarist susceptible to brooding.

The "*mwalimu*'s son", as he is still largely known back in his home parish, is otherwise genteel in his manners almost to a fault as well as being of singularly up-right behaviour. While his mates at St. Paul's are continually fighting to control their impulses in order to reduce their apparently innate resistance to the practice of such virtues as obedience and charity, Innocent Kintu's punctilious observance of the Rule seems to come to him naturally, and he easily stands out as the most exemplary seminarian in a community of over two hundred souls. In some respects things even appear to have been arranged by Providence in advance to his advantage. The ignominious "Key" is a case in point.

Consisting of a rugged piece of metal about a foot long and worn suspended from an equally rugged and coarse chain, the hideous Key was Father Campbell's idea of how to persuade the minor seminarians with their diverse linguistic backgrounds and tribalistic tendencies improve their spoken English and at the same time promote the much wanted community spirit on the campus. According to established lore, the Key is a relic from Father Campbell's discarded auto!

The Key derives its effectiveness from the connotations of degeneracy and degradation that are associated with wearing it. The student body regards the instrument with what amounts to abject fear. Each morning a student selected by Father "Rector" at random and as surreptitiously as possible takes charge of that object of opprobrium and infamy and, concealing it careful in a pocket or under the shirt, snoops around seeking out his prey, namely the vernacular speakers.

It is never a problem catching someone in the process of talking to a fellow mate in a vernacular tongue. The snooper's duty is to approach the offender and put the Key around the culprit's neck. It is a part of the Rule that the culprit turned victim wear the demeaning instrument over his shirt or cassock as the case may be and, thus attired, continue with the

157

day's normal pursuits until he in turn alights on another transgressor of the vernacular precept. In the event, the former's guilt is considered fully remitted thereupon, with no further need to expiate for his sin. The transfer of the Key to a new "carrier" becomes increasingly difficult as the day wears on, and predictably so since the Key carrier at supper goes without the meal! A seminarian who misses his supper three times during a school term as a result of the operation of the Key is liable for dismissal from the seminary.

While Kintu's spoken English is good by African standards and stands to benefit from his study of Caesar, Virgil, and other works of the literati of Ancient Rome, his tribal language is neither spoken nor understood by any other person on the seminary campus. Since he himself cannot speak any of the half dozen or so vernacular languages encountered on the seminary campus, he is automatically precluded from being a Key carrier! Thus, even were he to wish to do the highly improbable - namely break the vernacular precept deliberately - the circumstances clearly would deny him the opportunity of doing so.

Beginning with his very first term at St. Paul's Minor Seminary until the very last exactly seven years later, Kintu is consistently rated by the seminary authorities as a bright seminarian of outstanding promise. The boy shows, throughout his Minor Seminary career, that he likes everything the seminary seems able to offer. Few seminarians look forward to the Manual Labor Hour for instance. Kintu on the other hand, notwithstanding his lanky form, which is a far cry from the husky shapes of the majority of his colleagues, invariably heads the column of students as they march from the last afternoon class to the dormitory to change their clothes for the unpopular period.

Shortly after his promotion to High Figures, Kintu is relieved of even that "welcome" chore! Father Choirmaster discerned early that the lad possesses a gift for music in addition to his many other endowments. In order to foster this latest gift, Father Choirmaster arranges to have the lad, who indeed surpasses all other trainee organists in his mastery of the keyboard, take additional music lessons during the Manual Labor Hour.

A contributing factor to the decision to have the gifted young man concentrate on developing his inherent harmonic skills was the abrupt end of Innocent Kintu's singing career. An enthusiastic member of the seminary's renowned choir from the beginning, the starry-eyed Welekha youth let himself be carried away by his exuberance during choir practice just as his last term in Low Figures was coming to a close to the extent of ruining his once melodious voice irreparably. Father Choirmaster had almost no option but to have the youthful and budding organist concentrate his energies on manipulating the keyboard!

It is thus that Kintu, in what has become an everyday scene, is always seen to head to the side chapel, where a well-tuned harmonium is located along side an equally well-tune piano for his convenience, gripping his favourite music manuals with dutiful affection at the first sound of the bell announcing Manual Labor Hour.

By all counts the speed with which Kintu learns to play the piano and the church organ seems to everybody to justify the special privilege of remaining in-doors during the period everyone else is out toiling in the fields. It is no secret that the Manual Labour Hour, more than the Key or anything else, is responsible for the steady and continuous diminution of the student population at St. Paul's.

The youngster's love for music knows no bounds as Father Choirmaster, himself an accomplished pianist, introduces him to everything ranging from the Preludes of Chopin, the Sonatas of Mozart and Chorales of Bach, to the Polyphonies of the Palestrina, and the famed Gregorian chant. Kintu's own choir accompaniment in time develops into a sweet concatenation of sounds that is destined to soar with celestial majesty into the spires of many a church. The sweetly flowing accompaniment, from fingers suitably long and slim, causes many a congregation to explode in prayerful hymn as they sing from the depth of their bosoms.

Innocent Kintu became entrenched as his parents' most beloved child long before he set foot in the seminary. His rising reputation as a seminarian of exceptional promise and a polished church organist only confirms what they suspected from the day he was born, namely that their son was ordained to be a saviour of a sort, not just of his tradition bound tribesmen, but the entire Dark Continent!

As far as they know, Africa is the only place where the Word of God is being preached for the first time ever. It would have come as a surprise to the couple to learn that St. Augustine, Bishop and Confessor and Doctor of the Church, and perhaps one or two others amongst the fathers of the Church were sons of Africa, not to mention Pope Victor I (Nkharanga's own patron saint) who is credited with making Latin the Church's official language.

Convinced that their is the continent's very first truly Christian home, it comes as no surprise to them when an exception is made in Innocent's case with regard to the application of the Diocesan rules relating to seminarians during the periodic breaks in their training.

That no less a personage than the His Worship, the Bishop of the Diocese, calls at the couple's humble place of abode to communicate to them the welcome piece of news is a surprise however. And great is the rejoicing that ensues from their knowledge that their boy, instead of spending all his holidays at the Mission Headquarters under the watchful eye of his Father Parish Priest, was free to spend his week-days with his parents, provided he traveled to the Mission Headquarters at least three times during the week to attend Holy Mass.

In the words of His Worship, there is no doubt that the couple's home is free from the bad influences that have prompted the Diocese to restrict seminarians to residence at their Mission Headquarters in the first place. And so it is that young Kintu comes to represent the hallmark of his parents' success in the evangelizing business in particular and life in general.

As a trailblazer, Innocent Kintu somewhat unexpectedly finds that he is an object of envy to his brother Gideon and sisters Josepha and Francesca. They have grown, probably unwittingly, to detest the apparent ease with which he commands the respect of even the most disreputable elements of the populace in their neighbourhood, and their envy has very nigh turned into hatred for their supremely successful brother. They have, first of all, not been able to enjoy the fun they see other children enjoying. They have had to forego all of that as children of the walimu. And they now find themselves having to deal with this!

Neither Kintu's apparent lofty regard of himself and what his siblings perceive as his rabid authoritarianism nor the couple's habitual harrying of the trio at each and every turn does much to improve this situation. While they have as yet

161

far to go before they turn into open rebels and finally ease from their lives the burden of their once vaunted sublimation, the cleavage that now only exists on the subconscious level is clearly already there nonetheless, waiting to be confirmed with the passage of time.

There is meanwhile never a time when Kintu becomes overwhelmed or piqued by the adoration he receives from the more devout elements in the parish. Whereas seminarians elsewhere, who find themselves objects of sentimental or undue admiration or adulation, gradually manage as a rule to evolve tongues of speech that at least keep at bay the temptations inherent in exposure to false piety, Kintu as his parish's sole representative at St. Paul's misses the benefit of learning from his pals. He therefore continues to be flatly doctrinaire and to believe that there is merit in not concealing the fact of his having left all to follow Christ. For, as he reflects often times, did his loving Master, addressing the multitudes from atop a mountain, not say: "Neither do men light a candle and put it under a bushel, but upon a candlestick, that it may shine to all that are in the house."

If any scruples make to surface, they undoubtedly are stilled by the experience Kintu regularly has each succeeding Sunday morning after High Mass at the Mission Headquarters. As he threads his way from the organ to the church's steps, resplendent in his spotless white cassock, to join the celebrant at the church's front as is his custom, parishioners in their multitudes surge around him eager to say how inspiring to prayer the sounds of the organ are, and to acclaim him as the only church organist they have met whose accompaniment and musical interludes are so conducive to contemplation and prayer - and how they can't wait to see him ordained the first Welekha priest!

Invariably, memories of the spontaneous display of joy and exhilaration remain with Kintu for long after the resumption of the school term, and even haunt him whenever he learns that someone has dropped out from the seminary.

10.

Damn the Old Man

St. Barnabas' Major Seminary to which Innocent Kintu proceeds on completion of his Minor Seminary preparation exudes a special mystique in the eyes of the infant church's laity. The seminary community has always taken the hordes of visitors who flock in from near and far for granted. As far as the "pilgrims" themselves are concerned, however, St. Barnabas' is a worthy place of pilgrimage as much for the sciences of the mind (Philosophy) and of the soul (Theology) taught there as for the fact that, out of the many aspirants to the priesthood who succeed in joining minor seminaries, few indeed survive to reach the Major Seminary.

Finally, the sight of the major seminarians darting nimbly hither and thither, uninhibited by their full-length garb, is a sight to be remembered both for its novelty and for its inspirational value.

Nkharanga is pleased with himself as he and his son pick their way around the seminary campus at the start of his major seminary career on this bright sunny afternoon. Innocent Kintu is one of the lucky few who has been admitted to the august institution upon his promotion from minor seminary; and by the look of it, as he checks into his cubicle, which has a window that overlooks the seminary chapel, he is enjoying what has to be a bright and cheery experience. It is evident from his mien that this has been a long time coming.

Not to be outdone, Nkharanga has been here before on a pilgrimage with his entire family before; and he too feels exhilarated. He would have agreed that when the family came

164

here three years ago on the pilgrimage, they were making what was the equivalent of a metaphorical journey into their beliefs as pilgrimages are sometimes described. This time around, however, there is nothing metaphorical about their visit to St. Barnabas'. Once his son checks in and officially becomes anointed as a "major seminarian", the countdown, Nkharanga feels, will be on; and, within the short space of seven years, a member of his own family will have realized his vocation to the holy priesthood; and, as far as he is concerned, his own work as a catechist, devoted to the evangelization of his people in Welekha-land, will be all but done.

Nkharanga knows from his own training that when a candidate for the priesthood in the Catholic Church receives ordination, he is ordained a "priest according to the order of Melchizedek". That is because he too will offer the bread and wine at each Mass for consecration. Nkharanga has even memorized the text of the "doctrine of holy orders" that was promulgated by the Council of Trent, and that states: "Sacrifice and priesthood are by the ordinance of God so united that both have existed in every law. Since, therefore, in the New Testament the Catholic Church has received from Christ the holy, visible sacrifice of the Eucharist, it must also be confessed (*tateri etiam oportet*) that there is in that Church a new, visible and external priesthood into which the old has been translated. That this was instituted by the same Lord our Saviour, and that to the Apostles and their successors in the priesthood was given the power of consecrating, offering and administering His Body and Blood, as also of forgiving and retaining sins, is shown by the Sacred Scriptures and has always been taught by the tradition of the Catholic Church".

This is the doctrine that is also affirmed with anathema in the Church's canons, one of which states that "in Holy Orders a character is imprinted".

And Nkharanga also easily recalls the teaching of the same Council concerning sacraments in general which laid down that "If anyone shall say that in three Sacraments, namely Baptism, Confirmation and Orders, there is not imprinted on the soul a character, that is, a certain spiritual and indelible mark (*signum quoddam*) . . . let him be anathema"!

At the time Nkharanga and his family came here on their pilgrimage, the seminary was in recess; and apart from the occasional sight of a member of the faculty pacing to and from while reciting the Holy Office, there was no life in evidence. Nkharanga now realizes that he did not until now have any real idea what a major seminary looked like; and he is overawed at the sight of so many people in clerical garb, all of whom seem caught up in a perpetual flurry of activity! When an individual is not hastening this way or that, he invariably is pacing to and fro, eyes glued to a breviary or some other meditational manual.

Unfortunately it has always been Nkharanga's weakness to cower at the sight of priests when they make their appearance in clerical attire of one sort or another, as is their custom. The sudden discovery that his company includes a Catholic priest has usually sent shivers through his system the way the sight of a cobra sends shudders through a person who finds the reptile in his path unexpectedly.

There has invariably followed, in the wake of such a discovery, an uncontrollable surge of scruples of conscience having as its well-spring his manifest anxiety that the reverend one might conceivably be exposed to indignity of one sort or another as he mixes with the catechist's countrymen -

Nkharanga has always supposed that his countrymen are far too superstitious and incorrigible!

And so, seeing all those people who are mostly clad in thick textured, satiny white gowns - the monotony broken only by the occasional appearance of a figure gracefully attired in the formal canonical dress consisting of a conventional black suit plus Roman collar, Innocent Kintu's father feels small indeed. He can hardly believe that his son is about to join that truly adorable set whose mien appears to radiate the virtues of humility and obedience just as their attire seems to symbolize charity and chastity!

For an instant Nkharanga allows memories of a visit paid by him a while back to what he regarded as the only other Welekha family of "true" fame to flood his mind. The visit that took place a month or so following upon their pilgrimage to St. Barnabas' Seminary, and when Kintu was in Syntax at St. Paul's, was to a family that appeared in the Nkharangas' view to have gained fame over-night and whose reputation now all but overshadowed their own in Catholic circles!

Up until that time, Nkharanga imagined that his was the leading Christian family in all of Welekha-land. That belief was to be shattered by the news he received from Father Campbell one day that Samuel Kwentindio, a catechist serving an outpost of the only other mission in Welekha District, had a son whose admission to St. Barnabas' Seminary direct upon his graduation from the high school he had been attending had received the Diocesan Bishop's assent and blessing! Father Campbell had gone on to inform the astonished Nkharanga that the Kwentindios also had an only daughter who had taken the final solemn vows of poverty, chastity and obedience for cloistered nuns hardly a month earlier! Nkharanga had listened in disbelief as the priest explained that the convent where all this had taken place was the very same convent where his own wife Annamaria had spent some time as a young girl!

At the priest's suggestion, the Nkharangas accompanied by Gideon, Francesca and Josepha, Kintu's siblings, had traveled with him to the Kwentindio homestead for a courtesy visit. Innocent Kintu and Moses Kwentindio, who was the Kwentindios' only son, were both away at St. Paul's and St. Barnabas' respectively, and the two did not therefore get an opportunity to meet and get introduced.

From the date of his discovery that old Kwentindio's Moses, and not his own Innocent Kintu, was poised to become the first Welekha priest, Nkharanga secretly espoused what amounted to envy for his counterpart at the distant and to all appearances little known outpost. But it was envy that from the beginning was tampered with feelings of apprehension and even sympathy.

Nkharanga felt that the years spent by seminarians at the minor seminary served a very essential purpose, namely keeping the future priests insulated from the world and its wiles during precisely that stage in their development when they most needed the "protection". It seemed to him unthinkable that a loyal member of the church's hierarchy could be fashioned from material that had not had the benefit of such protection; and even his wife Annamaria agreed with him and said it in so many words!

In the couple's view, the loftiness of the priestly order that saw candidates become transformed from ordinary humans into *alteri Christi* (other Christs) demanded it. And they considered this especially fitting for Welekha candidates for the holy priesthood. In short, Innocent Kintu's parents had serious misgivings that the son of their "rival" could make the grade!

During their visit to the relatively unknown Kwentindios, Nkharanga was only able to see a photograph of Moses Kwentindio, the "high schooler" turned "major seminarian" and reportedly already a Subdeacon! He was neither impressed by the Reverend Kwentindio Junior's bearing nor felt any regrets at not being able to meet him in person.

But now, as Innocent Kintu's father prepares to leave for home, he is suddenly desirous of meeting the Reverend Moses Kwentindio because he senses that there might be some merit in leaving his son under the charge of the boy's tribesman. Nkharanga's experiences during his brief visit to St. Barnabas' have caused him to review his attitude to the Kwentindio family; and his fellow catechist's son looms in his imagination as virtually a priest already.

The Reverend Kwentindio Jr. has no forewarning of the famous catechist's trip, and is not on hand to meet Innocent Kintu's pa. What is more, he still has to meet Innocent, the prodigy whom members of the seminary choir appear so keen to meet.

As the old man bids his son goodbye, he does not at all need to add to the many injunctions he has already given his young charge whom, now more than ever before, he is inclined to regard as his sacrificial lamb. But he suddenly feels constrained, in view of the spiritual re-awakening he experiences, to include in his parting remarks something to the effect that if and when the boy ever gets himself dismissed from the seminary, he should consider himself no longer their child! Nkharanga even feels he has to point out that if and when Kintu becomes tempted to change from the nice, exemplary and promising youngster that he has until now been into something else, instead of considering retracing his steps home, he will be better off getting himself drowned in the strategically placed great River Mpogoro!

Although the seminarian keeps his cool as he lends his ear to that extraordinary message, he in fact feels angry with his old man beyond telling. First of all, the message that his dad was communicating was superfluous. Much more than his father, Innocent Kintu longs and literally hungers for the priestly state with all its encumbrances, namely celibacy, blind obedience to the bishop, etc. Innocent is additionally well aware of the untenability of his father's position. His minor seminary preparation, and his study of the Lives of Saints which he undertakes for the joy of it, have given him an adequate grasp of the fundamentals and left him in the know to the extent that he can no longer be bamboozled by such mumbo jumbo!

It is, moreover, not the first time that his father has shown his ignorance in a sphere as important as that in his blind attempt to lord it over him. Innocent Kintu, having gradually overcome the scruples that previously bedevilled his recognition of this fact, has long concluded that his father, autocrat though he is, in fact knows much less than he himself does not just in the secular spheres of knowledge, pre-eminently the sphere of music, but indeed even in such life and death matters as those that pertain to faith and worship!

Ever since he made that discovery, the seminarian has often wondered why the old man sometimes seemed to flinch when it came to according him the respect he, Innocent Kintu, was due. There was no doubt, given the exemplary life he had led since his childhood, that he was due a lot of respect by all - his own father included!

Innocent Kintu has, of course, also noted that many others amongst his so-called superiors, whose very behaviour showed them to be incorrigible and irredeemable in his estimation, put on airs in an even more glaring fashion!

The young man experiences a peculiar feeling of relief as soon as his father, whom he has hitherto adored almost as if he were a deity, disappears round the bend in the road on his homeward journey. The feeling of relief is mixed with elation and, strangely, also fear. But it is fear of an extraordinary kind - it is not fear of pain but of the unknown! Although Innocent Kintu knows the former like the back of his hand, he feels like a fish out of water now when confronted with the latter. The blind trust he previously placed in his parents insulated him from that type of fear.

The youngster has never experienced such a feeling before and finds himself pretty confused in its wake. Ordinarily he has always felt emptiness akin to weightlessness at the moment of parting with anyone of his parents. This is because he grew up trusting that their presence and visibility somehow caused all his needs, both physical and psychic, to be fulfilled. Even when they were not present bodily, the feeling of awe that came from just knowing that he was their son has always ensured for him a sense of security that he well knew was far from ordinary.

On this occasion, Innocent Kintu actually feels the reverse! While the old man is still around and pouring out his "nonsense", something springing from the core of his inner being sends a clear signal to the effect that from now on his dad's continued presence is not going to promote his physical well-being, and even much less his spiritual well-being, any more. As if timed to react on the spot, Innocent Kintu's imagination just then rallies with the strangest portrayal of a

171

wholly changed, almost insane, Nkharanga who even seems ready to force his son to do precisely those things that would go against his inclination like skipping his prayers, gormandizing, etc. just so he can indulge in the pleasure of seeing Innocent Kintu carry out his conjunctions!

Thus, as the old man departs, Innocent Kintu feels relieved and seems only too pleased in spite of his sudden "fear of the unknown" as he begins to sense that it is his father's absence as opposed to his presence that now holds out sure promise for his self-actualization in direct contradistinction to his customary experience! For the first time in his life, he seems patently more self-fulfilled and secure left on his own! The very image of his father now looms up as a threat.

From Innocent Kintu's point of view, the first term at St. Barnabas' Major Seminary passes quickly and uneventfully. There are the usual problems of adjusting to new faces - faces of members of the seminary's staff and faces of the seminary's other inmates. But it is adjustment with a difference. With his arrival at St. Barnabas', the seminary in his view acquires among other things a remarkable organist who is besides imbued with what is decidedly the right attitude to the holy priestly vocation - not at all a minor thing judging from the emphasis placed on it by the spiritual director during the three day retreat that kicks off the seminary year. The task of adjusting can, not just in a manner of speaking but in point of fact, be said to have shifted to the establishment and its inmates!

The only real thing of significance that occurs as far as the young enthusiast is concerned is a dream he has towards the term's end - a dream so nightmarish that it threatens to mar his entire term's work. In its aftermath, the first year

172

philosopher (as "Brother" Innocent and others in his class are referred to) is extremely conscious of the fact that other lesser mortals would surely succumb to the temptations inherent in the dream and probably lose their faith as a consequence!

Brother Innocent dreams that it is Games Hour on the campus. But instead of finding himself on the lawn tennis court where he excels with his nimble forehand and backhand volleys, volley hits with backspins, topspin shots, lobs, slice backhand shots, cross-court shots, forward thrusts and down-the-line shots, and deceptive half volleys when he was not delivering unstoppable smash hits with his fore hand, he finds himself transported in his dream to the edge of a lagoon on the shores of the Sea of Galilee.

There, his hands are crossed in prayer as is always the case with him when no other soul is in the vicinity; and, borrowing the words that were used by the polygamous King David who ruled over the Houses of Israel and Judah exactly a thousand years BC, he prays thus: "My God, my God! Look upon me. Why dost Thou forsake me? Why cannot my sinful supplication reach Thee who art my salvation? Thou dost not answer, my God, when I cry out to Thee day and night and I am patient still. Thou art there, nonetheless, dwelling in the holy place; my ancient boast. It is in Thee that my forefathers trusted, and Thou didst reward their trust by delivering them. They cried to Thee and rescue came; no need to be ashamed of such trust as theirs. But, I, poor worm, have no manhood left. I am a by-word to all, the laughing stock of the rabble. All those who catch sight of me fall to mocking; mouthing out insults, while they toss their heads in scorn. He committed himself to the Lord, why does not the Lord come to his rescue and set his favourite free? They stand there watching me, gazing at me. Am I, any more, one of Thy people?"

So saying, Brother Innocent thinks to leave and join his colleagues on the sports pitch. But in that instant, his entire frame seems to be encased in an iron cuirass, and he feels like he is standing on loadstone that clasps and holds him bound fast to itself through its magnetic pull. He can neither move or swerve, nor turn this way or that. And in that moment, whilst held fast in the magnet's embraces and helpless, he hears a booming voice that comes crackling over the airwaves. The voice addresses him by his first name.

"Innocent, what have I done to you - or wherein have I aggrieved you? Answer me. Because I guided you forth through the desert, through all that span of time and fed you with manna, and brought you forth into a right good land, you have smitten me with blows and scourges! What more ought I to have done for you that I have not done? I, even I, planted you to be my fairest vineyard and you have slaked my thirst with vinegar, and pierced with a lance your Saviour's side. I went before you in a column of cloud; and you have led me to the judgement hall. Oh, innocent, what have I done to you? Wherein have I grieved you? Answer me!"

The resonance of the Voice's final words hardly clears from the eerie atmosphere than Brother Innocent's sensation of being manacled vanishes! But as it does so, something else that is as equally strange overtakes him. The physical part of him suddenly appears to be in revolt as, without any warning, his mouth turns into a cavernous gap that stretches from ear to ear. His jaws, wrenched apart by invisible hands, remain stuck at the axles. Then out shoots the tongue, the full slithering length of it; and his eyes, contorted beyond recognition, shut. The neck begins too twist slowly of its own accord and continues to do so until the eyes appear to be protruding from the back of his head.

Thus grimacing, Brother innocent attempts to moan; for these events are accompanied by a terrible sensation of pain centered somewhere in his skull. The only sound that comes out of him, however, is that of his jaws creaking under the pressures that converge about them. He can sense that he is in the process of tumbling helplessly to the ground now, and he braces himself, in spite of his already pitiful condition, for the devastating fall. But he is mercifully aroused from his uneasy slumber by the waking bell just before he hits the ground.

11.

Innocent Joke

Of all the facets of life at the *Seminario Nkuu*, as ordinary folk in the outlying areas refer to St. Barnabas' Major Seminary, there is none that strikes the visitor as does the cordial relations that hold sway between the different individuals who make up its community. A good many of the students are clerics already in their Minor or Major Orders. It is therefore not surprising that charity should be emphasized. The emphasis is most evident in the way the seminarians address one another. Everyone, reverend or not, is hailed as "Brother". Thus, even if one is not a reverend so-and-so, one is always able in the theocentric atmosphere that prevails to recover at least some dignity from hearing oneself addressed as Brother So-and-So!

A most jolly atmosphere in fact reigns everywhere as the Deacons, Subdeacons, and even the Lectors with their freshly shaved and still shiny *tonsurae* bend over backwards in their efforts to indicate to their lesser brethren that canonical titles actually mean nothing. Meanwhile, the as yet untitled members of the seminary "brotherhood", not to be outdone in humility, are usually glad to take the opportunity thus provided to show in devious but supposedly consistent ways that even if there might indeed be equality all around, its distribution van never be in equal measures for any two individuals; and they will proceed to cite passages from the *Summa Theologiae* and other "standard" works in support thereof!

Brother Innocent has been in the *Seminario Nkuu* only a fortnight when he points out to a senior Brother who seems overly argumentative that he does not have to wait to master St. Thomas Aquinas' voluminous work before he can prove the same point. George Orwell, he posits, has figured it all out for the benefit of unlearned brethren like himself: "They are all equal, but some are more equal than others!"

Arguments such as these are commonplace. Still, nobody has been known to take that as an excuse for resorting to anything that might even approach or be akin to an *argumentum ad hominem* since the rules of logic do not call for it. Consequently few, if any, breaches of decorum at St. Barnabas' Major Seminary can be directly associated with a lack of charity.

The observance of "the Rule", which like the British constitution is an unwritten one, is the focal point of all that one does in that august environment. This also explains why the new arrivals find it relatively easy to integrate with the rest of the community. Since a freshman is compelled to seek directions from his senior or titled brethren regarding the Rule's requirements, he soon finds himself on talking terms with both the longer established brethren and his fellow freshmen who, like himself, are frequently mystified because of their ignorance as to what they may or may not do.

It is customary for each freshman to be allotted a "guardian" from among the senior students to provide the novice with the continuing guidance he needs in his observance of certain aspects of the Rule, for example the Precept of Silence; and this tends to reduce the mystification experienced to that which is unavoidable or at least manageable.

177

Brother Innocent encounters no difficulty in mastering the fine points of the Rule and in time blooms into the Rule's most exemplary observer. By the end of the first term, he likewise already stands out as the most diligent member of his class. It also becomes common knowledge that Brother Innocent never lets his own comfort be a hindrance to a favour someone else might stand in need of. That he suffers from intense scrupulosity goes without saying. But then who is not scrupulous in the observance of the Rule now and again, particularly during those times when the Rector is suspected to be lurking around - as he, indeed, often does!

Innocent Kintu's mien has something about it that makes one think of a recluse - the type whose blissful countenance conceals a fascination for the life of rigorous asceticism. That Brother Innocent's asceticism may be as rigorous as all that is, of course, discounted. As everyone with perhaps the exception of Brother Innocent knows, being married to blind obedience is a far cry from the ability to withstand the rigours of monastic asceticism. Besides, the spiritual conferences conducted nightly by Father Rector are strongly biased against ascetical practices that do not have the formal approval of one's confessor.

What is not known is that Brother Innocent, who has never allowed his feelings on the subject to surface even in private, intensely dislikes Father Rector's seeming inclination to demean ascetical practices. And - of course - no one would have believed that, in his determination to follow in the footsteps of saints, Brother Innocent secretly engages in self-flagellation from time to time using a lash; or that he plans to fashion for himself a coarse belt to be worn under his pants as part of his penance and mortification.

As far as Brother Innocent is concerned, it is imperative for true followers of Christ to heed His call which is very clear: "Whosoever will save his life shall lose it, but he that shall lose his life for my sake shall save it." In Brother Innocent's view, the importance of that call, which is contained in the Gospels in all the synoptic gospels, and which the evangelists Luke, Mark and Matthew attest to by quoting the same exact phrase that was employed by our Lord and Savior, cannot be gainsaid.

Innocent Kintu does not at all understand how the Rector can justify his position, which he naturally promotes under the guise of urging that prudence and caution must be exercised when engaging in mortification. He has to know that Saint Francis of Assisi, who must have suffered tremendously from the stigmata that he had received, practiced frequent flagellations and fasts, and did not hesitate to use a hairshirt to mortify himself further. Then there was St. Teresa of Avila, a Doctor of the Church, who had as her motto: "Lord, either let me suffer or let me die."

Thumbing through the thick volume of the Lives of Saints is something that Innocent Kintu does often; and he has no doubt that it is the one tome that the Rector must have read from cover to cover at some point during his own preparation for the priesthood. Surely the Rector must know what it says about Saint Thérèse of Lisieux; for instance that she used the "discipline" vigorously, "scourging herself with all the strength and speed of which she was capable, smiling at the crucifix through the tears which bedewed her eyelashes", according to one of her biographers! And the Rector cannot have missed the reports that St. Pope John Paul used to beat himself with a belt and sleep on a bare floor as a way of dying

179

to the self! Brother Innocent is therefore quite perplexed by the Rector's attitude to penance and mortification.

It comes as no surprise that Brother Innocent's favourite biblical passage on the subject of mortification is none other that the Apostle Paul's admonition to the Galatians: "They that are Christ's, have crucified their flesh, with the vices and concupiscences."

And Brother Innocent also just loves the way Saint Alphonsus Maria de Ligouri, Bishop and Founder of the Congregation of the Most Holy Redeemer, put it when discussing the necessity and advantages of exterior mortification in *The True Spouse of Jesus Christ*. The seminarian feels that the saint could not have said it better when he wrote: "As the indulgence of the body by sensual pleasures is the sole and constant study of worldlings, so the continual mortification of the flesh is to the saints the only object of their care and of their desires."

Because there are only two sets of *The Complete Works of Saint Alphonsus de Ligouri* in the library, until such time as he is done studying the tome with its absolutely enthralling and quite insightful spiritual material, Brother Innocent is tempted to deliberately misplace one of the tomes on the shelves to assure its availability, and he falls for it.

All these things notwithstanding, there is no question concerning the fact that the brother is single minded, as perhaps no other other is, in his resolve to become a priest. But the resolve never seems in any way to hinder his ability to crack the most amusing jokes! His sense of humor, combined with the fact that he is unbeatable and quite unmatched as a stage character, makes him an immensely popular and admired figure on the seminary campus. In his enthusiasm to please, Brother Innocent often comes close to annoying his colleagues. This more than happens one day with repercussions he lives to remember.

Concealed round a corner on the occasion in question, Brother Innocent mimics the voice of Father Rector with such precision that a group of deacons and subdeacons, among them Brother Moses Kwentindio, recently appointed Dean of Students by Father Rector, though engaging in nothing untoward, feel quite shaken at the thought that their superior, unknown to them, is so close at hand. The Reverend Brothers are convinced that Father Rector, a short-tempered Irishman whose perpetual sermons on the virtues of hard bore everyone except Brother Innocent, is approaching and, led by Brother Moses, snap to attention!

Ever since he joined his new community, Brother Innocent has consistently noted that his fellow students and the seminary staff alike display a certain hard-to-define attitude in their dealings with him. This attitude approaches what you might call "sympathetic regard", and is clearly incompatible with a show of anger. Perhaps not entirely unexpectedly, this attitude has been interpreted by Brother Innocent as their spontaneous expression of administration and praise - an affirmation of their belief that he, Innocent Kintu, is the seminary's premier hope in its efforts to render Holy Mother Church obedient service! It has been only natural that he should also see it as an acknowledgement of their own "fickle mindedness" in the matter of observing the injunction to obedience and self-sacrifice.

Brother innocent has further noted that while the Rule invites all to practice obedience - that noble virtue which prompted the Godhead to come down from heaven and to dwell among men - the importance of its observance has never seemed to strike anyone else in the place apart from himself.

This is more than evident from the appointment of Moses Kwentindio as Student Dean, charged with the all-important task of "catching Rule breakers and reporting them to Father Rector" as he would put it! While he himself would have been only too proud and happy to serve as Student Dean, he still does not understand how the Rector, lukewarm though he is, came to appoint an individual of the calibre and metal of Brother Moses to that position.

Nicknamed "The Rod" not long after the commencement of his "reign" as the Dean, Brother Moses is about the only one in the entire seminary brotherhood whose regard for Brother Innocent has from the first lacked any hint of admiration or praise. By the same token, Brother Moses' standing in Innocent Kintu's estimation has never been on the high side; and it has sunk to the lowest end of the scale on Moses Kwentindio's accession to the coveted position.

Innocent Kintu is only slightly acquainted with the Kwentindio family. But he exerts the air of one who knows the Kwentidios and their offspring thoroughly well. He has somehow formed the idea that the Kwentindio family is some kind of fortress for "liberal" Catholicism, a notion he associates with lukewarmness. He consequently feels an instinctive dislike for Brother Kwentindio, the only member of the family he has met.

Innocent Kintu's opinion of the Dean has not been helped by the fact that the latter is his tribesman, belonging to the Welekha tribe whose pagan tendencies are in his view irredeemable! All these things notwithstanding, Brother Innocent has always delighted in the knowledge that most of the seminary residents at least seem to know which one amongst them is destined to save the situation. The Dean's fright, as Innocent Kintu mimicked the Rector, is evidence enough that not even he can deny that fact!

Brother Innocent at first feels like he must laugh at the manner in which the surprised reverends react to his mimicry. But seeing them seethe with anger at having been thus exposed, he sees at once that it was a mistake on his part to give his seniors the fright.

Everything might stop there but for the fact that brother Innocent takes exception to the irrational, indeed wholly unjustified as well as uncontrolled reaction that his innocent joke provokes. Contrary to his usual tendency to condescend to the wishes of his seniors, he adopts thereupon an aloofness that his irate comrades at once mistake for insolence.

While those who see him take it to be a temporary fixation, his strange aloofness persists and soon takes on what on close observation suddenly seems to have all too great a resemblance to a severe depression or some variant thereof! All the outward characteristics of the dreaded condition seem to be there at any rate. It is all the more extraordinary given Brother Innocent's usual jolliness and seeming insatiable hunger for sympathy.

That evening while at supper, one of the victims of Brother Innocent's joke turns to the "young punk" as he calls him and tells him to stop at once carrying about the "melancholy expression" on his face. It is at that moment that Brother Innocent, caught unawares by the remark, experiences what at first appears to be a normal hiccup but soon finds he is chocking on the food that he was in the process of swallowing. What everyone at his table sees, however, is a distraught and angry Brother Innocent expectorating, for no reason, and sending the food that he was chewing spewing in all directions, in the full view of everyone, including the Dean!

183

After that truly unheard of performance, he continues to sit at table with his arms folded and face wrapped up in a stony stare.

The table prefect is one of the few seminarians who has been to Brother Innocent's home as a guest of the latter's parents and is also the brother's allotted guardian for the purposes of familiarization with the myriad points of the unwritten Rule. The prefect has therefore believed that if there is anyone who knows Brother Innocent very well (excluding Brother Innocent's confessor that is), he did.

He decides that the young chum's attitude and behaviour on this particular occasion are evidence of wounded pride. Pride being a sin that cannot be countenanced within the community of a *Seminario Nkuu*, the prefect feels perfectly justified in springing up from his place at the head of the table and administering to the surprised Innocent Kintu what he considers a suitable slap across the face! Whereupon, his small silvery eyes glistening, Brother Innocent calmly turns the other cheek in a silent, mocking gesture of resignation. There is dead silence for an instant before the assembly of students, led by Brother Moses, break out in an uproarious bout of laughter!

This incident in the refectory marks the beginning of a strange new life for Brother Innocent. He thenceforward loses all capacity to cooperate effectively with anyone in his community. He neither talks with fellow mates nor listens to their bidding to the effect that he be the good boy he always previously was. He no longer cleans his cubicle – a serious breach of the Rule. Although outwardly he observes meal times, he now appears to have lost all appetite for food as he only stares at it.

Brother Innocent also takes to keeping long vigils by night before a picture of the Blessed Virgin Mary that is normally tucked away in between the pages of his missal. This particular aspect of Innocent Kintu's budding insanity naturally does not escape notice for very long since it involves keeping the lights in his cubicle on beyond the time allowed by the Rule. As if that was not bad enough, he is soon observed to wander about in the dead of night switching lights on and off and can also be seen doing other "funny" things by day – as if determined, in the Dean's words, to break all seminary rules. But, strangely, he continues to attend class and to keep chapel hours with his customary regularity, and to play the church organ with his customary gusto in spite of the insomnia that now appears to be getting the better of him.

Meanwhile Innocent Kintu's colleagues, the reverend Brothers in particular, begin to develop a habit of seeking him out during period breaks for the purpose of "disciplining" him. Finding him, they stand over him and bawl out expressions such as "Snap it, Brother! Be a man!" or "What is the matter with you, now?" A few call him a hysteric, while others call him a praying mantis! Others still tauntingly refer to him as a "silly and quietist". As their mutterings invariably draw a blank, they at first fake the fury with which they react to his "intransigence". In the end, however, it is real and fairly implacable fury that seizes hold of them, driving the reverends to box the Brother's ears. As the days go by, this becomes a pattern for "correcting the erring lad".

By this time every member of the student body, to be sure, has each his own theory regarding both the cause of Brother Innocent's ailment and its cure. Admittedly not everybody is able to try out his particular curative theory on the Brother. A first year student with his smattering of

Philosophy and little or no acquaintance with Moral, Dogmatic, Ascetic or Biblical Theology, Canon Law—and the rest, simply could not have succeeded in pushing his way past the Subdeacons and Deacons to the poor fellow.

Brother Moses, while appearing on the surface to care less about the startling developments, is deeply interested in the events that are taking place. Born, like Innocent Kintu, into an intensely Christian home, he is one of very few people on the African continent whose family can boast a nun. Now a Subdeacon himself and scheduled to be ordained a priest in just under three years' time, he is on the brink of adding his family to the small number around the world that have made themselves history by giving the human race an *alter Christus*.

The appearance in his life of Brother Innocent, also reputedly having a deeply Catholic family background and thoroughly taken up with his special brand of piety, at first caused the normally reflective and fairly stable-minded Kwentindio to begin doubting the tenets forming the foundation of his own devotions and spiritual life. But Brother Innocent's apparent meltdown - or whatever had got ahold of the Brother - has in time led to a re-appraisal by him of his own Christianity, including a review of the Christian roots of not just his own immediate family but of the Welekha people as a whole! Thus, as Brother Innocent is getting mired down in his relations with members of the seminary community, the Dean is himself battling to keep his suddenly questioning conscience in check.

12.

Three-Horned Dilemma

In the short time it takes Brother Innocent to have virtually the whole brotherhood at St. Barnabas' Seminary turn against him, Brother Moses' preoccupation with his own past grows from what at first seems like a passing interest to a veritable obsession that threatens to become unmanageable. Finally, distraught and unable to extricate himself from his alarming obsession with the manner in which Kintu and himself - two wholly contrasting individuals - came to be set on the same road to the priesthood, the Dean finds himself caught in a triple dilemma!

As the Reverend Kwentindio's reasoning goes, the vocation to the priesthood and indeed the very practice of religion itself are all indisputably founded on obedience—a readiness to submit blindly and unreservedly to the Diocesan Bishop on the one hand and total allegiance to a creed on the other. Ever since he met Brother Innocent, he has had a nagging feeling that his tribesman, despite his "posturing" and renown for being an extraordinarily attentive and docile seminarist, would actually hate to hear the orthodox position of the Church and is married bodily and spiritually to what is in effect an heretical position!

The Dean has for sometime now already had the distinct feeling that Brother Innocent's very practice of the virtue of obedience left no room for the role of the Holy Spirit. The practice of virtue - any virtue - was meritorious only to the extent that the practitioner acted in response to the motion of divine grace. Without the grace of the Almighty, man was

187

incapable of any good works. The "Rod" is almost convinced that all the actions of Brother Innocent are "wilful" and probably entirely lacking in merit! It does not seem probable that his tribesman's behaviour and attitudes even prior to the meltdown could be compatible with these dogmas of the Church!

For sometime now, Brother Moses has been conscious of what appears to be an unmistakeable streak of unruliness at the core of Innocent Kintu's behaviour, and he doubts very much that his tribesman can actually ever do anything he is told that goes against his sentiments and express liking. In the Dean's view, there is only imaginary collaboration with grace in every instance in which Brother Innocent "practices" virtue in general and obedience in particular. On the face of it, therefore, their individual attitudes to Christianity are to all intents and purposes at complete variance!

It all boils down, the Dean initially notes, to something really simple - if his tribesman's brand of Christianity is the right one, then his own practice of religion, the sophistication of his arguments notwithstanding, is ill-founded and indeed sham as well - and vice versa. But it gradually begins to dawn on him in the course of time that the matter isn't that simple!

The underpinnings of their piety, his own brand supposedly liberal and unpretentious and Innocent Kintu's essentially sentimental and showy, are somewhat like a thesis and an antithesis. There is in the event a synthesis of which neither of them is a part! The "Rod" grows increasingly troubled as he contemplates the possibility that Innocent Kintu and himself might both be fakes!

No, there can be no question that he, Moses Kwentindio, might be a fake! Whereas his tribesman is deep in trouble with virtually everyone on the seminary campus, he himself isn't in any sort of trouble with anybody. The Reverend Kwentindio ends up reflecting musingly that his own head at least seems to be working! As for Brother Innocent, everything he does - the way he genuflects in chapel, grips the rosary or intones the responses during Holy Mass, etc. - somehow seems to fit him for the bill of an ingenious counterfeit and a hoax!

Watching the Brother as he was serving Mass on the High Altar on one occasion about the time he perpetrated his "innocent joke", and fell out with his fellow seminarians, the Dean was convinced he saw signs that his tribesman, an actor first and foremost in his view, was starting to lose faith in his own ability to continue with the scheme of self-deception. Innocent Kintu's movements, although largely screened from view by his gown and mantle, appeared to point to a disposition that was suddenly vacillating and uncertain. Previously rigid and sure of himself, the young lad looked as if he finally was about to disown his posturing self once and for all!

Still, it takes the Rod prolonged thought and a great deal of introspection to reach his final damning verdict; namely that Brother Innocent is a rank conformist and nothing more! The Dean has come across many hypocritical individuals both in and outside the bounds of the seminary before, many of them quite adept, as it turned out, at putting on empty displays of blind, supposedly selfless, submission to authority. He is convinced now, however, that he had not met any individual whose conformism is total to the point of seeming impulsive like that of Brother Innocent!

The Dean rationalizes that the aberrant Brother is determined, just like everyone else in the small world of St. Barnabas' Seminary, to play to the tune that promises not merely acceptance in the new circumstances in which Africa has found itself, but also respect and honor in the "backward" surroundings. The prospect of filling the role of an *"alter Christus"* promises all this - and more! While the alternative in the case of Innocent Kintu's compatriots on the one hand is an obscure life in a village whose insignificance would be underscored by the fact that it most certainly won't be represented on any map, the alternative for Brother Innocent is completely different - something, the Dean guesses, akin to alienation from one's God-given nature and self!

The Dean recognizes that he too has conformist inclinations. But they are inclinations to which he succumbs more or less as a matter of convenience. His conformism is above all not deep-seated and certainly not, he feels sure, impulsive. If it comes to it - if his confessor were ever to look him in the eye and declare that he, Moses Kwentindio, didn't look as if he had the priestly vocation, he would neither be tempted to spit in the confessor's face nor feel like showering the Lord's minister with words of praise and thanksgiving either. The Dean thinks he has a pretty good idea what Brother Innocent's reaction in these circumstances would be.

His mind already in turmoil, the Rod is not about to stop there. His reasoning, whilst seemingly sound, in time gives way to a new and contrasting train of thoughts. The underlying logic is soon forgotten as his mind becomes buried under an avalanche of qualms and misgivings. Isn't he, Moses Kwentindio, not merely jealous of Brother Innocent's success and popularity both of which completely overshadow his own lacklustre image, and now finds himself unable to rest until he has proved that his rival's works are empty and undeserving!

At one point, he even persuades himself that it is the devil tempting him to discover in Brother Innocent imaginary symptoms of a sick soul, and that it is he and not Innocent Kintu who is likely to turn out an impostor!

Brother Innocent is at least seventeen by the look of him, and the dean has somehow come by the fact that the Brother is still uncircumcised! Cognizance of this otherwise unimportant detail causes Moses Kwentindio, who has himself already undergone the circumcision rite in accordance with Welekha custom, to become more and more convinced that Innocent Kintu and not he himself is likely to be the impostor. After all, the poor confused Brother has yet to attain manhood!

But a nagging thought persists - could it, perhaps, be that he, Moses Kwentindio, is going haywire? He suddenly realizes that he has not given the idea a reasonable amount of thought. Brother Moses has always been powerless to stop a variety of ideas, a few of them merely conflicting, but the great bulk plainly outlandish, from invading his mind. As he deliberates within himself, a certain idea, propounded by René Descartes and condemned by the Church, does invade his mind in a manner in a manner that seems equally outlandish.

Virtually out of the blue, the famous words of the philosopher pop into the Dean's head: "I think, therefore I am!" This is followed by a test of Brother Kwentindio's faith in the form of a suggestion. But if - just suppose that Descartes was right and it turns out that "being" at least in so far as the human race is concerned in fact draws its essence from "thinking"! The Dean sees the unavoidable conclusion: he is breaking the first commandment of the Modern Philosophers, viz. "Live and Let Live", by rationalizing the way he is doing. Breaking this commandment, at least in the eyes of Descartes' followers, is tantamount to being crazy!

Years earlier, during discussions in Philosophy class centering on the subject of neurosis, Moses Kwentindio always experienced feelings of uncertainty and unease. His recollection of this and the implications of the Cartesian position on reality now together make him shudder to think that the probability of going insane is indeed there! To boot - why is he so bothered about how people, Brother Innocent for one, practice their religion? Why otherwise does he feel so overly concerned about whether people live their lives aright according to him? Finally being a priest - and he is still no more than a candidate for that holy state - surely does not mean being a judge of others!

Going hand in hand with Moses Kwentindio's engrossment with his mental health is his bewilderment at the fact that until lately Brother Innocent ostensibly had left everyone in the diocese irrespective of ecclesiastical rank mesmerized and virtually ready to pay him homage as a budding saint! That engrossment, morbid and unsettling at first, eventually gives way to an ever growing curiosity concerning the first beginnings of his tribesman's spirituality.

The Dean's memories of his own childhood rekindle feelings of youthful pride in the fact that religious practice in his on home, ardent as it has been, has remained essentially a matter of personal choice with little moral compulsion if at all. The Rod become curious a no person can be to discover the factors that have led Brother Innocent to live as he does. He is determined to pursue the investigation as any cost even if it means the suspension of traditional value judgements and lifting a self-imposed moratorium on the ungoverned play of his mind.

Thus, by the time symptoms of serious anomalies in Brother Innocent's comportment begin to surface, the Dean already prefers to stay well on the side-lines, content to play the role of observer albeit a keen one. As far as he is concerned, there is a problem here and a big one—bigger, possibly, than either he as Dean of Students or the seminary authorities can handle. And so the field is left to his colleagues to do as they deem fit in their eagerness to put an end to Brother Innocent's mysterious and far from dignified behavior.

13.

The Devil's Claw

Neither the members of staff nor the students think the idea of much significance or worthy of thought. For one, they have their ready-made modern-day jargon that seems to explain all that takes place under their noses: quietism, acute depression, or a combination of them. The moralist and philosophical overtones of their diagnoses just match the mood that prevails on the campus. It is thus left to the faithful back ion Innocent Kintu's home parish to revive the classical name of the "thing" to which their standard bearer fell victim...the Devil's Claw!

The bulk of the faithful are always biased in favour of the instantaneous and the dramatic - just like their counterparts in other parts of the world. Whilst some of the stories they hear relating to their hero's tragedy conflict, everything seems to point to one thing: Innocent Kintu has been stricken down by the "malady" in a momentary space of time! It does indeed transpire in the end that they are prepared to fight with all might any notions that seem to go against their belief that the Devil, enraged beyond imagining, somehow found the opportunity, perhaps as the lad's guardian angel was having a snooze, and administered his *coup de grace* by his usual means—a single blow from the ugly claw he spots on his hairy paw!

The view held seems all the more plausible because the misfortune comes just as Kintu has embarked upon the final leg of his hunt for Holy Orders and takes place in the enchanting, mystique-filled surroundings of the *Seminario*

Nkuu. As it happens, the seminary's playgrounds provide the improbable setting.

Ever since he starts to be beset by hiss weird misfortunes, Brother Innocent regularly skips lawn tennis, which has hitherto been by far his favored game; and he can be seen bolting, with arms upraised, from his cubicle to the football ground instead at the sound the bell. But soccer never having been one of his favorite games whether as a player or as a spectator, he passes his time wandering about aimlessly on the soccer pitch until the bell signaling the end of the games hour sounds and saves the day.

The pitch is busy as usual during games hour on the day it all supposedly happens. Brother Innocent starts by giving the impression that he really wants to be allotted to a specific team. The referee, a balding Deacon, rising to what looks like an obvious challenge, proceeds to appoint him center forward.

Brother Innocent, however, lets down his team mates miserably by relapsing into his by now well-known habit of longing about aimlessly in complete disregard of the soccer game in progress. Since his buddies on the football pitch, by and large, are soccer lovers who are automatically keen to concentrate their energies on the game, Brother Innocent finds himself left to his own devices as has been the case hitherto.

Following the two-week long fast, he looks abysmally pale and lean-faced that afternoon. It is nearing half-time; but Brother Innocent, whose skill at playing soccer has clearly never been remarkable, hasn't been able even then to as much as get his foot to brush the leather. And now he stands there in mid-field, arms akimbo and trunk heaving as if he has just participated in a sprint for the ball and is panting in its immediate aftermath. His team's goalie brings off a brilliant save at precisely that moment. Obviously excited and

195

beaming, the goalie rises from the ground still grasping the ball, and then with a kick sends it rolling into Brother Innocent's vicinity. There is no other player nearby and Brother Innocent gallops for the ball.

Until then, a virtual silence has reigned on the football field broken only by the occasional shouts of individuals clamoring for the ball and the sound of leather being booted around. But in that instant, the voices of all the players, led by the coarse, rough-hewn and rasping voice of the referee, rise and shatter the peace as they all with one accord bombard the colleague with a flood of exhortations to the effect that he must get that ball! Lunging forward to meet the ball and sparred on no doubt by the naked awe aroused in him by the prospect of having to bear the yells that burst in on him from all directions now, Brother Innocent not only is seen to miss the ball but also to fall to the ground with a thud - and to remain there spread-eagled and open-mouthed as if struck by the proverbial but fearsome Devil's Claw!

Brother Innocent is a shapeless heap and remains quite still as his startled playmates gather about him. His eyes are wide open and he maintains a fixed gaze ahead of him as if in a trance. The stare is shorn of all emotion just as his face, for the first time ever, does not bear the slightest trace of the vivid smile and shy look that has characterized it from his cradle days.

The staff at the Kijiji General Hospital are used to handling strange cases involving maladies that are quite uncommon. When Innocent Kintu is wheeled into the hospital's casualty wing that afternoon, he outdoes himself as the strangest case of them all. Everything registers normal - his pulse, temperature, color of the tongue, blood pressure, hemoglobin, etc. Although Innocent Kintu's eyes are dilated

196

and he looks a bit starved, he looks relatively healthy in every other respect and even robust particularly when his physical condition is likened to that of the continent's famished and afflicted millions.

Innocent Kintu's affliction remains a mystery even after a week of intensive, wide-ranging physical checks. He behaves exactly as if he is bereft of willpower to do such simple tasks as eating, raising an arm or sitting up - until someone makes a move to assist! As it happens, a minimum force of seven robust people is required for the patient's meals, four to pin down his arms and legs, one person to wrench open his mouth and teeth as well as steady the head taking care not to be bitten or spat in the face, a sixth person to hold down his torso, and the seventh to serve the food which, of course, has to be in liquid form. The food itself must be served down in quantity as it is otherwise liable to be spat out entire by the patient who does it without ceremony or the least regard for those waiting on him.

When a bed sheet slides off the patient, he seems to consider it none of his business to stretch to stretch out an arm and restore it to its original use of covering his person. Innocent Kintu likewise appears to have stopped being concerned about hygiene when nature calls. He neither gives notice of the fact that it is about to happen nor displays any particular interest in the matter after the fact. When the eyes shut for the rare moments of sleep he has, they do so as if they verily and truly are the windows of his soul - a soul albeit with a difference.

A soul is defined as a "body incorporeal". Were Brother Innocent consulted on the matter and were he disposed to speak his mind, he unquestionably would emphasize - or so it would now appear - that a human soul is closer to a "spirit corporeal" than a "body incorporeal"! The significance of it all lies in the brother's apparent tendency to now regard all bodily substances as bastardized and degrading, and he likely would be hard put to it to concede that one can talk of a "body" incorporeal when referring to the soul with a clean conscience!

Actually Brother Moses suspects that Brother Innocent's view of the reality around him - or worldview if you will - has flipped a hundred and eight degrees and possibly irreparably, and any attempt by ordinary folks like him to understand what is going on is akin to trying to trying to see with the naked eye and without the help of a mirror things that are around corners and effectively blocked from view by other objects without the benefit of a mirror!

Not long afterwards, Innocent Kintu begins a practice that is as irrational as it is strange - and that almost drives everyone crazy. It consists of prodding himself in the palm of his left hand with the pointing finger of his right. This threatens in no time to spring a sore, and it becomes necessary to have his arms roped to the bedframe to reduce the harm he seems determined to inflict on himself.

Then, denied the possibility to move his hands freely, Innocent Kintu starts a new habit of making what appears to be the sign of the cross with his head every now and then. By this time the nurses are also pretty well occupied with the additional task of applying talcum powder at frequent intervals to their patient's sides and back in a fruitless attempt to prevent the bedsores from developing into wounds!

When they are alerted to their son's condition, Nkharanga and his wife react with surprise and a curious wonderment. They both tend to infer from the verbal reports the messengers bring that whatever it is that afflicts their son, it has something

198

to do with the increasingly ramified struggle between Beelzebub and the Deity in Whom they have placed their hope and trust. Nkharanga's matronly wife even secretly hopes that her son has in fact been chosen by Providence to serve as the continent's first example of a luminary of unwavering asceticism! The grisly nature of the reports lends credence to her hopes.

All the same, the catechist makes it to Kijiji General Hospital with great haste. On arrival there he is totally saddened by the sight that meets his eyes. His sadness is not diminished in any way by the avowals of the hospital's physicians to the effect that his son appears to be mentally and physically well.

14.

Payment in Kind

There are some at the *Seminario Nkuu*, for whom Brother Innocent had come to represent a dream of what they themselves would have liked to be - seminarians of great promise admired by everybody for their humility. His life, consciously for some and unconsciously for others, has up until now been an ideal that, while perhaps difficult to emulate, was a vital source of inspiration. In their eyes, if Brother Innocent couldn't make it to Major Orders for any reason, it became doubtful indeed whether they themselves had a calling to the elevated priestly state. For such as these, Brother Innocent's unseemly departure is now bound at the very least to have a shattering effect on morale.

The situation is a lot trickier for Innocent Kintu's juniors back home. Their brother's rather peculiar homecoming on a stretcher is something none of them is prepared for. Their initial reaction on seeing the wreck to which he has been reduced is that their brother, heroic precursor in the long line of God's brides with possibly themselves as his immediate runners-up, is a saint! His emaciated form easily reminds them of St. Francis of Assisi and other saint whose spotless lives enable them to share directly in the suffering of their Blessed Savior.

The tortuous struggle to keep him alive loom up as a cross that their Shepherd and Pastor no doubt has determined as the most suitable for their parents and for them as well to carry. These sentiments, which cause tears to well up in their eyes, find ready and fairly strong support in the attestations of many of the visitors who call to commiserate with the family. "To them He loves, He gives the heaviest crosses to carry" say some. Others still: "With great sufferings come comparable rewards!"

What however bolsters the spirits of the couple and the three-some most of all is the devotional practice of regularly sprinkling Innocent Kintu's prostrate form with water in a vial brought all the way from Lourdes. They do it stealthily since the "patient" is clearly apt to react viciously to the indirect suggestion that he might be possessed of the Evil one and hence the attempted exorcism using holy water! This furtive practice contrasts sharply with the couple's habit of praying openly to God, not for their son's recovery, but for the forgiveness of their own sins. This is in accordance with the advice volunteered by father Campbell to the couple in view of Innocent Kintu's less than ingratiating performance.

All these things have at least one beneficial effect on the couple and their siblings. They help to ensure that certain jarring things to which some of the couple's visiting kindred give utterance in their general anxiety for Innocent Kintu's wellbeing do not disturb their equanimity. Instead of getting upset by the things that are said, the couple and their children now fall into the habit of looking upon the treatment they receive from that quarter as a humiliation that is merely additional to the cross they are supposed to help Innocent Kintu carry!

The irate elders of Namwikholongwe in particular, having been so long ignored by Innocent Kintu's parents, now want full access to the kid. It is clear from the message carried by the emissaries they despatch to the couple on learning of the youngster's affliction that their objective is to take over control of the lad for the purpose of administering a certain medicinal concoction that alone, they believe, can restore his health.

The tribal elders have been greatly outraged all along by the behaviour of the so-called "*walimu*" in hindering their social commingling with the youngsters and they do not comprehend how, even at that late hour, two individuals in their proper wits can continue to disregard their advice in the face of the events that have transpired. Innocent Kintu's malady is in their view the result of the couple's unbridled lust for power and, above all, the subsequent wanton flouting by the Nkharangas of the sacred mores of traditional Welekhe society.

The elders readily acknowledge that they knew all along that the *walimu*'s worship of the white man's Deity was going to bring them no good. For the spirits of the dead to have merely laid back and suffered indignity of the proportions perpetrated by the couple would have been uncharacteristic of them and, in any case, quite unusual. It was to be expected that the revered spirits would sooner or later exact from the accursed perpetrators of such gross and unspeakable misdeeds payment in kind!

These views, although actively propagated by dwindling number of hard-core traditionalists constituted largely of elderly ancestral spirit worshippers, still command widespread respect even amongst the Christian membership composed, strangely enough, of a fast growing number of sects. A goodly number of the converts to Christianity evidently sought baptism on grounds that were more mundane than spiritual – the desire to be known by a name that reflects "the times" or the need to assure foe one's offspring a good education in a missionary school, etc.

202

The delegation sent by the elders from Namwinkholongwe arrives at the walimu's homestead intending to stress that its views have widespread currency even among those who publicly claim to belong to the newly ennobled generation. The delegates regard this argument as powerful enough to move even the thick-skinned Nkharangas, and they accordingly plan to hold it in reserve until all their other arguments fail to induce a change in the couple's attitude. These hopes are nipped in the bud, however, by the unexpected move on the part of the *walimu*.

On learning of the purpose of the visit that his kinsmen organize, Innocent Kintu's father rebukes the leader of the delegation and insists that they leave at once. He is worried above all lest the patient, whose comportment looks like it is getting more and more benign by the day, will get wind of the visit and its intended purpose and become disturbed afresh and uncontrollable.

But even as they turn to leave in the face of the practical problems that beset their mission, the representatives of the tribal elders in Namwinkholongwe predict that worse will befall the lad. They are supported in their prediction by not a few of the practising Christians who watch them leave.

15.

From a Wreck to a Wretch

Like the philosopher he is, Father Campbell never lets his true feelings surface, let alone unnerve him. The fact remains however that he feels miserably disappointed at the realization that Innocent Kintu, adjudged a star amongst his people by not just himself but the great bulk of the diocese's hierarchy, is a freak! As the *walimu's* confessor, the *Omukhulu* lets them know each individually in the privacy of the confessional that he has their trial at heart every morning when he celebrates Holy Mass. He otherwise continues to act as though nothing untoward has happened. As and when his schedule permits, he makes a stopover at the increasingly forlorn-looking homestead. But he conducts himself so casually that onlookers are tempted to think that he does not care less about the couple's tribulations. The number of times he stops over never adds up to anything in any event.

Now, two months after Innocent Kintu's ignominious return to his birthplace, Father Campbell himself comes to Khalolweni to celebrate Mass on the feast of the Martyrs of Uganda. He no sooner concludes the solemn High Mass than he doffs his crimson vestments and ambles down the terraced slope from the dingy little church towards the Nkharanga's homestead. Taken by surprise, Innocent Kintu's parents tear themselves away from the clusters of regular sympathisers and wellwishers to race after the priest. They later relate in a thoroughly changed atmosphere how the clergyman asked to be left alone in the room where their son lay chained to his sickbed.

No one, least of all the couple, can guess the trend of the priest's thoughts as he makes a beeline for the house. Regarded with awe by the great bulk of the faithful and almost as a demigod by the Nkharangas, no one supposes that Father Campbell, a white man and priest of God as well, can ever be troubled in spirit! They have always considered the possibility of a white man getting into a fit of weeping, for instance, as very remote. They indeed would sooner have mistaken the whimpering sounds of a distressed white man for grunts of joy - and, correspondingly, his tears of joy for tears of sorrow - than they would those of a beast.

In actual fact, even as he celebrated High Mass on this bright morning in the church with its overflow congregation, Father Campbell was sorely troubled in mind over the "Innocent Affair" as the Secretary of His Worship the Bishop is already calling it. The P.P. would readily admit to being, indeed, the person least likely to pretend that understood the lad's train of thoughts since he became a mental case. It has troubled the missionary very much to think that prior to that time he felt cocksure about Innocent Kintu being a lad of exceptional promise!

As he hurries towards the Nkharanga's humble place of abode clutching the end of his sash, Father Campbell feels he knows one thing for sure now; even if the young man, regarded until three months back as the diocese's most promising candidate for the priesthood, got cured of his insanity that minute by some miraculous occurrence, it would not affect the rating he had arrived at anew after serious mindboggling reappraisal of the situation. Father Campbell is of the firm conviction the *walimu's* son is exactly the sort of individual can cause a schism in the Church for whatever ideas he espouses. He hates to think that Innocent Kintu might, in the process, wreak   havoc on whatever good work he himself can claim to have accomplished over two and three decades as a missionary in Africa!

The lad, a prodigy of the virtues of obedience and charity outwardly, quite clearly has in him a streak of obduracy such as Father Campbell never suspected could exist in a person of Kintu's background…just the sort of stubbornness that drove the German monk Martin Luther to usher in the Reformation! The priest knows what he now does about his young charge instinctively, and cannot explain it beyond the fact that the treatment of the lad by his parents whilst he was a child in all probability had something to do with it.

The priest now feels a great dislike for Innocent Kintu - he cannot see how the upright and respectable *walimus* can be held to blame for the boy's decision to throw away common sense and suddenly embark on a strange, inexplicable new way of life! It is as he brushes aside the screen that hangs in the doorway to the darkened room that a curious thought occurs to him and causes the muscles of his massive heart to sag under the load of emotion: once ordained a priest (if he had gotten that far), Innocent Kintu's homilies on hell fire and devotions to the saints would be unending!

If it were not for Innocent Kintu's subsequent "relapse", what happens during the brief moments Father Campbell remains alone with him would probably go down in history as a miracle! Since the mysterious happenings on the football pitch, Innocent Kintu has never once shifted his gaze or blinked as a reaction to the goings-on around him. Neither has he ever uttered a word. Keeping him alive with sustenance is a thankless task that the couple, with assistance of neighbors and well wishers, now undertake more out of sympathy and mercy than a sense of obligation. And, of course, Innocent

Kintu has never once supported his weight on his own legs or as much as tried to walk upright.

The unexpected, however, happens shortly after Father Campbell's "talk" with the patient lasting no more than a couple of minutes. For Innocent Kintu, suspected by the multitudes of visitors who have been streaming into the homestead to see him of being everything from a victim of a rare form of insanity to a simple case of physical possession by the Evil one, is suddenly seen walking upright, if stiffly and somewhat unsteadily, out of his sickroom with the lumbering figure of the missionary looming in the background! Eyes glistening and appearing to enjoy the whiff of fresh air he undoubtedly has missed while confined in his dingy room, Innocent Kintu faces his startled parents and startles them even more by asking for a chair as well as something to eat!

As the *Omukhulu* tells it to His Worship a few days later, he sauntered casually into Innocent Kintu's room and, without any warning, set about berating the youngster for a variety of things, principally the boy's apparent lack of respect for him as the *Omukhulu*. Addressing the emaciated figure shackled to the bed, he yelled that he expected Kintu to rise as he walked in! H followed that up with the remark that his recommendation for Kintu's readmission to the seminary would simply not be forthcoming in circumstances such as those.

Thereupon he noticed a slight stir as the shrunken and wasted figure attempted to raise its shrivelled head and to focus its bleary gaze on him. Father Campbell, oblivious to the fact that his addressee is manacled to the bed, offered his hand in greeting. The response was uncharacteristic. "They have tied me to the bed!" was the reply given in a weak tottering voice. As soon as the shackles binding his wrists to the bed frame were undone by the missionary, Innocent Kintu seized hold of his former superior's right hand and attempted pumping it the way one would pump the hand of a long lost friend. A beaming Father Campbell went on to describe how Innocent Kintu made several feeble and predictably unsuccessful attempts to get up on his own before accepting the priest's helping hand.

Following Innocent Kintu's sudden and wholly unexpected recovery, Father Campbell arranges to have the young man spend as much time away from his home and parents as possible. The priest, who suspects that the causes of the youngster's depression are rooted in his parents' mechanistic approach to reality and their notable lack of psychological training, also believes that Innocent Kintu is better off far away from what he characterised as their idle capriciousness and tempestuous and above all tendentious disposition. It is thus that Innocent Kintu comes to share the spacious, though far from comfortable, quarters of the Mission cook.

Father Campbell is delighted to see Innocent Kintu fully engaged and busy. Something tells him that as long as the youngster is kept preoccupied, he stands very little chance of suffering a relapse. On no account should he be left the opportunity to dwell on the fact, pretty obvious now, that a substantial part of his ego has been subject to inordinate repression. The priest imagines, rightly or wrongly, that this has been the case; and hence the inclination to rebelliousness on Innocent Kintu's part. Such brooding is certain, in the priest's view, to precipitate a relapse into his peculiar madness! As time passes, the priest even arranges for his charge, who still chafes at any suggestion that he has been mentally sick, to learn carpentry. Innocent Kintu does have any "muscles" to speak of or that could even be described as flagging, and the *Omukhulu* has hit on the idea that carpentry is good exercise for him and also a timely antidote.

After a while, Father Campbell alters the schedule so that the ex-seminarian can spend his weekends at home. But it is not until after a good six months elapse that he decides on some form of compensation for Innocent Kintu's labors in addition to the free accommodation and food he receives.

All this goes well until one Friday afternoon, just as Innocent Kintu is about to sign off and head off home, he confronts the *Omukhulu* and asks to talk about his delayed vocation to the priesthood! Father Campbell at first pretends that he hasn't heard what Kintu is saying; and then he tries prevaricating. But Innocent Kintu is adamant and suggests that the priest is planning to go back on his promise. He is well enough to go back to the seminary, he says; and he wants to do so before the Latin he has learnt completely evaporates! He complains, besides, that the priest no longer appears to believe in his ability to play the harmonium. In his view, the harmonic sounds created by the mission organist of the day, a Franciscan nun, are just rubbish!

The priest's replies proving to be all too unsatisfactory, Innocent Kintu's mien changes from one of joyous accommodation to that of an impersonal, affect-laden and non-descript weirdo. And, instead of heading home for the weekend as usual after work on that Friday, he takes a path in the opposite direction, and one that happens to lead into a thick woodland and wild animal sanctuary.

Were it not for the fact that Innocent Kintu has come to be well known throughout the length and breadth of St. Peter's Parish as a result of his "mental" problems, he undoubtedly would have made it to the forest's inner sanctuary and probably got himself eaten up alive by one or other of the wild beasts with which the forest is infested. As it is, the forest ranger is one of he numerous people who have heard about the strange malady with which the *walimu's* kid had been stricken in the days Innocent Kintu had been bedridden. Like many other wellwishers, he took time off his job to travel to the famous home of the Nkharangas in order to satisfy his curiosity.

With accustomed alacrity, the forest ranger makes out Innocent Kintu's human form in the descending gloom of night as the latter approaches the fringes of the forbidding jungle. Innocent Kintu clearly doesn't even seem to be aware that he has ventured off the beaten track and is as good as lost already; and he comes struggling along with what strikes the ranger as an unsteady and rather awkward gait. On his part, the ranger recognizes him almost at once and is astonished when the young man not only fails to answer his greeting but also appears ready to bolt.

It strikes the forest park ranger that something is very much amiss, and he correctly surmises that the malady has again struck the *walimu's* hapless kid. With his mind made up, he makes as if to let Innocent Kintu pass, but he instead grabs both the lad's arms and twists them behind the struggling Kintu's back in a firm lock. Without once relenting his grip, lest Innocent Kintu with his command of a madman's strength break away from his clasp and lose himself in the impenetrable forest, he walks his reluctant prisoner the twenty kilometers or so to the walimu's homestead on the edge of the school compound.

It is well after midnight when Nkharanga opens the door of his cottage to let in a dishevelled and thoroughly flustered Kintu with the virtual stranger acting as his escort. With the realization that their boy has suffered a relapse also comes consternation and puzzlement. It is an eventuality that the *walimu's* household are least prepared for. On the contrary, the faith which members of the Nkharanga family have had in Father Campbell and his ability to perform miracles ever since he had his way with Innocent Kintu on the feast of the Uganda Martyrs has until this moment been boundless.

To be sure, there are a scant few souls if any in the neighbourhood who have doubted that this missionary from *Bulaya* would see Innocent Kintu - and perhaps his up and coming brothers as well - re-established on the road to the holy priesthood in due course. But the sight of Kintu being herded into the house against his will by the forest park ranger shatters the faith the *walimu* have had in the priest! Still, it is not lost on them that, but for the forest ranger, they might never have seen their boy again. And so, even though shaken to the core by the unusual manner of Kintu's homecoming, their trust in God's mercies remains as firm as ever.

Innocent Kintu has maintained an unbroken silence whilst being matched home by the stern-faced stranger. As they come to their journey's end, it starts to look as if he has in fact been engaged, during that time, in plotting and designing his life's course anew. He continues to maintain a dead silence; but the glint in his eyes, which are half closed most of the time, is fiery and fearsome. The curl of his mouth has about it an unmistakable twist that hints at total defiance!

It is clear that Innocent Kintu's consciousness is disturbed in the extreme as he goes about attempting to settle in and to forget about his employment at the Mission headquarters. His senses grow increasingly numbed by the sheer weight of his listlessness - or so it now appears. As it is, everyone coming within Innocent Kintu's reach has now to observe a curious new law that he or she ignores at the risk of being sprung upon by a suddenly rabid and quite demented Kintu and maimed!

In the days that follow, Innocent Kintu bodily charges all and sundry whose bearing seems to hint, even remotely, at reproachfulness; and he does so without any regard to the age, sex, social status or kinship of the party he assaults. Naturally, due to their ignorance of the reason behind these assaults, the victims and their sympathisers tend to think that Innocent Kintu is being driven to behave as he does by one or other of the variety of things their imagination conjures up - a troublesome demon, a tumor in the brain, or perhaps a chigoe embedded in Innocent Kintu's skull!

Unlike on the previous occasions when he just lay back on his sickbed with the apparent intention of making it his deathbed as well, Innocent Kintu now actually stirs to help himself. The scope for doing so turns out to be rather limited.

Innocent Kintu's parents now recall the old days when they were used to seeing their son happily do things in response to their intimation and parental commands - before his fortunes took an unexpected nose dive whilst away at the *Seminario Nkuu* in mysterious circumstances - with nostalgia. There was, of course, a time even after that when they were eagerly looking forward to the time when their son would resume being his old good self again. During those good old days, Innocent Kintu had, to all appearances, grown accustomed to putting his self interest last and the satisfaction of the will of others first.

It should, of course, have become clear to them by now that it does not behove them to tamper with his "autonomy". But it is precisely this that they all seem bent on doing, unaware that it is at the heart of his "rebellion" - if one can use that word to characterise Kintu's new mannerisms. The fact is that they do not now need to do anything to alert their son that this is what they are up to.

And it doesn't really matter what they do at this juncture. That is because, in the good old days when he was the "exemplary kid" they had always wanted him to be, he had himself come to expect them to treat him "condescendingly" then. He not only had enjoyed it, he had grown up believing that it was the way to go for any "decent" or "responsible" parents who "loved" their children; and he pitied the youngsters who were "left to their own devices" (his acronym for what others saw as the autonomy that children growing up actually needed to become self-actualized).

While Innocent Kintu still doesn't know any better, he definitely dislikes anything they do now. He just believes that life itself is cruel and a hoax, and that none of those he had looked up to as his "guardians" - and this includes his parents, Father Campbell, the staff of St. Augustine's Seminary and his "dissembling" fellow seminarians - will now come to his succour and help him realize his dream of following in the footsteps of the Messiah in the only way he knows.

Although Innocent Kintu will at this juncture eat his meal, for example, if satisfied that he does not do so at anyone's urging explicit or otherwise, any slight suspicion that any of the people around might in any way be attempting to influence or direct his action promptly rouses his fury. And it is not because he chooses to vent his anger on anyone. He doesn't consciously choose to vent his anger on anyone, and he doesn't see himself as someone who could do such a thing.

The "fury" is the result of an uncontrollable reaction, and he vents it in the same way someone who is being strangled to death fights back and throws punches. At this stage, the

213

inevitable desire of folks around at mealtime to see the "patient" eat his meal thus constitutes the gravest obstacle to his proper nourishment. And that is the catch Innocent Kintu's parents find themselves in without habing the slightest inkling of what is at play.

Not surprisingly, Innocent Kintu ends up on the worst terms with everybody. His eating habits deteriorate. He soon leaves off bathing altogether, abandons all aspects of personal hygiene, and even takes to answering calls of nature while fully clothed. In the end, physically emaciated and trailed by a vile smell, he resorts to spending most of his time in corners of the house picking bugs from the dirty and horribly tattered clothing he wears in preference to clean ones.

Part Three

16.

Shock Therapy Center

It is two thirty on this Sunday afternoon. With the exception of Father Rector, who is spending the afternoon with His Worship, the Bishop, for briefings on the state of the Apostolate, the rest of the seminary staff consisting of British, Irish, Dutch and German priests, are having their afternoon siesta. The telephone caller identifies himself as Professor Claus Gringo of the Livingstoneville District Hospital. He asks to speak to Moses Kwentindio, a final year student.

As the hunt for Brother Moses is mounted, the stage also becomes set for excitement of a rare sort to seize a community. Ever since the student body was permitted access to the telephone located in the Rector's Office a year ago, no member of that body has been known to use the facility for receiving or making a telephone call. Predictably it is a sizeable crowd of seminarians, curiosity stamped all over their eager faces, who herd the reverend Brother towards the Rector's Office.

To the more aloof, the scene created looks silly because the object of the manhunt has, not surprisingly, been found in his cubicle. It is the time of day when most students would be in their rooms! The fact that Rev. Moses Kwentindio's room was littered with sheets upon sheets of papers that bore scribbling in his short hand has escaped everyone's attention.

An almost tangible sense of expectancy pervades the throng of onlookers who have split up and now appear to man strategic points in the vicinity of Father Rector's Office. They stand or lean expectantly, their upraised eyebrows bearing additional testimony as to their intentions, namely to eavesdrop on the telephone conversation or, failing that, to apprehend the Brother for a briefing immediately afterward.

There is at least one outstanding feature about the composition of the group - they consist largely of first and second year students, so well known for their unbridled curiosity and lust for knowledge. The group easily reminds one of the Sophists of ancient Greece about whom they even now read. They seem to be interested in knowledge for its own sake - while their curiosity lasts, that is!

If the curiosity of certain of Moses Kwentindio's fellow seminarians for a hint as to the big event in the outside world necessitating the call is deep, the disappointment they are destined to suffer is deeper and more grievous. Following upon his conversation with Professor Gringo over the phone, Rev. Moses Kwentindio, as it happens, will remain the closed book he has been for a couple of years now, the please of his junior colleagues notwithstanding.

The more seasoned brethren would still remember that time three years back when Brother Moses, then only a Subdeacon, made history by stepping down voluntarily from the exalted and highly coveted position of Dean of Students before his term as Dean was up. This followed closely upon the departure from the seminary of one Innocent Kintu. Brother Innocent's departure sparked off, rather inexplicably, a series of resignations from the seminary of students one hardly expected could leave of their own accord.

Innocent Kintu was subsequently found to be a mentally disturbed individual according to the stories passed on to the new generation of students, and reportedly was still making the rounds of the country's mental institutions! Just as no one at the time suspected that any connection existed between Bother Innocent's departure from the seminary in mysterious circumstances and Brother Moses' resignation from the post of Student Dean, no one now suspects any connection between the telephone call and Innocent Kintu's misfortunes.

The Brothers who are close enough to eavesdrop on the telephone conversation find the exchanges plainly enigmatic. Their readiness to share what of it catches the ear with others merely adds to the confusion.

After the greetings and the all too brief introductions, the caller's voice, emboldened, comes crackling through like the determined hum of a bee that suddenly finds itself prisoner in a jar: "I've received the message you left with my secretary. Innocent Kintu is in my charge, and I can assure you that the information you in your possession, if made available to us, is bound to affect his prospects for a cure…"

"Actually, Professor" says Brother Moses nervously; "It is a tremendous relief to me and a lot of Kintu's friends that the poor fellow has finally been committed to proper psychiatric care. I am personally delighted that you yourself will be in charge of the patient. I have been trying to compile what you might call a dossier…"

"Sorry, dossier - did you say? Like the Donald Trump–Russia dossier?" The speaker at the other end of the line sounds quite excited.

"I have been attempting to compile a dossier on the Brother since his first mental breakdown three years ago, Professor. It's been my fling at Gestalt Psychology!" The former Dean winks, and smiles, as he speaks.

"Oh, I see!" the stranger hums in a dry professorial voice.

"In my own amateurish fashion," pursues Brother Moses, his tone somewhat relaxed now; "In my own amateurish fashion, I have been trying to crack this case! T's possible I may have broken new ground. The problem is, however, I don't know what the old ground covers! I do believe nevertheless that I have succeeded in reconstructing the pattern of events leading to the tragedy. I think I can explain…"

"You can?" echoes the Professor Gringo.

"Yes, yes, professor. The dossier…unfortunately it is still in my short hand and quite illegible."

At the other end of the line, the professor holds the receiver level with his flat, permanently sweaty nose, and seems to be laughing at it as he breaks out into a chuckle. For his part, Moses Kwentindio lets his face become distorted with a wide grin while he stares ahead of him into space.

"Jamila, my secretary, said you were wishing for an early meeting. If you tell me when you can make it to Livingstoneville, Mr. Kwentindio…" Professor Gringo has a definite way of making himself sound nonchalant.

Brother Moses winces nervously meanwhile at hearing himself called "Mister". But he quickly rejoins, his voice faintly hesitant. "Our holidays start a week from now. I might just be able to complete the dossier before then."

"Excellent. I should then expect to see you in roughly a week's time?"

For the eavesdroppers, the most confusing part of the conversation comes when the Rod, as brother Moses is still referred to, inquire on a sudden impulse after the condition of the hapless Kintu. He is anxious for a response from the other end of the line and for a moment or so fears that the line has bas already been cut. When the dry professorial voice finally comes crackling through, he seems well pleased with himself.

"The lad's behaviour is quite baffling. His mental faculties have virtually ceased to function. He is fast losing his eyesight besides. When he arrived here, the eyes were no more than tiny slits and were covered with grime. There is just a chance that we might succeed in keeping them open. If we fail, the young man's dependence on others will become complete..."

"Oh my God!" ejaculates Moses Kwentindio with surprise.

"Sorry, dear! I thought I might give the position to you exactly as it is." Professor Gringo's voice assumes musical style as he goes on to say: "Until I received your message, I didn't think your brother - am I right?"

"In a religious sense, Doctor - that's right!"

"Well, I didn't think your brother had a chance," said the Professor. "He hails from a little known part of the colony and - if you will pardon me - members of the Lekha tribe have a reputation for being inscrutable! My colleagues too consider the case hopeless - unless additional useful information on the patient's background becomes available to us!"

"You mean he isn't undergoing any treatment?"

"Oh yes, he is," the other party cuts him short. "The usual fare for patients in his category - electric shocks to keep him reasonably restrained."

There is a pause before Brother Moses says distractedly: "Did you say his dependence on other people is almost complete?"

"Well, yes. He will be totally blind soon...I mean," crackles the voice hoarsely. "Your brother's finger-knuckle joints also appear to have been denied the opportunity to maintain their resilience for quite sometime. They won't, for

220

instance, now permit his fingers, which are firmly locked in a bent position to either stretch…"

"Dear me!"

"His other bodily joints aren't in any better shape," continues Professor Gringo as if no interruption took place. "But, worst of all, his fingernails, which haven't been pared for a while, are literally piercing…they are digging into the palms of your brother's hands as they grow! The wounds are fairly deep and well - bad. The knuckles themselves…they have begun to form themselves into two creepy fists that are growing tighter and tighter by the day. The set-up, Moses, is akin to that which is known to apply to grown foetuses when they become starved of vitamins and other nutrients…"

"Oh, God! What a pity!" the Rod is heard to exclaim. In a subdued voice that is scarcely heard by the other party, he mumbles on: "And yet it is all taking place just as I thought it would. The problem is now biological - not just mental! Yeah, the *Second Childhood*!"

Moses Kwentindio, who had momentarily lapsed into soliloquy, is now suddenly all astir. He forgets himself in his state of frenzy and begins to bellow into the telephone, obsessed for the moment with the desire to establish contact with the party at the other end which he dearly hopes has not been cut: "Professor - are you there? Are you there, Dr. Gringo?"

"Yes, yes! Go on!" comes the comforting crackle. "I am listening. You do seem to have quite an idea there…"

"Oh!" sighs Moses Kwentindio, plainly relieved. "Excuse me for thinking aloud, Professor. When you mentioned a while ago that the patient's physical condition is comparable to that of a starving fetus, it struck me that Brother Innocent, without saying so explicitly, is in fact now craving

221

for a *second childhood* - one that will permit the autonomous man in him to develop afresh. I can well imagine the patient experiencing a subconscious need now to exercise his birthright to an autonomous existence - if you know what I mean.

"I don't for once believe that the Brother is deliberately inflicting martyrdom on himself. This isn't self-immolation. It would be rather quaint, indeed totally bizarre, for one to endure such severe martyrdom at one's own hands..."

Moses Kwentindio, who has once more relapsed into soliloquy, comes to with a start when the professor's crackly voice interrupts his monologue: "Moses, I guess we shouldn't be discussing all this over the phone. People could be listening in, and I am not just referring to the CIA!

"That's right, Moses Kwentindio confesses, looking about him at the upturned faces of his fellow seminarians. "Guess I will see you next week then, Professor..."

"Good day and cheers!" croaks the psychiatrist.

As the silence that follows on that final crackling sound shows, the eardrums of Moses Kwentindio, and of the eavesdroppers no less, have tended to magnify the sounds transmitted over the telephone line. The line itself is now cut with what seems to be a resounding "click".

Moses Kwentindio's heartbeat races at several times its normal pace as he makes his way back to his cubicle. Drawn there as if by a magnate, he lets his legs bear him along effortlessly as if the rest of him was a mere load. But no sooner is he there than he begins to gather up the sheets of paper littered on the floor purposefully, scouring the length and breadth of the room like a determined chess player studying a chessboard.

For Brother Moses, as he braces himself for the impossible task of transposing the pages upon pages of his shorthand into a dream dossier on his tribesman in the short space of a week, the rest of that afternoon flies by faster than the minutes and seconds of the ancient rustic clock that a parish priest gave him as a Christmas gift (to remind him that life was short and was getting shorter with every passing moment) on the mantelpiece. As far as things of world at least go, nothing he can think of even comes close to being as paramount to him now as his forthcoming meeting with the famous Livingstoneville shrink. He is, besides, determined to have the dossier rewritten and legible for the meeting. As far as the former Dean of Students is concerned, his meeting with the Professor just has to end up as a watershed moment for his buddy (who had already lost it) and for himself (if he was going to escape ending up in the same boat as his buddy)!

Predictably, the Brother is close to a physical as well as a mental wreck when the bell signalling "lights off" goes later that night. Yet, by that time - by the close of the first of seven days in the countdown - he barely manages to organize the numbered pages in their numerical sequence and does not even start on the exacting and arduous task of producing a fair copy of the dossier.

For a good two hours, brother Moses lies awake on his back, staring into the darkened ceiling. As he turns over in his head the contents of the dossier represented by the pile of scarcely decipherable papers in a corner of his writing desk, his concentration, defying the extreme weariness he feels, is able to sleep at bay - until his mind turns from contemplating the causes of Brother Innocent's illness and begins conjuring up imaginary scenes of his forthcoming meeting with Professor Claus Gringo.

223

His eyes finally close shut as implausible images of the personality of the psychiatrist he has spoken to over the phone but has never met begin to crowd his mind. And as they shut, they do so as if they too are veritable windows of his soul shutting off the outside world, and with it the distractions that stand in the way of an unfettered play of the higher faculties of reason and the imagination.

Brother Moses' nightmare has him confronting a Livingstoneville psychiatrist by the funny sounding name of Dr. Schizof Quack. His interview with Dr. Quack suggests that everything that could go wrong has gone wrong from the very first.

"My dear Innocent Kintu" screams the loathsome, absolutely creepy looking fellow who looks more like a sorcerer than a member of the psychiatric profession. He regards Brother Moses for a second or two before adding: "I gather you hoodwinked the warder into releasing you from your cell and you even succeeded in gaining freedom by pole vaulting over the barbed wire fence! Clever of you, eh! I've first class medicine for types like you. From here you go for the shock therapy - you know from your experience what I mean better than I do!"

Dr. Quack snarls and indulges in a hearty, braying and quite loud horselaugh. He then adds: "I hear you want to be called by different names now - Moses Kwentindio!"

Brother Moses realises presently that he is chained to two robust nursing orderlies who look more like thugs than hospital staff. He has nothing on and his first thought is to get himself something - anything - to cover his nakedness. He would go for the drapes he sees hanging from the windows if only he could drag the orderlies close enough. They however misunderstand his intentions and do not budge an inch.

Brother Moses has no recollection whatsoever, in the meantime, of the events that have led to his present predicament. He is all but resigned to his grisly fate and has even left off staying beseechingly at his savage-looking captors when memories of how it all came about begin gradually to light up his mind.

He arrived in Livingstoneville that morning armed with the dossier and ready for his meeting with Dr. Claus Gringo. But on reaching the hospital, he decided on a sudden impulse to test an idea he had nursed ever since he first considered writing the dossier on his tribesman. If the patient himself could be persuaded to read the dossier through, that should, he imagined, be a sure trigger for his cure as any he could think of!

With Brother Innocent's psychic roots laid out clearly in black and white, it would be only a matter of time, so Brother Moses's reasoning went, before his tribesman became aware of his limitations; and, as far as he was concerned, such an eventuality would assure Innocent Kintu's recovery. What would remain after that would be normal self-administered psychotherapy aimed not so much at healing as at ensuring successful social intercourse.

Brother Moses was convinced as he approached the prison-like ward where Innocent Kintu reportedly was incarcerated that even if it meant facing the professor without the dossier, it would pay to leave the one and only copy he had with his fellow tribesman if he indicated interest in reading it through.

Brother Moses has a good recollection of the unexpected cooperation he received from the patient notwithstanding his ravaged physical condition. The brazenfaced warder, amazed at what the brash young man in a clergyman's attire achieved with the patient in a very short time, even granted them leave to continue their chat outside the special enclosure beyond which patients in Innocent Kintu's category were ordinarily forbidden to wander. So long as their walk was confined to the hospital grounds, the fact that Innocent Kintu was naked to the skin did not even seem to matter.

Brother Moses's power of recall is unable to take him beyond that point, leaving a gap that makes him unsure of himself now. When he inquires about Dr. Claus gringo, his captors merely snarl and lead him on. A door is thrown open - the door of the Shock Therapy Center; and in the same instant his terror and feelings of anxiety turn to rage.

Brother Moses recognizes everything in the Shock Therapy Center: the writing desk with the pile of papers still scribbled in his short hand - the pile that he hopes to transform into a sleek dossier; the ancient clock on the mantelpiece; and all the other familiar items in that belong to his room at St. Barnabas' Major Seminary. Awakened by the unreality of it all, Brother Moses suddenly finds himself wondering if he should direct his rage at Dr. Claus Gringo for having started it all with his telephone call or at himself.

17.

Dr. Claus Gringo

Moses Kwentindio, optimistic as ever, has been looking forward expectantly to this hour. But he never dreamt that he would be permitted so much indulgence! Finding himself now, all of a sudden, locked in a scarcely veiled philosophical sparring session with his host - a session that brings back to him those early years in the major Seminary when arguing for argument's sake was the order of the day, he is beside himself.

"I have always had the feeling," he intones with enthusiasm, "that what others think of a person isn't all that sacred. Professor, I know it is like confusing disciplines; but of late I have even come to believe that social acts tend to be harmful. I believe this to be especially true in circumstances in which considerations of decency and decorum rule. The only social acts that are perhaps harmless are those that actually are sham or acted. They permit the individual to maintain not just some but all of his wits about him - he remains master of the situation!"

In comparison to the racy sophomoric voice of Moses Kwentindio, the voice of Dr. Claus Gringo, MD, M.Sc., D.P.M., Consultant and Professor of Psychiatry, is slow and measured: "There should be nothing special about what others think of an individual", he begins. "Come to think of it - actions that are oriented to other people or done with others in contemplation…what, in other words, are called social acts are bound to be harmful to the development of one's personality when the actor feels inadequate or wanting. As regards other instances - well, I had left these open to question!"

The voice of Dr. Claus Gringo is in fact always slow and measured - except when he is talking on the telephone, in which case the voice becomes brisk and dry. Indeed the professor's voice otherwise varies very little when he speaks - whether delivering a lecture to students, giving dictation to his secretary, presenting a scientific paper at a symposium, chatting with his Anglo-Saxon wife or, as in the present instance, during a consultation. On this occasion as on all others, Dr. Gringo speaks without notes. His head, with its crest of shaggy black hair, which is its trademark, tilts to this side or that meanwhile as he rumbles on.

A squat man, Dr. Gringo, a native of neighboring Uganda, is given to dressing in a finicky manner. This morning he is turned in a white pair of slacks, a collarless short-sleeved *kitenge* shirt whose crimson tinge lights up his shining black face, and a pair of matching brown leather sandals. Seated stolidly in the wooden armchair by his work desk, he seems unable to stop fidgeting with his fountain pen as he speaks.

Dr. Gringo is very well respected in intellectual circles, and serves as an External Examiner at the Stanford Medical School (his alma mater) and the Johns Hopkins School of Medicine amongst others. Those who know him well are aware of his notorious and rather favourite practice of misleading his audiences into thinking that he is a fool while he simultaneously temps them to come out with their definitive views on matters at issue.

The professor's gaze is fixed on the young man in clerical garb who sits over across the desk leaning against one arm. The fluorescent lighting causes the freshly sheared tonsure spotted by the cleric atop his crown to gleam like a polished coin. It looks outlandish amid the thick tufts of hair on other parts of his head! His poise nonetheless reminds the man of medicine of a statue of St. Anthony of Padua that he remembered seeing in the sanctuary of a Catholic church in his hometown where he occasionally served as an altar boy when he was growing up.

"Psychiatry" says he after a slight pause, "has ceased being primarily occupied with genetics and has entered the field of Microbiology. We could very well be placing too great an emphasis on such things as brain nerves…"

Moses Kwentindio's interjection is brash and unexpected. "I am a layman in these matters even though my interest is consuming!"

"Ahem!" exclaims Dr. Gringo. During the lengthy pause that follows, he tilts his head to one side, clears his throat once again with a blaringly fake coughing fit, and then settles back in his armchair.

"The Orientals are right" pursues the churchman, "in saying that religion is like opium. It embodies within it that stuff which, to many, is decency at its best - or perfect decorum! Religion thus merits to be regarded with the greatest suspicion. Although it may in itself be harmless, it must be considered harmful in as much a it provides such wide scope for stifling the development of the human personality…"

Dr. Gringo's left upper eyebrow twitches and then flickers up and down. "In other words" he gasps, "People are better left to do and act as they wish - is that it? I am sure that isn't what you mean! "

"Yes and no" Moses Kwentindio retorts. "It is about time in my view that a start was made to see religion for what it really is and not just what it idealizes. I mean…it should be taught dissected and cold like the physical sciences - if it is

229

worth what it is supposed to be worth! People learning to believe should be left to live the religion according to their whims - if you like!"

"I get you" Dr. Gringo rejoins hoarsely, snapping his fingers simultaneously for emphasis. His voice a shade hoarser he continues: "It's...well...sort of obvious. From what you say, I conclude that religion was kind of rammed down your brother's throat!"

"More than that," Moses Kwentindio snaps in reply. "It is the one thing I've strive to bring out in my dossier, although I still have to learn with what success. If I may just run ahead, Professor - when your patient says "I", it is always his submissive self speaking. Brother Innocent has never had the opportunity to develop a sense of personal autonomy in my view. I submit that he has had no other experience..."

"Mr. Kwentindio" the older man breaks in, totally focused on the substance of his guest's statement and seemingly unconcerned by the fact that the clerical collar that forms a part of Moses Kwentindio's attire signifies that he is a reverend and needs to be addressed ass such; "There is a thesis which says that autonomy represents a point of focus to which our actions tend as a natural consequence, and which the individual ignores at the risk of condemning oneself to an inane aimless existence. I am starting to think there may be a lot to be said for your thesis - I have, of course, still to hear the rest of it!"

Without pausing, the balding professor adds as an aside: "I keep telling my students that insanity could well boil down to a trait of the mind - an aversion for thinking in cheerless straight lines or an avowal that one's thinking will be in abstruse vicious circles!"

230

Dr. Claus gringo is in an unusually gregarious mood and finds himself laughing at his own joke before his listener does. The seminarian, who struggles to hold back his laughter, is quick to chime in with a blockbuster of his own: " My math teacher used to kid us that insane people's thoughts came discrete and hence abnormal, while the thought of sane people, naturally his own included, formed a continuum! I can only suppose that he was right…"

The psychiatrist's laughter is represented by a fitful guttural sound that he dispenses in measured doses as if it were, so that it resembles the fretful bleating of sheep in the midst of a munching session.

Such moments are infrequent occurrences during discussions that attract his participation and he secretly gives the quiet-spoken cleric credit for the achievement. That this laddie with the eerie tonsure atop his crown is no beatnik has already become more than apparent to the western trained "mind reader".

Moses Kwentindio has impressed his host with the ease with which he grapples the socio-psycho issues that, he is now more or less persuaded are fundamental to his patient's case. It of course remains to be seen whether the information he has come to volunteer will be of exceptional value. One thing though is already certain - the young churchman has more on his mind than just to volunteer information.

When he resumes his poise following his rare fling at vigorous laughter, Dr. Gringo cocks his ear in his visitor's direction and raises his eyebrows as if to emphasize that he is not about to turn caviller.

For his part the Rod fingers his Roman collar with one hand and the buttons of his sky blue double-breasted waistcoat with the other. "I have taken to browsing through medical

231

literature of late" he announces casually after what seems an eternity; "The other day I was leafing through an old copy of *The Healing Arts*..."

The mention of the words "Healing Arts" causes Dr. Claus Gringo to jump from his seat. "That's the world's leading journal of mind-reading! It is still published as a supplement of the *Stanford Observer*. I received my Diploma in Psychiatric Medicine from Stanford!"

"I've heard of Stanford," his guest rallies with unexpected enthusiasm. "Supposed to have the greatest concentration of inventors and Nobel Prize winners!"

"Of madmen" Dr. Claus Gringo adds quickly. Too much of anything is bad. Too much scholarship makes one look like a numskull to the rest of the world, and it becomes worse when there seems to be a concentration of them. Stanford would make an interesting tourist spot for Africans especially..."

The laughter takes a while to die down. When it does, Moses Kwentindio resumes his story: "I was leafing through a copy of this journal and all of a sudden I came upon the term 'autonomous nervous system'. Although the accompanying text was bristling with mathematical equations and made little sense to me, that expression did! Having heard what you said a while ago, I am now convinced that autonomous nervous systems do exist. Their mere existence also somehow seems to vindicate my own crazy theory, although I started off from very different bases. As of now, Professor, my authorities are the likes of Teilhard de Chardin and Julian Huxley! Perhaps I should have gone to study psychiatry instead of taking a crack at the priesthood - and then my authorities..."

"Hold it!" bawls the psychiatrist. "Talking about authorities, Pierre Teilhard and his English counterpart Huxley are not exactly my favourite. These people seem to thrive on metaphysics and nothing else. Quite frankly, metaphysics and I have never been bedfellows!"

The seminarian winces and then quips: "In that case, I will restrict our consideration to just one quote from each of these foolhardy metaphysicians as my philosophy tutor liked to refer to the pair."

"Only one, please" his host pleads jokingly.

"Let's begin with Teilhard's finding that that as we humans fumble with religious mysteries in our endeavour to comprehend them, more often than not we end up taking as the essence of the matter under study what in fact are mere reflections of our own thoughts!"

"I don't quarrel with Pierre Teilhard sometimes" rejoins the professor. His mood visibly changes from sombre to jolly as he adds: "Pierre was still down to earth there, I suppose..."

The small office reverberates with the cacophony created by their laughter for a while. Dr. Gringo reclines back in his seat and wipes his nose as the laughter peters off. But he continues to indulge himself in producing little throaty animal like grunts - almost as if he were a sheep - even as Moses Kwentindio resumes his speech.

"Sir Julian Huxley pointed out something quite different but complementary. To use his own words - it isn't possible now any more to maintain that science and religion must operate in thought-tight compartments or that they concern separate sectors of life. They both are relevant to the whole of human existence..."

"Mmm!" Dr. Claus Gringo is assuredly surprised that his guest is so well read. His own lips part slightly as Moses Kwentindio pursues unabashed.

"The religiously minded can no longer turn their backs upon the natural world or seek escape from its imperfections in a supernatural world; by the same token, the materialistically minded can no longer deny importance to spiritual experience and religious feeling…"

The psychiatrist's short stubby hand shoots up: "All my Christian friends would contradict you there" he growls. "As a matter of fact they advocate that a good Christian must shut his/her eyes to the world! I also think that you would find it a thankless task to try and convince my agnostic friends that spiritual experience and religious feeling should be given any importance in the natural run of things…"

"That's precisely the point, Professor. We are dealing with two things in either instance: religion as a set of cut and dried dogmas and logical - or illogical - network they constitute together, and religion as a collection of empty devotions and pious practices on the one hand; and science - or, more specifically, materialistic thought - as an integrated body of scientifically proven facts, and science as an instrument for self-serving propaganda.

"Science, like religion, does occasionally sink to the level of an opiate. Religion plainly was the intoxicant in the case of Brother Innocent; but quite obviously we must leave room for science as well to serve as opium of the people!"

"A round about method but interesting results…"

"But that is not all" Moses Kwentindio mutters with a smack of the lips; "There appears to be a curious link between these and some of your own theories. My material is probably out-dated…"

"No matter! Shoot right on" snorts Dr. Claus Gringo, leaning forward so that he strikes the pose of a hunchback.

"I recall reading somewhere that the awareness a human being can have of an object is two - and apparently only two - types," mumbles the cleric uncertainly.

"Sense perception and imagery" volunteers his host, a discernible note of interest in his voice.

"That's right! Apparently we are faced in either case with the object as something apart from ourselves. In sense perception, the object exists tangibly and is real; in imagery, the object of our perception is pictorial and subjective..."

"Correct." The psychiatrist seems to be listening with his ears and with his eyes as well.

"The object in sense perception exists in real space with the sense perception itself remaining constant and independent of the will. In imagery, on the other hand, the object appears in our subjective inner space and has to be continually recreated, being entirely dependent of the will..."

"Sounds as though you took the material from a standard text-book," the older man growls hoarsely.

"The dossier draws heavily on this concept of human awareness" says the Rod, his manner voluble and confident.

"I do not need to tell you, young man," says Dr. Gringo interrupting; "I find many of your ideas provoking and a few quite engaging. I once wrote a paper on 'Theories of Human Awareness' for a symposium; I have been interested in scenarios representing dynamic situations in this area ever since, but must confess that I have never gotten very far..."

"Well," splutters his guest; "It apparently is possible for an individual to grow up able to perceive objects say, only in imagery. The upbringing of that individual never permits him or her to behold anything except in an inner, continuously recreated space with the will of that person playing the essential part. But the will itself in this case is unlikely to free from some powerful exogenous influence…"

"Say that again!" grunts the professor.

"Exogenous influence - the influence associated with the power of those responsible for the formation of the collective conscience."

"You mean, the parents?"

"Exactly," chimes in Moses Kwentindio, lowering his gaze so that his eyes meet those of his host.

Almost immediately, however, the cleric's gaze is back to the Makonde carving on the ledge besides the large portrait of Her Majesty the Queen of England. The carving depicts an enthusiastic drummer of Welekhe origin. Unlike the icons of ancient Rome or Greece that mainly survey or stare at a scene, the carving depicts a drummer in action. The oversized head reveals no face, and certainly no eyes, of significance. But the head itself is thrown back in a manner suggestive of sheer wild abandon. The muscular arms of the drummer sweep out on either side of his bare rugged chest and above the distinctive line-up of drums to his left and right, where they stay poised to beat rhythm out of the drums' crusty hide.

"The parents - or elders - represent for the victim from the outset a spectre that is at once fearsome and desirable! Assuredly their attitude has been uncompromising and yet preferred to anything else. The victim, finally, has always regarded the elders, unwieldy though they be, as a beneficent and immensely admirable lot!"

Tranquility reigns in the snug, daintily furnished office. After the seminarian's monologue, neither the host nor Kwentindio himself seems eager to break the silence.

The Rod is unruffled when he finally resumes his speech. "More specifically, it is possible for one to grow up accustomed to attaching - indeed nailed to the habit of attaching - motives or intentions to one's every act on the conscious and ultimately also unconscious level..."

"What do you mean exactly?" Dr. Gringo interjects breezily.

"I mean...grow up accustomed to a setup whereby one's every gesture and action is induced so to speak by considerations outside of the self and not autonomous in that sense" explains the churchman, with an animated waive of the hand.

"I see the possibility," his host chimes in. "Although still more of a hypothesis than a proven fact, it does appear that external influences and pressures, of consistently applied to children, do sometimes have the effect of narrowing what we call the range of their object awareness. The victim's ability to discern certain things can be severely affected as a result - it is supposed that the object awareness would be only dim when the awareness relates to objects that are either irrelevant and of little consequence to the directed responses to which the victim is subject. It is thus very possible for an impressionable little one in an extreme case to grow up having no choice but to submit continually to the control of a domineering elder's psychic omnipresence..."

"Just what I have been attempting to verbalize," the young man begins to mutters. "Forgive me if I sounded like I was preaching instead of..."

Moses Kwentindio is cur short by a suddenly impatient Dr. Claus Gringo. "Never mind. Proceed with what you were saying!" he squawks.

"In discussing the spectrum of society," Moses Kwentindio says, lowering his gaze and speaking directly to the psychiatrist, we obviously have to allow for different degrees of internalization as well as variations in the sequence of learning and unlearning processes. However, in general and certainly in our extreme case, the extent to which moral compulsion (as I would call it) leads one to think that human acts must satisfy the collective conscience - the extent to which an individual is drawn to conform with society for the sake of it - seems to me to represent a measure of the degree of that individual's mental imbalance or insanity if you will!"

Dr. Claus Gringo seems more interested than ever. As he shifts his gaze from the fountain pen on his the desk and concentrates on the figure in the apparel of a travelling clergyman on the other side of the desk, his eyes glow bright red like he had light bulbs for eyes!

"I'm not quite getting you," he stutters, heaving his hulk closer to the desk.

"Well, it's this," stammers Moses Kwentindio. "One can be so preoccupied all through one's formative years, and eventually one's entire life, with seeing the will of other people fulfilled that he or she never has the opportunity, time or inclination to perceive anything in what you shrinks call real space! It is perception that Thomists at least would be inclined to think ought normally to proceed conceptualization and its handmaid imagination...imagery, if you like."

"Ah, Ha!" exclaims the professor exuberantly.

"Outward harmony," the churchman pursues unsmilingly, "cannot be rightfully accorded precedence over an unfettered and clear conscience!"

"But you are not suggesting, I am sure, that the speech and mannerisms of the mentally disordered - I mean of course those still capable of producing a semblance of spoken words and displaying recognizable attitudinal traits - are misleading by design?" The professor's tone is serious all right; but his expression has all the traits of someone about to burst out laughing.

The seminarian's features relax just sufficiently to disclose a faint smile as he announces: "I do. Not that the poor victims should be kept in leg irons for it, though! I just happen to think they are aware and conscious of the things they do, even if they have decided to let people other than themselves be the dictators or prime movers of everything they do. One can even say that until they are able to figure out ways of casing off the yoke, they do not know any better…"

The buzzer goes off just as Moses Kwentindio is concluding his speech. Dr. Claus Gringo, blear-eyed, leans toward the intercom and lets escape what sounds like a grunt. He simultaneously depresses a green button on the wireless gadget.

A woman's voice belonging, Moses Kwentindio supposes, to the chocolate coloured receptionist cum secretary who accosted him in the front office on his way in, reverberates throughout the small hut well appointed precinct. It says: "Professor, will Father what's-his-name like a spoonful of sugar in his tea? I know you like yours just spiced Indian-style and unsweetened."

The seminarian's face is deadpan as he flashes what looks like a "V" sign. With a sheepish grin, the psychiatrist, who has momentarily looked up in his guest's direction as the question was being asked, grunts and turning dutifully to the intercom says: "Two spoonfuls will be alright, Jamila."

Dr. Claus Gringo hardly completes the sentence when his guest and Jamila in the anteroom explode with ecstatic laughter. The secretary's voice, bursting into the office via the intercom, is magnified several times over and so completely transformed that her laughter now sounds just like the whine

239

of a Vespa scooter! The hilarious laughter proves quite infectious as the psychiatrist, unable to resist any longer, joins in. His delighted chortle is loud and raucous and in baritone, and complements the chorus just perfectly.

During the tea service, the mercurial Jamila several times attempts to steal glances at Moses Kwentindio. She is however caught at her every attempt by her intended prey. He looks inobservant and harmless enough; yet he seems determined that no glance of hers will go un-noticed. As their eyes meet, they both invariably turn their gaze on the psychiatrist who pretends he sees nothing!

A Muslim by upbringing, Dr. Gringo's secretary, who is well aware that Catholic clergy do not marry, has never been confronted by a "clergyman" of so tender an age and who, besides, is so very handsome; and she feels quite intrigued. Hidden from her is the fact that the object of her admiration, now in his final year at the major seminary, is unlikely to be elevated to the priesthood. Since Innocent Kintu's mental breakdown three years ago, the former Dean of Students has just been marking time whilst compiling his "dossier" on the Brother, and intends quitting the seminary before the year is out - at least he thinks he will have completed this task by then!

While the real reasons behind Jamila's burning curiosity are seemingly hidden from the cleric, the fact is concealed from both of them that in under a year's time they will be united in wedlock as husband and wife!

The balding don waits for is secretary, who lingers on with the obvious intent of catching the gist of their conversation, to leave before he addresses his guest. "Well," he croaks when she finally disappears into her office, "You can expect that I am in the literal sense dying to see how the thesis you just propounded relates to my patient's predicament…"

Like an interviewee who knows the answer to a question but is unable for the moment to muster words for a reply, Moses Kwentindio sits there open-mouthed and stares stupidly at his host.

18.

Theory "R"

"Well," Moses Kwentindio says at long last, fingering his Roman collar and the buttons of his coat. "There was a time when I was what you might call a square. At that time there were things I used to observe and wouldn't care less about their underlying significance. When Brother Innocent with his peculiar problems burst in on me, I had not quite graduated from that status yet; but I finally did - and very fast - thereafter! I still do not know whether to rejoice that he did or not. But, whatever is the matter with him, I have little doubt in my mind that he represents a polar case..."

"Polar cases are rare, to be sure," Dr. Claus Gringo breaks in with a nod of his head. "If this is one of them - and I dearly want it to prove one - I dare say you owe this Brother of yours a bundle. If I tried to reason my way into some of the obscure things you have raised, I would be liable to drift off in my thoughts and not find my way back to reality in the absence of an actual observable caricature of humanity of the same genre. Going off on a tangent, I would probably end up haywire myself!"

"I myself am adrift," Moses Kwentindio concedes in a faltering voice. "I guess I will continue on this course until my hypothesis is proved one way or the other. It is a crazy hypothesis, but it is the basis of the dossier I have spent myself trying to produce..."

"Come on, I'm all ears" Dr. Claus Gringo mutters impulsively.

'Well! O.K." The seminarian sounds hesitant at first. Then, after a pause: "Just try to fancy yourself, Doctor, in somewhat different straits from your present - you are eleven still or even younger. Hunger is gnawing at your middle, and you are at table. Instead of enjoying the meal before you, however, all that you are concerned with is the gratification of your parent's announced desire to see eat! Sounds a little out of this world, Doc, doesn't it?"

"When put in words, it certainly does, laddie," says Dr. Claus Gringo slowly and gravely, and biting his lips as if to give added emphasis to his comments. "You know as well as I do that we humans find nothing harder than hearing the truth about ourselves. Truth, a bitter pill that is capable of healing a stricken mind, isn't the easiest thing on earth to come by in any case…"

"Well," Moses Kwentindio quips in a cutting rejoinder; "I suppose that's right. Now then - if, as I suspect, fear is at the bottom of your desire to please, you will do everything to appear a great connoisseur of food and of fastidious taste, and so on. Depending on the extent of the compelling desire - of which you are an unwitting victim - to conform to your elders' wishes, you will even believe that you *are* a great connoisseur of food and of fastidious taste. But there will obviously be moments when you will forget yourself and will be gobbling food in a manner that you yourself wouldn't have imagined!

The seminarian pretends that he doesn't notice the psychiatrist's eyes widening in a frozen stare, and continues: "It turns out, surely enough, that you've never thought of yourself or contemplated your being except in imagery in the sense we spoke about. And you certainly cannot - nay would not with your life on it - be brought to agree that you are by upbringing such a crude fellow! The picture you have of yourself has never been anything but rosy - you are an altogether acceptable person, possessed of the highest integrity and having a natural prepossessing manner!

"The question 'Why do I eat?' cannot easily cross the mind of someone in those straits - except may be to the extent that an individual's participation in the institution of eating is or isn't deemed to be in agreement with the will of superiors.

"Coming back to you - you fancy, with a gleam in your eyes, that your upbringing could not possibly have left anything to be desired, or room for improvement even! Indeed, as your sharp memory will bear you out, everybody - certainly that section of the human race that was blessed with the privilege of coming into contact with you, and never mind that it was largely faceless and nameless – has always seemed to regard you with deep unwavering admiration, a reflection no doubt of the singular manner in which you were brought up!

"Unlike the upbringing of most other humans, yours was characterized by, shall we say, your parents' high visibility, an all too extreme anxiety for you that they almost certainly were in the habit of expressing aloud (for the benefit of other poor folk) at each and every available opportunity, and your parents' utter impatience with you, as the willy child you constantly were inclined (and have long ceased) to be - and so on.

"You are alive to the fact that the imprint of the will of those who hold sway over you is on your every act and motion, and your feelings of self-satisfaction and sense of pride have been duly reinforced on countless occasions before by the spontaneous words of praise you have heard uttered in your favour - not to mention the opprobrium you knew to lie in store for the good laddie that you always were in case the devil in you, now happily dead, thought to resurrect. The more you have been - and presumably continue to be - subject to domination and influence, the more you are inclined to believe your fantasy!"

"That makes a good deal of sense!" exclaims Dr. Claus Gringo, suddenly alert. According to the expression on his face, he might as well have been saying: "You seem to be madder than Innocent Kintu except, thank God, that you are endowed with such an amazing capacity for introspection!"

Speaking impersonally, Dr. Claus Gringo's guest says: "Thank you." A far away look on his set expression he continues: "Your parents at the other pole have never been able to count their lucky stars and cannot count their spouse the belief that they have made a real and quite splendid person of you by raising you in the way they did - quick to obey and to learn, or rather to parrot! It is the next thing to impossible to get either you or your mentors to see that you have all along been treated virtually as chattel, with no independent will and little or no intelligence of its own; and fit to be only that which they want to make of you - namely an object for their own self-aggrandizement! A good question, indeed, would be: What if it should somehow transpire that that which the devoted members of such a one want to make of him or her cannot come about, and this situation arises at a time when everyone's expectations are high? But you, Professor, are as unlikely to make a good model for my typical case as Aristotle…"

"Well, who then - Oliver Twist?" growls Moses Kwentindio's host, starting from his chair.

"Not the likes of Oliver," intones the churchman in the wake of the latter's exclamation. "Having become worldly-wise through manly experience with the hard realities of life, the chappie understood life as well as - if not better than - Tolstoy himself! Although Twist looked every bit like excellent meat for this world's 'Pharisees and Scribes' if I may borrow the master's phrased, he seems to have from quite early on how to discern the imposters and quacks from a crowd. No, Charles Dickens' hero wouldn't have fit the bill any better!

"I agree' Dr. Claus Gringo says resolutely. Then, after a moment of deliberation within himself: "You assign degrees of responsibility - as between the vexing and the vexed, I mean?"

"And among the rest of the actors in the 'Renegade Model' as I like to call it," declares Moses Kwentindio breezily.

"Hmmm...how so?" his host grunts.

The reply is instantaneous and angry. "They relegate Autonomous Man - Autonomous Man in the sense in which Aristotle would have understood that phrase - to the rank of an Automaton! A robot. They renege on Man's most dignified instinct!"

The two men face each other in silence. As they do so, the younger man rests both his elbows slowly on the desktop and forms his knuckles into a "ball". Carefully balancing his lower jawbone on the "ball", he resumes his speech, ostensibly taking no heed of the fact that his head too now moves in a bizarre pattern albeit in sympathy with each freshly spoken syllable.

"Take the formal mentors," says he. "More likely than not, a headstrong couple so as to be more efficient as mind benders. Could have them fill the role of leading citizens in their neighbourhood. Or let them be pillars of their Church in addition - for good measure! Whatever you do, they must be respectable - you see!

"Then let's take the admirers of those 'elders', 'handlers', '*walimus*' or what have you. There are outright admirers, who, unlike 'wannabes', may or may not practice what they admire. And, the larger group of mixed admirers represented, by and large, by the undefined, hugely gullible and admittedly ignorant masses whose combined regard for the ideals of the victim's mentors looms in the eyes of the victim as the *Vox Populi*!

"There is the small force of hard-core traditionalists who consider it a misnomer to use the term 'elders' when talking about the type of mentors I just referred to. They regard these people as a sore that society would be better off without having to endure! Typically, the relations between the traditionalists and the new breed of elders will be at cross-purposes. The former want to ensure that their offspring participate from as early as possible in traditional cultural activities such as *n'gomas* and ancestor spirit worship so-called, whereas the latter may feel constrained to take special measures to ensure that their children remain unsullied by the 'ignominies of a heathen past'!

"There is that powerful clique that holds the cards for survival - real or imagined - in both the spiritual and secular realms, and from which the 'elders' in our present instance take their inspiration. There is also that ever-changing composition of disciples - largely contemporaries of the candidate for the mental asylum - whose admiration for one or other of the above apostles of salvation, subject as it will be to a myriad enticements and pressures including the calls and demands of Mother Nature herself, can hardly fail to impact on the personality complex we wish to design for the candidate…"

Rocking with subdued laughter, the psychiatrist, his head inclined to one side, is staring with open mouth at his young guest.

"And, finally, there are what you mighty call the circumstances of the candidate himself which go hand in hand with the powerful, all pervasive if unrecognized force represented by the 'fear of the unknown', certainly not an inconsequential force in our highly illiterate society…"

The hawkeyed professor is of course already convinced that, more than anything else, Moses Kwentindio has come to court his reaction to the provocative if somewhat peculiar, theory of madness he might well have spent a lifetime developing. Dr. Claus Gringo is now inclined to think that it was a pure coincidence that his patient's situation came to a head while attending the same institution where the extremely imaginative Kwentindio happened to be studying. He sees the cleric's acquaintance with Innocent Kintu as providing the sharp-witted fellow the excuse to unload on him the results of a lifetime's work! He doubts very much in the light of this finding if Moses Kwentindio will go on to become a priest.

But the psychiatrist is also stung with curiosity to hear the remainder of the ingenious theory. He grins widely and gasps: "And the candidate himself…it isn't quite clear to me what you would make of him - a dunderhead?"

"Oh, no!" Moses Kwentindio shoots back, his face a mirror of serenity. "The candidate and principal actor, far from being the quietist, fool or whatever may be imagined, up until the point in time when his life's dreams become shattered; when the prospects for the fulfilment of some cherished ideal finally melt away never to return and his life's plan derails; prior to all that, he is likely to come across - and Innocent Kintu certainly did - as a devastatingly personable and cute and imaginative individual, if short on facts and prone to being duped by what David Hume - I think it was - appropriately called 'logical illusion'!

"Incidentally, my dossier sets out to show that the patient was drilled to distrust and to hold in disdain our basic natural instincts and, of course, the materialistic conception of the world as proclaimed by the irreligious!"

Dr. Claus Gringo belches loudly and, too late, pats his thick lips with a handkerchief he whips from the top drawer of his desk. Intrigued, the churchman pauses to look. As he does so, the psychiatrist uses the opportunity thus afforded to interject.

"And if science, not religion, were the intoxicant..."

Moses Kwentindio's face suddenly becomes drawn, "Yeah," he shrieks; "According to the theory, parallel results should be expected. Whether you are dominated by a hell-bent Newton or by an archbishop, if the domination is effective, you should become a prey of Hume's illogical illusion and wind up with a split personality as you people prefer to call it just the same!"

It all happens in a flash. One moment the man of medicine is settled at his desk following the churchman's words intently; and the next moment finds him standing on top of the desk hollering: "One up for your Renegade Theory!"

A thought crosses the seminarian's mind that, his own theories aside, everyone, including the reputable man of medicine now dancing on top of his desk's flat top with a face writhed in an expansive grin, might have in him or her a grain of insanity in embryonic form that, unknown to mankind, was capable of sprouting into seething madness on an impulse!

Winking mechanically, he suddenly finds himself yearning that human nature is fashioned differently from what he had just imagined, and that Dr. Claus Gringo is not about to become another victim of a cruel Nature!

The psychiatrist, his voice once again a mere growl, continues unabashed under Moses Kwentindio's intent gaze: "The thing seems to clinch! This equation of the split personality that you have elaborated—I dare say there is a lot to be said for it."

He slides to the other side of the desk and starts pumping his guest's hand as the latter squeals inquiringly: "Well?"

The seminarian seems to take it that it is now his turn to grin, and he grins from ear to ear!

"I must give it to you straight," the older man rumbles on, "that you appear to have successfully outlined here the grand picture of what madness is all about! I have, of course, still to hear details of what really happened in Innocent Kintu's particular case. But given the demonstration you just gave, I do not doubt your ability to trace the development of my patient's problem from the perception stage right up to the point when symptoms of his abnormality begun to show in his makeup.

"The movement from a confusion of subsets to a unitary whole is something Psychiatry has attempted to pinpoint and describe with little success in the past. As you know, the very language of we 'headshrinkers' as some prefer to call us has traditionally hampered development from what consists largely of semantics to an objective treatment of the subject of mental disorders. It is against this background, Mr. Kwentindio, that I find myself viewing what I sincerely believe is a great leap forward…"

Moses Kwentindio, whose attention has fast diminished with a growing in ability to refrain from laughing, stops holding back and bursts out into an ecstatic fit of laughter. His sides ache painfully as his host rumbles on.

"It has only just struck me," says the professor brazen-facedly, "that while the actions of a psychopath during his so-called lucid intervals look just the sort one would expect of a normal person, they in fact must be appearing so only on the surface! I must grant you that, under closer scrutiny, they do invariably prove to be as mystifying as those done by the patient when in an agitated state of mind!"

The seminarian stops laughing and instead flushes helplessly as his host goes on: "We are habitually faced in our profession with missing links as we attempt to plot a delinquent's train of thoughts in a give situation. I venture to predict, my friend, that your Renegade Theory - Theory 'R' if you don't mind the twist - will greatly facilitate the discovery of those missing links!

"The ingenious model you have constructed, with its revolutionary parameters for measuring the socio-psycho forces at play in society, is certain to prove invaluable when it comes to grasping the pitiful endeavours of patients as they try to hold their own particularly at those times when bouts of the disease are severest!"

The seminarian's face wears a quizzical air. His wide-eyed stare is briefly interrupted when he becomes overwhelmed by an unexpected urge to yawn. His struggle to stifle the yawn is futile.

"Oh, now! You flatter me there, Professor!" he gasps weakly. Then, after refilling his lungs with fresh air, he stutters: "It was important in my view that we discuss the basic approach and principles before launching into a discussion of the dossier…"

"You haven't brought it along by any chance?" The tone of Dr. Claus Gringo's voice is urgent.

"I am afraid it is still no more than a jumble of untidy undecipherable notes. Anyway, the time I am taking to render the notes into something more legible is probably no different from that which I would take writing them anew!"

Moses Kwentindio sounds sincerely regretful up to this point. Then his voice changes: "Since we spoke over the phone, I have been turning the subject matter over in my mind pretty thoroughly, you can be sure. Doctor, with luck and a bit of accommodation from yourself, I might just be able to act the griot and give it to you straight from the head…"

The psychiatrist does not laugh. Instead, he eyes his visitor with a half wary half affectionate regard, causing the latter's half-hearted laughter to fizzle out.

Intending to speak in a soft whisper, Dr. Claus Gringo, his aspect suddenly grave, finds himself growling in a rough grating voice: "Sonny, I have to confess that I was at first very nearly stupefied by your untempered indulgence in Metaphysics. Not that I saw anything vainglorious or unreal about what you were conveying - I simply had never thought to carry on a prolonged discussion in such terms! Is metaphysics one of the subjects taught at what-do-you-call-it?'

"St. Barnabas' Seminary…"

"Is it one of the subjects they teach?" The psychiatrist speaks with what seems to be a deep and genuine interest.

""It is one of the compulsory cram courses offered to First Years," replies Moses Kwentindio, indifferently.

All the same, the reply causes the professor to squirm and guffaw helplessly. The churchman himself smiles sheepishly

252

the while. The prevailing mood is plainly mischievous, and the seminarian seems to have the field.

"I can hardly believe," he quips after a pause, "that the only task I have remaining is to render the material for the dossier legible! My long shot, Professor, is to expand it into a book I can publish. When finally available in print, the dossier will be embellished, you can be sure, with a lot of mythical nonsense. People generally prefer myths to reality, and it seems most can't even tell reality from myth!" The churchman speaks with obvious relish.

Jamila Kivumbi bursts into the room with a tray loaded with coffee and sandwiches just as. Claus Gringo is saying: "Although I have still to heart you narrate the events ensuing in Kintu's present unfortunate condition, you might like to know that if you ever get the dossier in print, I could help spur on sales od the book by making it compulsory reading for my students. Come to think of it - it would be a pity if I missed some important details as you run through the catalogue of events for me. Would you mind if Jamila here bugged you with her dictaphone while you were at it?"

"Hey, ho! Wait a minute!" yelps the cleric amid giggles. "Well - may be, may be not! Can I be sure I will retain the copyright?"

While his audience, consisting now of the psychiatrist and the woman who would be his future wife rollicks with laughter, the seminarian calls out in mock seriousness: "Darling, you will have seek my permission prior to transcribing…"

The lunch break passes quickly. At the end of it, Jamila Kivumbi sets up the dictaphone on the desk and settles down in a spare chair facing the guest.

19.

The Vatican Tape

Moses Kwentindio hardly begins to speak when Dr. Claus Gringo's secretary becomes conscious of the strange, highly erratic manner in which her heart is throbbing - as if she is about to have a heart attack. She knows that his proximity to her is the cause. She soon becomes bored with the subject matter of the story and finds herself increasingly becoming engrossed in the study of the seminarian's features and the gesticulations he employs in punctuating his narrative.

By a most strange quirk of nature, Moses Kwentindio himself suddenly finds he has to struggle just so that his mind does not wander from the story; for Jamila Kivumbi, simply attired in a loose-fitting midi, seems to be acquiring the look of a fairyland queen. The bright glow of the garment she wears accentuates the chocolate tone of her skin to a point that mesmerizes him.

It is with great difficulty that the cleric succeeds in remaining coherent as he describes the *walimu's* disastrous attempt to turn their son into an instant saint. His host's gaze is fully upon him throughout nonetheless, and the psychiatrist even jumps up involuntarily from his seat as Moses Kwentindio describes how the neurotic Kintu made the slip but for which the pent-up neurosis might have eluded detection until too late!

The professor is clearly seized with fright at that moment at the thought that the Roman Catholic Church had been about to be saddled with mad priest! Since, according to Kwentindio, Innocent's ravings would have assuredly been mistaken for orthodox Christianity by a goodly section of the young African Church, even though a 'cultural' Catholic himself, he is clearly troubled by the thought that Kwentindio's tribesman would not only have been a hard nut to crack once ordained a priest, but defrocking him would have conceivably led to a schism!

The psychiatrist is apprehensive enough as he mulls over the fact that the Church of Rome would have found itself in a tight corner with Innocent Kintu's elevation to the priesthood. His apprehension turns to agitation when the "message" is finally driven home - the Church's central role in producing the wretch that Kintu now is surely made it deserving of all that and more!

As he reflects on this situation, he finds himself feeling extremely pleased with himself for having come up with the idea of a dictaphone for taping the chronicle of the events that led to such a miserable end for his brother African!

Wondering how many more people on the continent stood to suffer a similar fate, he is convinced that the taping will have significance beyond the present case - the first of its kind he had come across. The peculiar manner in which Innocent Kintu fell victim to the Church's teaching on the one hand and the enormity of Moses Kwentindio's task, he is certain, puts the taping on a par with the infamous Watergate Tapes!

The atmosphere is incredibly tense and Dr. Claus Gringo makes a mental note almost as a matter of course. He would have his secretary label the latest offering in tapes the "Vatican tape"! A virtual agnostic that he is, he hopes that sooner or later the Supreme Pontiff of Rome himself will be held to ransom for the havoc wrought by the likes of Father Campbell in their scramble for souls.

PAYMENT IN KIND
(2nd Revised Edition)

Payment in Kind | The Columbia Review: "A realistic novel that spans across borders, oceans and continents, yet succeeds in remaining solidly anchored in the lives of interesting, genuine, flesh-and-blood characters. Highly recommended!"

Mr. Joseph Luguya received his early education in missionary schools in his native Uganda. He studied philosophy and theology at St. Mary's Major Seminary, Gaba. Mr. Luguya later attended the University of Nairobi, the Stanford Business School, the CII College of Insurance in London and, for a brief spell, the University of Dar es Salaam. He has lived and worked in Uganda, Tanzania, Kenya, Canada and the United States.

Mr. Luguya is also the author of *Inspired by the Devil: Part 1 - The Gospel According to "Judas Iscariot"* (3rd Revised Original Books Edition 2007), *The Forbidden Fruit* (Original Books 2011), and the three volume thriller *Humans: The Untold Story of Adam and Eve and their Descendants* (Original Books / CreateSpace 2015).

Joseph M. Luguya

Made in the USA
Monee, IL
30 June 2020